ON FIRE

Caught up in the overwhelming desire to protect her, Lord Warwick's lips brushed over hers. It had been meant as an innocent kiss. But he had not reckoned on Maggie's frenzied response.

Her lips crushed against his, her mouth open and warm. Something snapped inside him as the kiss deepened and a searing heat bolted through him. He kissed her face. He kissed her graceful neck. His hands cupped her breasts, and she began to make soft, whimpering sounds. He freed her breasts and bent to taste them as she arched into him, tossing her head back, her smoldering eyes those of a woman drugged.

Then her lids lowered, her long lashes feathering against her cheeks. A gentle peace had settled over her.

God in heaven, but she was exquisite!

BOOK YOUR PLACE ON OUR WEBSITE AND MAKE THE READING CONNECTION!

We've created a customized website just for our very special readers, where you can get the inside scoop on everything that's going on with Zebra, Pinnacle and Kensington books.

When you come online, you'll have the exciting opportunity to:

- View covers of upcoming books
- Read sample chapters
- Learn about our future publishing schedule (listed by publication month *and author*)
- Find out when your favorite authors will be visiting a city near you
- Search for and order backlist books from our online catalog
- Check out author bios and background information
- Send e-mail to your favorite authors
- Meet the Kensington staff online
- Join us in weekly chats with authors, readers and other guests
- Get writing guidelines
- AND MUCH MORE!

**Visit our website at
http://www.kensingtonbooks.com**

The Counterfeit Countess

Cheryl Bolen

ZEBRA BOOKS
Kensington Publishing Corp.
www.kensingtonbooks.com

ZEBRA BOOKS are published by

Kensington Publishing Corp.
850 Third Avenue
New York, NY 10022

All Kensington titles, imprints and distributed lines are available at special quantity discounts for bulk purchases for sales promotion, premiums, fund-raising, educational or institutional use.

Special book excerpts or customized printings can also be created to fit specific needs. For details, write or phone the office of the Kensington Special Sales Manager: Kensington Publishing Corp., 850 Third Avenue, New York, NY 10022. Attn. Special Sales Department. Phone: 1-800-221-2647.

First Printing: January 2005
10 9 8 7 6 5 4 3 2 1

Printed in the United States of America

For two of the nicest people who ever walked the earth, my big brother Jerry Boyce and his wife Connie.

Chapter 1

As Edward, the Earl of Warwick, lay soundly sleeping in his dark bedchamber, his drowsy mind awakened to the sound of chattering females. But that same mind assured him of the improbability of such an occurrence. After all, he had no wife, no sisters, not even a mother to intrude on his gentleman's domain. He therefore rolled over with the firm intention of going back to sleep.

Then he heard a shrieking female voice, and this time—no matter what his mind told him—he realized she was *inside* Warwick House.

He jerked up and listened. Though the words he heard were indistinguishable, they were definitely uttered by one or more females who must have stormed into his home. He flung himself from the bed and jammed his legs into a pair of breeches, flying from the room and along the hallway to the stairwell. What the devil was going on down there? A blazing glow illuminated the great entry hall, where the candles had been extinguished when Edward had gone to bed not so very long ago.

From the top of the stairs he surveyed the ruckus below. And froze. What was likely the most beautiful female he had ever seen stood spitting out orders to *his* servants as if *she* were the mistress here. His mouth opened in dismay when he realized one of those orders was a demand to carry trunks to the "countess's"

chambers. His glance scanned the disarray in his
heretofore well-ordered townhouse. He counted no
less than fourteen trunks. In addition to the arrogant
Incomparable, there was a slightly more youthful ver-
sion of her with spectacles propped on the bridge of
her nose, a skinny hag dressed in servant's clothing,
and the fattest cat he had ever seen—all of them talking and shrieking at once, except for the cat.

Edward cleared his throat. No one seemed to take
notice of him. He began to move down the stairs and
cleared his throat again. This time all the intruders
glanced up and stared at him.

Completely unaware that he stood there shirtless,
he asked, "What is the meaning of this?"

The Incomparable stepped forward and he was
powerless to keep his gaze on her incredible choco-
late eyes when every part of her was a feast for any
man's eyes. His glance dipped along her creamy skin
over her pink-hued cheeks and along her graceful
neck and bare shoulders to settle on a remarkably
lovely pair of breasts that barely dipped beneath the
bodice of her elegant gown. The rose-colored dress
draped over the smooth curves of a body as perfect as
her stunning face. She absently stroked the enormous
cat as she looked up at Edward. "Who is this handsome creature?" she asked, then quickly cupped a
hand to her mouth in embarrassment.

"I might ask the same of you," he said.

"This is Warwick House, is it not?" she asked, a
hitch of uncertainty in her rich voice.

"It is," he said, moving down the stairs.

Her chin lifted. "I, sir, am Lady Warwick, and this is
my house."

"I, madame, am Lord Warwick and I'd be damned
sure to know if you were my wife!" For a fraction of a
second he wondered if the old earl might have secretly married the Incomparable, but Edward's

predecessor's movements—including his abhorrence of females—were well known to Edward.

He watched the beauty for signs of capitulation, but the proud woman gave none. "How long, my lord, since you succeeded?" she challenged.

What gave her the right to question him? "Eighteen months."

Now her shoulders slumped and her composure dissolved. Right before his very eyes, she slid into a graceful heap on his marble floor, her skirts fanned out beside her, that damned squealing cat arched on her lap.

And she proceeded to cry. Not that it was like any female hysterics he had ever witnessed before. For one thing, she kept shaking her dainty fists and saying the most vile things, and her curses seemed to be directed at a man she most *un*affectionately referred to as The Scoundrel.

Even if she was behaving in a most undignified fashion, the sight of a female (especially a beautiful female) weeping, softened Edward. "Now, now," Edward soothed, stepping toward her but not really knowing what to do. He could hardly hug a strange woman, nor could he give her any hope that this was her house.

"Why did I ever believe him?" she cried. "I knew he was a wicked, scheming, lying, perfectly o-o-o-d-i-ous scoundrel."

Her shoulders heaved with each wrenching sob. He felt deuced awkward just standing there when the woman was so obviously distressed.

"Hell's too good for the vile, lying, despicable scoundrel," she continued.

It was a given the man she abhorred was a scoundrel.

"To whom are you referring, madame?" Edward asked, setting a gentle hand on her trembling shoulder. That damned cat of hers—claws extended—slapped at Edward's hand!

Sucking a bloody finger into his mouth, Edward

realized he *knew* who The Scoundrel was. Hadn't Lawrence Henshaw been passing himself off as Lord Warwick when he fled England just ahead of the hangman's noose?

"My . . . late husband," she answered.

Henshaw was dead? England should be that lucky. "I beg that you quit crying, my lady." He used the title to appease her, though he *knew* she was no countess. "Let us go into the saloon where we can discuss your situation." *Damn that Henshaw!* He'd always had an eye for the ladies and had obviously tricked this woman into marrying him under the false impression she was marrying an earl.

The young woman he took to be the Incomparable's younger sister retrieved a handkerchief from her reticule and handed it to the weeping beauty, who promptly dried her eyes, then looked up at Edward and offered her hand. He was deuced happy to help her up, especially since she gave all appearances that her crying was ended. But when he reached for her, that damned gray cat slapped at him again. This time he snatched back his hand ahead of the fat feline's attack.

"Stop that, Tubby!" she said to the huge cat as she cradled the overfed ball of gray fur to her breast. "I'm sorry, my lord," she said, peering up at Edward. "Tubby's wary of strangers." Then she contrived to get up without his assistance.

Tubby? Edward had to admit the name suited the animal. As did Killer, Tiger, and Out-You-Go.

They walked to the saloon which Wiggins, ever the pragmatic butler, had anticipated would need candles and had accordingly brightened the celery-green room.

"Here, here, my lady," Edward said, tentatively putting an arm around the distressed widow, his eye peeled for a reaction from Tubby. "Come sit down." Edward cursed to himself. *Damn that Henshaw!*

As soon as she was settled upon the gold and green

striped brocade settee, he came to sit next to her. He had to know if Henshaw was really dead. He wouldn't put anything past the blighter. "About your late husband," he began. "Would he have been a black-haired man some four or five inches shorter than myself? Probably the same age as I?"

Her gaze swept over him, pausing discernibly at his bare chest.

That was when Edward realized the impropriety of his sitting there bare-chested with a woman who was an obvious lady. He moved to get up, to go fetch a shirt and coat when Wiggins, the butler, strolled into the room with a freshly ironed shirt and navy blue frock coat.

The widow and her female entourage had the decency to turn their heads while he dressed.

When he finished, Wiggins asked, "Should your lordship desire a fire?"

"Don't bother," Edward said. "We shan't be here long." Then Edward returned to the settee. "Now where were we?"

"I believe you had just described my late husband," she said. "You knew him?"

Edward's lashes lowered. "I believe so." Since Henshaw was last seen boarding a ship bound for the colonies, that probably meant the Incomparable was an American.

"You are an American?" he asked.

She shrugged. "I'm from Virginia, but my parents were English. Royalists. So it's difficult to call myself an American, though I suppose that's what I am." Her accent was upperclass British.

From the corner of his eye Edward saw that the younger woman whom he presumed to be the Incomparable's sister had plopped onto a Louis XIV chair and proceeded to lose herself in the pages of a book.

His attention returned to the beauty. It sickened

him to think Henshaw had abused so lovely a creature. He hoped to God the man truly was rotting in
hell. But he wouldn't trust the scoundrel not to have
faked his own death. "When did your husband die?"

"Four months ago."

"A natural death?"

She stiffened. "I'd rather not say."

She was hiding something, and he wouldn't put it
past that damned Henshaw to have forced this beautiful woman into his vile schemes. "What I need to
know, madame, is if you actually saw his dead body."

She nodded solemnly. "Fortunately, they had put
his clothing back on before they brought him to me."

What in the deuce was she talking about?

The younger girl looked up from her book and
spoke. "What my sister is reluctant to tell you, my lord,
is that her late husband met his end at a brothel."

Now Edward was convinced the dead husband was
indeed Lawrence Henshaw.

The Incomparable flicked an impatient glance at
her sister. "I didn't want you ever to know that!"

The girl had returned her attention to her book.

"Foul play?" he asked the widow.

"Not at all," she said. "Lawrence—in his cups and
feeling rather invincible after a triangular tryst—
leaped naked from a third-floor balcony. It's just the
sort of thing The Scoundrel would have done."

Yes, it was. "And you're sure the body was his? Could
his fatal injuries have obscured his appearance?"

She smiled. The most radiant smile he had ever
seen. Her teeth were even and a stunning white. He
felt as if he were in a sunny spring meadow. "I wondered the very same thing myself," she said, "for by
then I knew how his wicked mind worked. So I bared
his chest for proof."

He waited for her to elaborate, but she didn't.
"What proof would that be?" he asked.

A slight blush rose to her cheeks. "Lawrence was possessed of chest hair that formed a harlequin pattern."

"And the dead body was undoubtedly your husband's?"

Her lovely lips thinned to a grim line. "Undoubtedly."

"I see you've chosen not to wear mourning."

"To do so would be hypocritical, my lord. I was living apart from The Scoundrel at the time of his death with no intentions of ever going back to him."

He wondered why she had married the man in the first place since she found him so despicable, but Edward knew how charming Lawrence Henshaw could be—until he got what he wanted. He also knew how destructive Henshaw could be. His hands fisted with anger toward the dead scoundrel.

"Then it seems, madame, you are possessed of sound judgment. Your husband barely escaped England with his neck."

Petting the contentedly purring cat, she nodded thoughtfully. "I should have expected as much. When he courted me he vowed to bring me to London and give my sister a grand debut, but once we were married The Scoundrel changed his tune. He offered one excuse after another why we couldn't come to England. Soon his own stories were conflicting with each other, and I knew it was all just so much flim-flam. I even came to wonder if he already had a wife in England." Those huge brown eyes of hers quizzed him.

"He had no wife," Edward assured.

"So what was his real name?"

"Lawrence Henshaw."

She sighed. "I much prefer being Lady Warwick. Mrs. Henshaw sounds so . . . so mundane, and you must admit Lawrence was anything but mundane. The Scoundrel."

"No, I don't suppose he was."

"I suppose he was a thief," she said matter-of-factly.

"That would explain why he arrived in Virginia with a great deal of money."

"Worse than a thief."

Her eyes widened. "Oh, dear, was he a murderer?"

"He was a traitor. He used his position at the Foreign Office to pass important information to the French. That information cost the lives of thousands of British soldiers."

She winced.

"For this, he was paid handsomely."

"Oh, dear, I'm most happy that the money is gone, for I should hate to be living on blood money."

All that money gone? Then how was this woman to return to America? "Why, precisely, did you wish to come to London?"

"To be perfectly honest with you, my lord, I planned a deceit of my own. I thought I would come live at Warwick House and have a grand season for my sister before I contacted the man I thought was Lord Warwick's solicitor to notify him of Lawrence's death. I knew once it was known Lord Warwick was dead, his heir would be entitled to all of this. Being an optimist, I had hoped that by the time we'd had our season, Rebecca would be betrothed to a man of means." She glanced at her girlish-looking sister.

"And," Rebecca piped up, "Maggie knew that by that time her beauty would have secured many hearts."

Scarlet tinged the Incomparable's cheeks. "I thought no such thing!" she chided her sister.

Rebecca shrugged. "It's just as well I don't have a season. I have no desire to be wed."

After her sister's disastrous marriage, Edward could well understand Rebecca's aversion to matrimony. Besides, he peered at her youthful face, she hardly seemed old enough. "How old is Miss . . ."

"Miss Peabody," Rebecca answered. "I shall be eighteen next month."

He settled back against the settee, eying the pair. He needed to get these females out of his house. "Well, well. I'll summon the carriage to convey you ladies to Claridge's Hotel."

This announcement succeeded in refreshing the Incomparable's tears. Dash it all! Made him feel quite the brute. "Now see here, my lady, surely you realize this is not your home."

"Oh, I know that," she said, sniffling. "It's just . . ." She let out a sob. "We have no money for a hotel."

Or for the passage back to America, he'd guess. What was he to do? Anything to snuff those wretched tears. "Then I suggest you ladies settle in for the night. I know you're whipped from the long journey. Tomorrow, when you're refreshed, we'll see what we can do about your return to America." He was well satisfied with himself. Even if he was stuck tonight with these females. And one very fat cat. It wouldn't do at all for Fiona to get wind of this arrangement.

Between great sobs, the beauty favored him with another of her shattering smiles. "You're so very kind, my lord."

They all stood up, and he rang for the housekeeper to prepare rooms for the visitors, but Wiggins had anticipated that, too, and the rooms were in readiness for the ladies.

Edward walked with them to the iron-banistered stairway, rather pleased with himself because the lovely one's tears had stopped.

"Is there a Lady Warwick?" she asked, placing her hand on his proffered arm.

"Not as yet," he answered. "I'm pledged to Lady Fiona Hollingsworth, but nothing is official, owing to the sudden, unexpected death of her mother, which has plunged the lady into mourning."

"The poor dear," Maggie sympathized. "Our dear

Mama's death was even more painful than Papa's, was it not, Rebecca?"

The very bookish Rebecca Peabody had refined the art of walking upstairs and reading at the same time. "What?" she asked, annoyed to be distracted from her reading.

"Oh, never mind!" Maggie said. "Mind your step or you'll fall down the stairs and break into a hundred pieces."

The first rooms they came to on the second floor were for Miss Peabody. She did not even look up from her book as she bid them good night and wandered into the room.

Next they came to the countess's chambers. "Actually, a countess hasn't occupied these chambers in at least fifty years," he said, "owing to the fact that my uncle—the late earl—never married. I plan to redecorate before I wed Lady Fiona. The rooms are exceedingly outdated."

He swept open the door as two maids were putting fresh linens on the bed, and the Incomparable's maid was unpacking her mistress's valise. It was as if he were seeing the formerly scarlet room for the first time. It was not only outdated, it was faded and some of the fabric had become so fragile he could have read a newspaper through it.

"It looks clean, and that's all that matters, my lord," Maggie said, giving him her hand. "My sister and I are most indebted to you for your generosity."

"It was nothing," he mumbled as he started for his own bedroom.

Maggie waited until she heard the earl's door close, then snatching up her cat, she hurried to her sister's chamber. Though smaller than the long-dead countess's chambers, this guest room was spectacularly furnished in elegant ivory and gold with stunning gilt cornices and moldings. Still reading her blasted book, Rebecca glared at her sister over the rim of her spectacles. "You should be ashamed of yourself, Maggie."

"Whatever for?" Maggie asked as she sank onto the silken bed, her feet dangling far off the carpeted floor, her hand absently stroking Tubby.

"For abusing your gift of being able to cry at the drop of a hat."

"Oh, that." It was really the oddest thing that she possessed the ability to cry on cue, but when she was truly distressed—for example, when her Papa had died—nary a tear could be summoned. She supposed her tears—like her beauty—were gifts bestowed upon her for the purpose of making big, strapping men putty in her delicate hands.

And Lord Warwick was most definitely a big, strapping man. She had nearly lost her breath when she had stood at the bottom of the stairs and looked up to glimpse the tall, bare-chested godlike creature scowling down at her. Of course she was completely humiliated that she'd blurted out her admiration, a most vexing habit of hers, to be sure! Even now the vision of that sleek, powerful body and the handsome dark, brooding face that went with it made her throb in places she'd as lief Rebecca knew nothing of. "Is not Lord Warwick a most splendid looking man?" she asked casually.

Rebecca did not remove her eyes from her book. "Pity he's spoken for."

"My dear sister, 'spoken for' is not the same thing as actually being married. It's probably one of those engagements arranged long ago by meddling family. I daresay Lady Fiona is some horse-faced peeress Lord Warwick can barely tolerate."

Now Rebecca closed her book and gaped at her elder sister.

"Dear God, you can't mean to snare him! How could you when your last marriage was so disastrous?"

"Now, now, pet. Don't get so overwrought. I have not decided to snare him. After the last fiasco, you can be well assured I will never rush into a marriage without knowing—really knowing—a man." She shrugged. "But you must admit the earl is decidedly promising."

What she neglected to tell her sister was that a hasty marriage (that wasn't *too* hasty) would keep them from the poor house. Maggie was getting desperate. By the time he had met his untimely death, The Scoundrel had managed to squander away most of his ill-gotten fortune.

She had racked her brains trying to come up with some way to continue living in modest dignity with her sister, but no viable possibilities presented themselves. Being a governess was out of the question because she would have to leave Rebecca behind, and her little sister was hardly self-sufficient. Being a seamstress was also out of the question. Her needlework—as her own governess had been quick to remind her—was most inferior, and why shouldn't it be? Maggie had been raised to expect fine modistes to make her clothing. She had even thought of taking up her pen in order to eke out a modest living, but, alas, she was possessed of no talent in that direction, either.

When it came right down to it, Maggie had only one talent: the ability to attract men. Not just attract them. Men had been known to make complete idiots of themselves over her.

A pity she'd wasted her charms on The Scoundrel. But then eligible men in the Virginia farming community where she was raised were as scarce as English lords.

"One would think the association of the name War-wick with The Scoundrel would be enough to warn you away from the man, regardless of his handsome face. And body," Rebecca added.

"I should have known Lawrence wasn't Lord Warwick," Maggie said. "I'm so vexed at myself! I knew he was a lying, scheming, perfectly odious scoundrel."

"The real Lord Warwick, you know, is going to send you away tomorrow."

Maggie, her fine brows lowered, bit at her lip. "You must help me think of a way to stay here. Lord Warwick's bound to know hordes of eligible men—men whose character he can vouch for. A month should be long enough for me to find one."

Rebecca rolled her eyes. "I suppose one of us could feign an illness."

"That's it!" Maggie flopped onto her stomach. "Of course, I can't be the sick one. Then I wouldn't be able to be properly courted."

"So what illness shall we say I have?" a resigned Rebecca asked.

Maggie considered the matter. "Let me hear you cough."

Rebecca gave a fake cough.

"Can you not do better than that?"

Her sister gave it another try, this time a deep, bellowing sound.

Maggie's face screwed up, and she had a strong desire to clamp her hands over her ears. "No, that won't do," Maggie said, shaking her head. "Consumption's out." She bit at her lip some more, then sighed. "You'll just have to pretend to be suffering with fever. Don't worry, pet, I'll smuggle you all the books you could ever desire to read."

Rebecca's eyes brightened. "Did you see his lordship's library?"

"How could anyone possibly read all those books?"

"I could."

"Yes, I suppose you could."

"What if Lord Warwick sends for a doctor? He'd know at once I have no fever."

Maggie went back to chewing on her lip. "Let me sleep on it." She got up off the bed, cradled the cat to her bosom, crossed the room to the chair where Rebecca sat, and kissed the crown of her sister's head. "Don't read all night. You'll put undue strain on your already weakened eyes."

When Maggie returned to her own chamber, Sarah was laying out her nightshift on the faded red counterpane. Maggie's heart caught as she watched her aging maid. It seemed like only yesterday Sarah's hair had been brown and her step lively. When had her hair turned silver? How could the once strapping maid have become so frail? Maggie wished to reverse their roles, to wait upon the woman who had waited upon her since the day she was born, but Sarah's whole life had been spent serving the Peabody family and the maid bristled at the idea of relinquishing what she perceived as her responsibility. Would that she could pension Sarah off, Maggie thought bitterly. Nothing would make Maggie happier than seeing Sarah relieved of all her burdens, ensconced comfortably near Rebecca and her, the closest thing to family that Sarah had.

"You shouldn't have waited up," Maggie said. "I know you're exhausted from today's long journey."

"I'd rather be here than in my bed tossin' and turnin'," Sarah said. "Sleep don't come so easily when one gets older."

As much as Maggie wished it weren't so, Sarah was old. Maggie allowed Sarah to assist her into the shift, then she placed firm hands on her maid's fragile shoulders and ordered her to bed. "And don't you dare present yourself in my room before ten of the clock." Sarah did so need a good night's sleep after the grueling journey.

Maggie doused the candle and lay in the aged bed. It felt so good to be in a real bed after so many weeks sleeping on the ship's narrow cot. It felt good to be on solid land that didn't pitch and sway. Never mind that the room smelled musty from years of disuse. Never mind that her presence was as welcome to her host as the pox. Just to be in a warm home on a real mattress provided a comfort she had not known in a very long time. For tonight, she would allow herself to be lulled by the physical replenishing she had craved for so many weeks.

Tomorrow, she would face her demons.

As she lay there awash in contentment, Tubby purring beside her, she pictured the restrained power in Lord Warwick's wondrous physique. "Please, God, don't let him be another scoundrel."

Chapter 2

As difficult as it was to drag himself from his bed the next morning, Edward did. He had important French documents to decode at the Foreign Office. Thirteen hours of intense mental focus on the task yesterday had sent him home in a state of exhaustion. He had been too tired to eat and had fallen asleep as soon as his head hit the pillow, only to be awakened shortly thereafter by the arrival of Henshaw's widow.

Yet even after the woman was fast asleep in her bed, the problems her visit posed kept Edward awake for hours. He feared he might have revealed himself and his sensitive work at the Foreign Office when he disclosed Henshaw's treachery. For all he knew, she could be a French spy. Or Henshaw could still be alive, using his lovely wife for some diabolical purpose.

Edward tried to recall every word he had said to her and was certain he had not revealed his own position at the Foreign Office. But if the woman was half as mentally alert as her late husband, she would know only a man at the highest level of government would be privy to the information about Henshaw's spy network.

Then there was the suspicion that Henshaw himself might have told her about Edward and his function at the Foreign Office.

Edward's instincts were to believe her innocent,

believe that she had no prior knowledge of her husband's true identity. Edward's trust in her had nothing to do with the fact that she was beautiful. It was the little sister who prompted him to believe the counterfeit countess's truthfulness. From the similarity of their looks, they had to be sisters, and the sister—whom he really couldn't believe a part of any conspiracy—had verified Henshaw's death.

As Cummings shaved him, Edward sat motionless. His head throbbed with one of those dull headaches one gets when deprived of sleep.

The Incomparable still dominated his thoughts. Not because he was attracted to her. Quite the contrary. He only had eyes for Lady Fiona, and it wasn't fair to his dear Fiona for him to have the beauty as his houseguest. He had to get the widow away from Warwick House. If word ever got out he was entertaining two unmarried ladies, his future with Fiona would be at risk. Especially if the *ton* ever saw how beautiful Maggie Peabody-Henshaw-Lady Warwick was.

Maggie had determined she would not miss the earl that morning. Therefore shortly after dawn she had taken it upon herself to dress in a lovely saffron morning gown and had contrived to fashion her hair into an attractive Grecian style without Sarah's help.

Then she sat in her room, listening for the sound of Lord Warwick's tread outside her chamber door. Something told her the earl would be an early riser. Actually, that something was her hunch that he worked for the Foreign Office. Why else would he know about The Scoundrel's perfidy? And if Lord Warwick worked at the Foreign Office, he would probably appear there during the morning.

At nine o'clock she heard his heavy footstep as he strode down the hall. She knew it was Lord Warwick's and not a servant's because his step exuded masculinity and confidence, just as he himself did.

When she eased open her chamber door, he turned around to face her. A flicker of disappointment fired his eyes but was quickly replaced by a controlled smile. "Good morning . . . my lady. I would not have thought you an early riser."

Because most attractive women spent hours on their toilette? "I had hoped to speak with you before you left," she said as she moved to him.

He offered his arm. "Then join me for breakfast."

She walked with him to the end of the hall and down the broad staircase and into the well-lit morning room where they took their seats at a small, round table covered with a white cloth and set with a silver urn, teacups, and various breakfast offerings. Maggie poured coffee into fine porcelain cups and handed him one.

Despite his perpetually brooding countenance, Lord Warwick's face was as perfect as his athletic body. His face—like him—exuded masculinity. The cut of his square jaw, his aristocractic nose, his intense amber eyes, all underscored his unrestrained power. The casual sweep of his dark brown hair was at odds with the man's stiffness, but she could well understand his hair—like his impeccable clothes—embraced the prevailing fashion.

While she was gathering her courage, he cleared his throat. "How can I be of service to you, madame?"

She drew in a deep breath. "I should like you to find me a husband." There, she'd said it. She had even managed to blurt it out without allowing the violent trembling in her body to reach her voice.

He gave her an *are-you-a-lunatic?* stare.

Not at all what she had hoped for.

So she proceeded to launch herself into another fit of hysterics. "I know, your lordship," she managed between great, heaving sobs, "that you have no obligation to me whatsoever, but you seem such a fine gentleman." She paused to wipe her tears on the dainty handkerchief she had extracted from her pocket. "It's just that we are so alone here in England." A whimpering sob broke into her sentence. "I have no husband, no fa-a-a-ther to screen potential suitors."

"There now," he murmured, patting her arm with a big, steady hand. "Please don't cry. We'll think of something."

Sniff. Sniff. "As much as I abhor lying—and I would never tell a lie unless it was to help someone I care about—could we not say I am your cousin? I shouldn't like to put you in an awkward situation with Lady Fiona." Her crying tapered off.

"I'm not going to say you're my cousin!" he barked.

She sucked in a deep breath and stood up. "I beg that you look at me as a man would a horse at Tattersall's." Gracefully holding out her arms as if she were dancing a minuet, she slowly turned around. "Save for the wretchedly red eyes, think you I can quickly attract a husband? A man whose integrity you can vouch for?"

She did not remove her gaze from his as he perused her with fiery eyes. Then he averted his gaze. And coughed. "I wouldn't think that would be too difficult," he finally managed.

The smile that brightened her face obliterated all signs of her recent tears. "Then you will help?"

That brooding look that seemed as much a part of him as his magnificently broad chest, returned. "I did not say that."

With slumping shoulders and pouting mouth, she returned to her seat. "Of course, I understand you're not a man who's given to making rash decisions. Your solidness is what makes you so perfect for this office. I merely ask that you consider helping a . . . a penniless widow in this small matter. I shall, of course, give you time to consider the matter."

While she resumed eating, she watched the handsome earl. Such a pity he was betrothed to that horse-faced Lady Fiona. Maggie ate rather heartily. Yesterday's meals, due to her dwindling purse, had been most meager.

Lord Warwick hurried through his breakfast, then begged to take his leave. "There are matters I must attend to today. You and your sister are at liberty to stay here until I return."

At least he hadn't turned them out.

On his way to Whitehall he cursed the very beautiful Maggie Peabody-Henshaw-Lady Warwick. What did she think he was? Some procurer? Of course, he couldn't find a husband for the minx. The gall of her to ask!

But how was he to get rid of her? Perhaps Lord Carrington would be able to help in the matter.

When Edward arrived at his office, Harry Lyle was already seated at his desk in the office they shared. Papers were stacked, spread, and wadded up on the top of Harry's desk. Not that Edward could actually see the top of Harry's desk. Edward's glance flicked to his own desk which he had left entirely free of papers or clutter of any kind.

Harry spun around and gazed up at his friend and colleague, his eyes narrowing. "You don't look at all well today, old fellow. What's the matter? Breaking code keep you from sleep?"

Edward's chair scraped across the wooden floor as he pulled it out and sat down. "I was too exhausted to even think about code last night. I had a rather . . . peculiar intrusion upon my sleep."

Harry arched a brow.

"Lawrence Henshaw's widow came barreling into my house just past midnight."

"What the deuce?" Harry asked, nearly swirling from his chair.

"It appears Henshaw died in Virginia, though to know Henshaw is to know that even his death could be a lie. He secured his wife's hand in marriage by claiming to be Lord Warwick. The Scoundrel." He smiled to himself as he remembered the way the widow's cheeks dimpled in disdain when she said *The Scoundrel*.

"Good Lord!" Harry exclaimed. "So the poor woman really did think she was a countess!"

"Just so. The devious Henshaw picked his peer well. I know of no other peer of the realm who was more reclusive than the former Lord Warwick. Very few people would ever have met him, ever be able to identify him."

"But Henshaw's cleverness failed him one more time. He hadn't considered the old earl would die."

"Exactly."

"So what did you do with the woman?"

Edward shrugged. "That's the pity of it. She's still at Warwick House—along with a sister, a maid, fourteen trunks, and one very fat cat."

"Couldn't you send them to Claridge's?"

"I tried. The woman fell into hysterics. It seems she has no money."

"You'd best hope Lady Fiona doesn't find out you've two unmarried ladies at your house."

"It's all decidedly innocent, but I'd as lief Fiona never learn of it. I thought perhaps I could pay for the widow's lodgings at Claridge's, but it wouldn't do for Fiona to learn I had a woman under my protection. As discreet as they are at Claridge's, word would be bound to get out."

"Deuced difficult situation you're in, not to men-

tion that Henshaw's widow—if she *is* a widow—could
be lying about Henshaw's death. She could even be
a spy!"

"I've thought of that, too."

"You'd better discuss this with Lord Carrington."

Edward nodded thoughtfully as he got to his feet.
"I'll just pop in and speak with him now."

Lord Carrington's secretary, Charles Kingsbury, informed him that their superior was not in. Which was
really no surprise to Edward. A man as rich and well
connected as Lord Carrington could bloody well do
exactly as he pleased. The man even refused to accept
a salary from the government he served.

"A pity," Edward said to the stiff public servant who
was a couple of years older than Edward. "I had
hoped to tell him of my visit from Henshaw's widow."

Kingsbury's eyes widened. "Henshaw's dead?"

"Apparently so."

"Good riddance to foul baggage, I'd say. But whatever can his wife want with you?"

"The lady was under the impression she was Lady
Warwick."

Kingsbury's thin lips straightened. "So the blighter
didn't change."

"Apparently not."

"Lord Carrington would undoubtedly like all the
details. Why don't you try to reach him at Berkeley
Square?"

As Edward waited in the drawing room of Carrington's fine mansion on Berkeley Square, he
thought of how he would have liked to have known
Carrington when he was a younger man. As one of
the wealthiest men in the kingdom, Carrington had
been a favorite at the French court and had amassed
spectacular treasures of art and sculpture—and

beautiful women—during his Grand Tours of the continent some thirty-five years previously. A pity he had never married and had no heir to pass all this to, Edward reflected as he gazed at the Italian masters hanging on the silk walls, at the ceilings painted by skilled artists, and at the gilded moldings and cornices in the room.

Presently Lord Carrington himself, lean and fit and dressed as fashionably as a well-to-do young dandy, strolled into the room, examining the lace at his cuffs. "Well, well, Warwick, what brings you here so early in the morning?" Carrington asked as he came to sit in a French armchair across from Edward.

"Lawrence Henshaw's widow showed up at my house last night."

The marquis's face blanched. "Henshaw's dead?"

"Apparently so. I'm inclined to believe the widow."

"What, pray tell, could the woman want with you?" Lord Carrington asked.

"Oh, it wasn't me she was interested in. She thought my house was hers."

Lord Carrington's bushy brows drew together. "A singular error."

"Allow me to explain," Edward said. He proceeded to narrate the events of the previous night, leaving out nothing and concluded by saying, "Though I don't trust Henshaw, I believe the widow's telling the truth."

"What makes you so confident?"

"The younger sister. That she's related to the widow is impossible to deny. The girl's just seventeen and mad for reading. She verified Henshaw's death, and somehow I don't think she was coerced into doing so."

"You honestly think the widow came here solely to attract husbands for herself and her sister because she's destitute?"

Edward shrugged. "I don't know what to think. That's why I'm here."

"We have to learn if she knew about her husband's activities, his contacts with the French. She might be able to lead us to the men who paid Henshaw to betray his country."

"A man who lies about his own identity is hardly likely to have told the truth about his ill deeds," Edward said.

Lord Carrington did not speak for a moment. "You're probably right, Warwick, but we cannot afford to presume the woman's innocent. We need to keep her in London. She must be watched at all times."

Whatever Edward had hoped for, it wasn't this. His eyes narrowed. "What are you suggesting?"

"I'm not suggesting anything. I'm ordering you to allow the woman to stay at your house. Your mission will be to uncover any information she may have about her husband. Even unwittingly, she might know something that would be valuable to us."

"But, your lordship, I cannot have a pair of single women living under my roof. I'm a bachelor, and I don't wish to risk securing the hand of Lady Fiona Hollingsworth."

"There must be a way," Carrington mumbled to himself. He got up and strode one length of the Aubusson carpet to the other. "I've got it!" he finally said.

Edward shot him a quizzing glance.

"We'll say the previous Lord Warwick secretly married the woman before he died. She can pretend to be the Countess Warwick, and no one ever need know she's a counterfeit. As a gentleman, you will be obliged to provide for your uncle's widow."

"Then I can ship her off to Claridge's."

"You'll do no such thing! It's vital that you keep a watch on her at all times. When you're unable to do so, Harry Lyle or Charles Kingsbury will fill in for you."

This was easy for Lord Carrington to say. He hadn't yet seen the woman. "I don't think Lady Fiona would approve."

"Why? She'll believe the widow really is your uncle's widow."

"Because the widow is extremely beautiful."

There was a flicker of mirth in the old man's eyes. "What age is she?"

"I'd say about five and twenty."

"Oh, dear. Sorry to do this to you, old fellow, but you'll have to suffer the widow's company for king and crown." The touch of humor in the older man's voice did not sound sympathetic.

Lord Carrington was making it most difficult for Edward to refuse. "What would I tell her?"

"Say you're taking pity on her, that you've decided to help her find a husband. Think of it, Warwick! What better way to assure you're with her at all times? You can take her to Almack's and the theatre and various balls. During the day you can show her the city."

Bloody hell. Anyone seeing him with the Incomparable would never believe the relationship platonic. How long before Fiona got wind of it? "Why can't we say she's Harry's cousin? Let Harry deal with her. He's not promised to anyone."

"We don't know how many people she may have seen on the journey to London—people who already know the widow as Lady Warwick. It's also important that the other side associate her with Henshaw. All of us in the know—including the cursed Frenchies— were aware of Henshaw's use of the Warwick title when he fled England."

A very good point. Somehow, though, the thought of the French keeping a watchful eye on Henshaw's widow angered him.

Chapter 3

When Edward returned to Warwick House early that afternoon, Maggie was leaving her sister's chamber, a frown on her face. "Oh, my lord," she said as she looked up and saw him, "I regret to inform you my sister's quite ill."

She held that damned cat in her arms. Did she go nowhere without it?

His mouth formed a grim line. "A pity. I had hoped she would accompany us—for the sake of propriety—when I introduce you into society."

A spectrum of emotions flitted across that lovely face of hers. Then she smiled and said, "Perhaps she's not *that* ill."

"Won't you join me in my library?" he asked. "I wish to speak with you privately."

A moment later they were strolling into his sanctuary, a book-lined room of modest proportions. Because it was not too large and because he never allowed the fire there to go out, it was an incredibly comforting room that Edward preferred above all others. She took a seat across the cherry wood desk from him. The sun from the front window shone on her face, and he noted it cast a shadow beneath her luxuriously long lashes. His gaze traveled to her buttery muslin dress. Most becoming. Even if it did have a high neckline. Thank God the woman was possessed of good taste. Things could have been worse. What if Henshaw's widow dressed as a trollop? Or in rags?

"Is Miss Peabody really sick?" he asked in a stern voice.

She shook her head. "No, I'm afraid I was lying."

"But I thought you abhorred lying."

"I do, but I also told you I condone prevarication when it's used to help those I care about."

"How can the ruse of your sister being ill contribute to the well-being of those you hold dear?"

Her dark eyes flashed. He noted for the first time they were almond shaped. And especially large. "I had hoped it would prolong our departure from your home, my lord." Her voice diminished to a near whisper. "We're quite desperate at the moment."

He was prepared to dislike her. He disliked being forced to spend time with her, forced to have her—and her entourage—live under his roof. The woman had even admitted to being a liar! But, oddly, he thought she told the truth now. How difficult it must be for one raised as a gentlewoman to have to grovel to a stranger. Her present honesty touched him.

"Madame, I have considered what we discussed this morning and have decided to help you."

She did not answer for a moment. A puzzled look spanned her face. "But why, my lord?"

She was no simpleton, after all. She would never believe his assistance was offered purely from gentlemanly courtesy. More likely, she would think he lusted after her. Given her appearance, she would have spent most of her life repelling men's advances; therefore, he would make it clear his interest in her was in connection with her late husband, an admission Lord Carrington had approved. "You may have surmised my connection with the Foreign Office?"

"I thought perhaps you were." The tubby cat stood

up on her lap and stretched, then leaped to the floor and began to prowl around the library.

"We believe your husband may have said something to you, something that will help us learn who your late husband reported to."

"If I knew anything I would be happy to share it with you, but you must know The Scoundrel told me nothing but lies."

"Perhaps something will come to you. Some word, some action of Henshaw's that might be relevant. In the meantime I will contrive to introduce you into society."

"Under what name?" she asked.

"Lady Warwick."

Her fine brows arched.

"We shall say you secretly married my late uncle before he died. Given the fact no one knew the previous Lord Warwick—I never even met the man—no one will dispute your story."

"So that's how The Scoundrel was able to pass himself off as the earl," she said as if she were thinking aloud.

"Yes. Everyone knows the former Lord Warwick was a bachelor who had no interest in society."

Her face brightened. "So I really can stay Lady Warwick? How delightful!" Then her mouth puckered into a frown. "But I will have to tell the truth to my future husband."

"Of course." Edward found himself wondering what man would win the beauty's hand. With her extraordinary looks, her lack of fortune and family should not be too much of a hindrance.

"I must own," she said, "that having you call me Lady Warwick will make me feel decidedly presumptuous. Can we not think of something for you to call me when it's just us?" Her face screwed up. "But, please, not Mrs. Henshaw!"

"I could hardly call a woman who's been married Miss Peabody."

"I don't see why you couldn't call me Maggie—when no others are present. After all, I'm supposed to be your aunt." She giggled.

"It will be impossible for me to think of you as an aunt. I must be five or six years older than you."

"I am four and twenty." For that instant, as she looked up at him with those wide, innocent eyes, she didn't look a day over eighteen.

"And I am thirty."

"Perhaps I should call you uncle," she said with a laugh. "My lord, I am ever so grateful to you for allowing us to continue here." She paused, and her gaze went to the tall window framed in burgundy silk draperies. She watched a bird perched on a yew in the small courtyard behind his residence. "I do hate that people will think me mercenary for having married the old earl."

"Does that mean you won't consider marrying an old peer with one foot in the grave?"

Her lashes lowered as she considered her response. "I hope I don't have to. Despite that I've been burned, I'd still flirt with fire. I still believe in love, you see." She laughed. "I thought I was desperately in love with Lawrence Henshaw when I married him."

"Don't berate yourself," he consoled. "Many women were captured by Henshaw's charms."

She sighed. "That's why I need you. You can screen out all the ineligibles. And you must know, my lord, the prospective husband does not have to be rich. All I ask is to live comfortably, to have a home I can share with my sister and Sarah."

He presumed Sarah was the elderly maid. Most admirable. "What about love?" he asked.

A wistful look washed over her face. "I must first

find a man whom I admire. Admiration should be the foundation on which love is built. Do you not agree?"

He did. His love for Fiona had grown out of a deep, lifelong admiration and friendship.

Maggie's face brightened. "When do we begin?"

Despite that she was four and twenty, despite that she had been badly burned in her last relationship, she possessed a childlike enthusiasm. "Tonight. We shall go to the theatre. I've invited a few gentlemen to share my box." God help him if dear Fiona found out about his so-called aunt. He would write to Fiona straight away and apprise her that his uncle's secret wife had shown up. Later, when the business was resolved, he would tell Fiona the truth. "It's imperative that Miss Peabody accompany us."

"Of course," she said. "You won't wish your relationship with me to be misconstrued."

He nodded, then cleared his throat. "You have a suitable wardrobe?"

"Yes, quite. The Scoundrel—when we first married—insisted on purchasing all new finery for me. I hope the styles will not be too provincial."

He remembered how lovely she had looked last night in the rose-colored gown which was much more elegant than today's modest morning dress. Elegant, meaning it revealed the tops of her plump breasts. Really, it was not fair that one woman possessed so many magnificent physical attributes. "You dress with excellent taste, m—Maggie."

That wretched cat vaulted onto his lap, its claws hooking into Edward's thigh. "What in the blaz—"

Maggie leaped from her chair and circled his desk to pull the cat from his lap. "Tubby! You're being a very naughty boy!" She tried to hold the cat to her, but it went stiff-legged, then launched itself onto Edward's Turkey carpet and began to prance around the chamber as if he owned it.

Maggie's glance fell to Edward's lap which was covered in cat hair. "Oh, my lord, I'm so very sorry. Allow me to—" She reached toward his lap, but Edward quickly stood up. He would be damned if he'd let her stroke his thighs! "I can manage," he said as he began to brush the cat hair from his clothing. Then, grumbling, he sat back down.

She returned to her seat and folded her dainty hands in her lap.

"Now where were we?" he asked.

"We were discussing my wardrobe."

"Oh, yes. I'm sure what you'll wear to the theatre tonight will be adequate. Does your sister also have appropriate clothing?"

"Since she lived with me, I saw to it that she received as many new dresses as I."

Even though the sister was not yet out? "Henshaw must have been most generous, then. How long were you married?"

"We married almost two years ago."

"And how long before you found him out?"

"Six months after we were wed, I left him to reside with my half brother. It was really the most beastly timing. Had Papa died before I married, he would have divided his estate among the three of us, but he died after my wedding—thinking I was in perfectly comfortable circumstances and would also provide for Rebecca."

"And in so thinking, he left his entire estate to his son?"

"Yes," she said, frowning, "the son from an earlier marriage."

"You did not get on with your half brother?"

She shrugged. "James—my half brother—resented that Papa remarried after James's mother died, and his resentment, I'm afraid, extended to Rebecca and me. My brother and his wife made life quite impossible for my sister and me and, of course, they heartily disapproved of my separation from an 'English lord.'"

So poor Maggie really had no where else to turn. "Then I hope you'll be able to make your home in England."

"With an honest man!" she added with a laugh.

He stood up. "We dine at half past six. Then we'll go to Drury Lane."

Since Harry Lyle might be called upon to watch Maggie when Edward was unable to do so, Edward had invited him to be one of their number tonight. Rounding out their group were Basil Cook, who had been at Cambridge with Edward, and Lord Aynsley, a widower who was a dozen years Edward's senior. Since Edward's party was late arriving at the theatre—owing to the fact Miss Peabody (who dressed quite as elegantly as her sister tonight) had misplaced her spectacles—the three gentlemen awaited them in the Warwick box.

Edward introduced Maggie—as the widow of his late uncle—to the three, then said, "I hope you gentlemen can help me ensure Lady Warwick's first visit to London is agreeable."

The three men nearly knocked each other over while offering Maggie their services. Edward was rather pleased that Cook and Aynsley sat on either side of her, clearing him from culpability in reports to Fiona. He sat next to Harry in the row behind Maggie.

While Cook and Anysley vied for the lady's attention, Harry whispered to Edward, "You bloody, lucky dog."

Edward raised a brow. "What are you talking about?"

"I'm referring to your houseguest. Why did you not tell me she was a diamond of the first water?"

"Oh, do you think so?"

"Any man who is not blind would think so. Would that I'd drawn your assignment."

"I tried, old fellow."

"I will be most happy to keep a watch on the countess when you're unable to. I never thought filling in for you would be so rewarding a task."

Rewarding in what way? Surely Harry did not think to make love to her!

The theatre hushed when the curtains opened. Edward tried to concentrate on the production, but he was unable to do so. The elegant neck and bare, lily-white shoulders of Maggie, who sat in front of him, drew his attention away from the play, along with the immature antics of Cook and Aynsley, who were acting like a pair of schoolboys. *"Are you too cool, my lady? Shall I get your shawl? Is the light too dim for you to read the program? Have you seen* The Tempest *before?"* Edward was convinced neither man had absorbed a single word of the drama.

And for her part, Maggie was behaving entirely too charmingly. Did she have to feign such flattered interest in the pair of cads? It was positively provocative the way she lowered those lashes of hers when she spoke to them in that melodious voice.

Edward fumed. He should have known Cook would be the buffoon over Maggie. Because of his rotund appearance it was unlikely he had ever sat this close to such a beauty before. But for Lord Aynsley to make such a cake of himself! Had the man no pride?

By the fourth act, Harry bent his head to Edward and made a whispered declaration. "I believe I'm in love."

At first Edward thought Harry was referring to something about the play he himself could not get interested in. Then he followed the direction of Harry's glittering eyes. They never left Maggie.

"She needs a husband," Edward whispered, "and

you, my friend, are certainly in no position to take on the responsibility of a wife and her young sister."

Harry glowered. "I've been putting a little away."

A moment later, Harry added, "Let me come with you tomorrow when you go to the British Museum."

"You can't be spared," Edward snapped, seething. "You now have my work to do too."

"You bloody, lucky dog," Harry said.

On the carriage drive back to the townhouse Edward queried the pair of beauties who sat across from him. "How did you enjoy the play?"

"I've never enjoyed anything so much!" Rebecca said. "Thank you ever so much, my lord, for taking us."

He cocked a brow and met Maggie's gaze. "And you, Maggie?"

"I adored it," she said. "It was a most delightful evening, and your friends were exceedingly solicitous of me."

Rebecca scowled at her sister. "Men are always solicitous of you, Maggie."

"You shouldn't say such things in front of Lord Warwick. I declare, pet, you shall put me to the blush." She sent his lordship a humble look. Oddly, Maggie did not wish him to think her a practiced flirt.

"I believe you've made a conquest of Mr. Cook and Lord Aynsley," he said.

"And they are amiable men?"

"Honest men, yes. Cook is somewhat immature, and Aynsley, you must know, is a widower who seeks a mother for his seven children."

Why would his lordship have invited the men if he did not approve of them? Each of the men had been perfectly agreeable. A pity their appearances compared so poorly to Lord Warwick's. Maggie found herself wishing Lady Fiona had never been born. "He did not tell me he had seven children," she mused. "What ages are they?"

"How should I know?" Lord Warwick said with an agitated shrug. "I believe the eldest boy is at Eton. The rest must still be at home."

"Where does Lord Aynsley make his home?" she asked.

"In Shropshire. Why anyone would choose to live in that God-forsaken place I cannot tell you," he grumbled.

She felt responsible for Lord Warwick's ill temper. He obviously had not enjoyed the play, and he undoubtedly disliked having to ferry her and Rebecca around the city—almost as much as he disliked having the vexatious females invading his house. *The poor sourpuss.* "I shall ask Lord Aynsley about it tomorrow when he accompanies us to the museum. I'm sure there must be much to recommend the place."

Lord Warwick harrumphed.

"Since Mr. Cook and Lord Aynsley have so graciously consented to come tomorrow, you really don't have to, my lord," Maggie said. "You must have more important things to do than play city guide to a pair of colonials."

"I'm coming," he barked. "You—and your sister—are my responsibility, and I'll not be trusting you to a pair of buffoons."

"My lord," she said in a scolding voice, "how very unkind of you to malign your friends in such a way. Being very agreeable does not make them buffoons."

"I shouldn't have called them that. They are, both of them, fine men. And you'll meet more tomorrow night at Almack's. Expect to receive vouchers in the morning."

"Vouchers?"

He shrugged. "No one is accepted at Almack's who

has not been approved by its formidable patronesses, aristocrats all."

"Then you've obtained vouchers for Rebecca and me?" she asked, her admiration for him soaring.

"Actually, my friend Lord Carrington did."

"How very kind of him."

When they arrived at the townhouse, Maggie asked if they could eat a bite before retiring. What she did not tell him was that she hoped Lord Warwick would be in better humor once his belly was full.

They went downstairs to the kitchen and scrounged up three servings of plum pudding, then Lord Warwick walked with them as they mounted the stairs to their bedchambers.

When Rebecca reached her chamber door, she took the knob in her hand, then faced Edward, her eyes glistening with excitement. "Thank you again, my lord, for taking us to see Shakespeare."

"It was my pleasure," he said as she entered the room.

When they reached Maggie's door, she turned to him and offered her hand. "I'm ever so much indebted to you, my lord."

For once he did not speak to her as if he were the guardian and she the small child. "It's I who hope to be indebted to you, Maggie," he said with one of his rare smiles. Perhaps her ploy to improve his mood with food had worked.

She smiled and entered her bedchamber.

And screamed.

Chapter 4

"What the devil?" Edward spun around and raced to Maggie's room.

Her chamber door still open, she stood a few feet inside the room, a trembling hand cupped to her mouth as she surveyed the mammoth disarray in every corner of her chamber. "Someone's gone through all my things," she said in a quivering voice.

The linen press had been emptied, her entire wardrobe flung around the room as if by a cyclone. Contents of the dressing table spilled over its glass top; its drawers gaped open. Books fanned over the heaps of clothing, and all the coverings were stripped from her bed.

Grumbling a curse, Edward bolted to the adjoining dressing room and study in the hopes of catching the person responsible for this. "Bloody hell!" he cursed. Those rooms, too, had been completely ransacked.

And the intruder was gone.

When he returned to Maggie's bedchamber, that maid of hers, wearing a wrapper, her gray hair unbound, was attempting to sooth her mistress at the same time as Miss Peabody came flying into the room. Edward stalked to the windows and searched behind the draperies, then opened the casement to see if the perpetrator might be lurking outside. The sheer forty-foot drop to the pavement below convinced him no one could have come through these windows.

Next he went to the bed and looked under it. "Ouch!" he hissed, snatching back his hand.

Maggie raced to him, trembling all over. "What's wrong?"

"I believe your cat dislikes me excessively."

Maggie dropped to her knees and angled her head under the bed. "Poor Mr. Tubs," she crooned. "Did that bad man scare you?"

Edward was outraged. "I'm not a bad man. It's your damn cat who's the bad one."

"Oh, I didn't mean *you* were bad, my lord. I was referring to the intruder. He must have frightened poor Tubby out of his fur," she said after she coaxed the cat from beneath the bed and cradled it to her generous bosom. With a cracking voice, she added, "I was afraid whoever did this might have harmed Tubby."

Edward could be so lucky. "Whoever did this is long gone," he reassured Maggie. He had expected to find tears racing down her cheeks since his brief acquaintance with her had confirmed her propensity to hysterics. Surprisingly, no tears gathered in her frightened eyes now, even though she was more upset than he had ever seen her.

"See if Mama's pearls are missing," Rebecca instructed her sister.

Petting the loudly purring cat, Maggie strode to an open drawer of her dressing table and began sorting through the jewels it contained. "They're here," she said in a lifeless voice.

"Try to remember what jewelry you had so we can determine what's missing," Rebecca said.

The sisters' roles reversed, he thought. The trembling elder sister was nearly in shock while the younger sister kept a level head.

He came to set a gentle hand on Maggie's bare

shoulder. Fortunately, the damn cat didn't try to draw blood this time. "You've nothing to fear," Edward said in a low voice. "Whoever did this had no wish to face you. Rest assured I'll have a footman guard your room every night you're here." His voice gentled. "Sit down, pull yourself together, and try to determine what's missing."

She lowered herself into the chair in front of her dressing table which was illuminated by a pair of crystal lustres, and she began to more carefully examine the jewelry drawer. "I had very little in the way of valuable jewels," she said, her voice still shaking. "Here's the ruby ring The Scoundrel placed on my finger the day we married. He also gave me an emerald necklace I sold to finance our trip to England." She continued to examine what looked to Edward to be mostly worthless jewelry. "I don't think anything's missing," she said, looking up at him with sorrowful eyes.

"Now would you look at this!" the maid shrieked. She held up a green silk gown, its bodice slashed as if by a knife.

Rebecca rushed to the maid. "Why would someone do this to Maggie's clothes?"

Edward had a very good idea. Someone was looking for something. Something that Lawrence Henshaw must have given to his wife. Or something that someone *thought* Henshaw had given to his wife. "Sarah," he said, rather pleased that he had actually remembered the elderly maid's name.

She eyed him with a quizzing gaze. "Yes, my lord?"

"Will you be able to determine if any of your mistress's clothing is missing?" he asked.

"I most certainly can. Just give me a few minutes." She and Rebecca set about restoring the clothing to the linen press, both of the women muttering oaths as they discovered every dress slashed.

"There now, Miss Maggie, don't you fret," Sarah

said. "We've got just enough pieces of fabric left to repair these beautiful gowns, and no one will ever be able to tell that a madman went on this rampage."

"He certainly was a madman," Rebecca concurred as she folded a piece of gauzy linen—a nightshift, if Edward wasn't mistaken. Against his sorely tried will, he pictured Maggie in the soft, lacy shift. And cursed his traitorous physical reaction.

Maggie gave Edward a morose look. "Why would someone do this to me?"

He set his hand to her trembling shoulder. "Someone obviously believes your late husband left something valuable in your care." *Something valuable to the Foreign Office—or to the French.* That someone was aware that Henshaw's widow was in London, that she was staying at Warwick House, that she had gone to the theatre tonight. The very idea of someone sneaking into his house chilled Edward.

Almost as much as the realization that Maggie could be in grave danger.

Maggie's lashes lowered, a look of pain clinching her face. "What if I hadn't insisted Sarah not wait up for me? Would they have harmed her?"

He wished he could reassure Maggie, but he honestly did not know how far this depraved person was willing to go to get whatever it was Henshaw had. "You mustn't worry yourself over *what ifs*. All that matters now is my pledge to you that this will not happen again, that I will make sure you're always protected."

"And Rebecca and Sarah?" Maggie asked in a woeful voice.

"Miss Peabody and Sarah will be fine." *It's you they want.*

"Your lordship?" Rebecca said.

He met the girl's gaze. "Yes?"

"Nothing's missing."

"I wish something were!" Maggie exclaimed. "I'd

much rather this vile person be a common thief than a—" She looked up at him with a questioning gaze.

He wished he could lie to her, to reassure her that nothing like this would ever be repeated, but she was too intelligent to be deceived by empty promises.

He summoned a housemaid to make Maggie's bed, then he called for Wiggins. "Someone's entered the house tonight with the intention of stealing Lady Warwick's things," he told the butler. "Did you or any of the servants see anyone?"

"No, my lord, and I've questioned the footman. Hawkins had duty in the front hall, and he swears he did not sleep. No one came up the front stairs."

"What of the servants' stairs?" Edward asked.

Wiggins shrugged. "After ten o'clock—when we were in our beds—no one was stirring in the back of the house. Whoever did this"—he eyed Maggie's bed chamber—"must have sneaked in after we were asleep."

"Was the back door locked?"

"I couldn't say, my lord."

Edward cursed. "Please question all the servants and let me know if you learn something. And, Wiggins . . ."

"Yes, my lord?"

"Make sure the doors are locked at all times."

"Very good, my lord."

With the housemaid's assistance, Rebecca and Sarah were able to finish tidying the chambers in ten minutes, then Edward dismissed them.

Maggie still sat before her dressing table, the candlelight flickering in her dark tresses, her hand absently stroking the contented cat in her lap.

"Whether you are aware of it or not," he said to her, "your husband must have entrusted something to you. Something that someone here in England might be willing to kill for. Think, Maggie. Was there anything Henshaw gave you for safekeeping?"

From where he stood, Edward could look down at her and see that the bodice of her snow white dress barely contained her rounded breasts. Breasts Henshaw would have touched, might even have pressed his lips to. *Damn the man.*

Her eyes flashing, she suddenly leaped from her chair and raced to her dressing room, Edward on her heels.

"It's gone!" she said.

"What's gone?"

"The Scoundrel's things. I kept his effects in a small leather case."

Edward's gaze swept over the room. "What things?"

She sighed. "A ring, a pair of diamond spurs, a letter from a man in Greenwich, a Fielding book . . ." She bit at her lip. "There was something else . . . oh yes, a map."

"A map of what?"

She shrugged. "Some county in England. One of those that begins with an H."

"Hampshire? Hertfordshire?"

"Hertfordshire," she said.

"Was there any marking on the map?"

She shook her head.

"What about the Fielding book? Any markings on it?"

She thought for a moment. "In the flyleaf. There was a name. I thought it the previous owner of the book. There was a name and city."

"What name?"

She frowned. "I paid no attention to it, really. If you were to call it out right now I doubt I'd recognize it. But I remember distinctly the name of the man in Greenwich. It was Andrew Bibble."

The name meant nothing to Edward. "What did the letter say?"

She frowned in concentration. "It was only a sentence

or two. It seemed Mr. Bibble was going into mourning after having buried their mutual friend."

"What was the mutual friend's name?"

"The name was not given, my lord."

"Are you sure?"

"Quite. As I said, the letter was very brief."

"I'm so very vexed with myself," she said a moment later.

"Why?" he asked.

"Knowing The Scoundrel as I did, I should have realized he wasn't an earl. Wouldn't an earl have been in possession of a signet ring and have a solicitor's address? The Scoundrel had neither. I was so beastly blind!"

"Don't be so harsh on yourself. It's only natural to assume someone's telling the truth about his own name." He set a hand to her trim waist and fought the urge to draw her to him. Instead, he nudged her back to the bedchamber where she returned to her seat in front of the dressing table. Edward forced his glance to look no lower than her chin.

"Why did you not sell the spurs and ring?" he asked.

"Because I thought they belonged to the new earl."

How could such a dishonest person be so honest, he wondered.

"I wish, my lord, I could contribute in some small way to repairing the damage my late husband did."

"Perhaps you have."

"Andrew Bibble?"

"Most promising." He started toward the door. "I'll send notes around to Aynsley and Cook to cancel tomorrow's outing."

She spun around to face him, her brows arched.

"I'd prefer that you stay here until I can . . . learn more," he said. "I'll be better able to protect you—and your sister—here than on the streets of London." He had purposely thrown in her sister to ensure Maggie's compliance.

"Then I most certainly hope you can 'learn more' quickly, my lord. I am most anxious to see the capital."

"And secure a husband," he said with a smile.

"The sooner I do, the sooner you'll be rid of me and all the strife I seem to have brought into your home."

Now she was making him feel the curmudgeon. "Pray, don't spare a thought on such trivialities. Your presence here may turn out to be rather fortunate—for my work, you understand," he added.

She gave a false laugh. "Good night, my lord. I hope the distress of tonight's events doesn't rob you of sleep."

"That is my wish for you, Maggie," he said in a gentle voice.

When he left her room he came upon Wiggins, whose lanky body stood as sentry outside Maggie's door.

"I'll need you to rouse a footman to keep guard over Lady Warwick's chambers," Edward instructed the butler, "and I'll need a fire and candles in the library."

"Yes, my lord."

"And Wiggins?"

"Yes, my lord?"

"Arrange the servants' schedules so that one of them is available to guard the lady's room every night."

"As you wish, my lord."

A few minutes later Edward was pacing the Turkey carpet of his library. Something even more menacing than what had happened here tonight upset him. *Someone in the Foreign Office is a traitor.* A few minutes ago he had tried to block such an accusation from his mind. Surely Henshaw was the only traitor in their office. None of their work had been foiled since Henshaw left.

But the longer Edward reflected on it, the stronger his conviction grew.

Why had no one ever tried to find Henshaw's documents in the four months since his death? It wasn't until Edward told Lord Carrington, Harry Lyle, and Charles Kingsbury of Henshaw's widow that the woman had come into peril. He felt bloody responsible for her—and for anything that threatened her.

Everything in Edward wanted to believe tonight's intruder acted solely for the French, eager to get some kind of document that identified Napoleon's spies acting in England. But if that were the case, they would not have waited for Maggie to come all the way to London. How easy it would have been to accost an unprotected woman on the road from Portsmouth. That they had waited until she was under Edward's protection proved they did not know of her existence until Edward revealed it to his trusted colleagues that morning.

He must find out if the three men who knew of Maggie's situation had told anyone else in the Foreign Office.

Otherwise, one of Edward's three most trusted coworkers was a traitor.

That person was desperate to get something Henshaw had. But what? Had Henshaw not acted alone? Could he incriminate someone in the Foreign Office?

Who in the hell was responsible for tonight's break-in? Certainly not Lord Carrington. He was too great a patriot. Besides, what could the French give him that he did not already possess? And the culprit could not be Harry, who was Edward's closest friend and as fine a man as he had ever known. Edward was more inclined to believe the traitor was Charles Kingsbury, a loner who was not especially well liked, though his intense passion for his job had always impressed Edward.

Edward determined that a document of some sort

was being sought. Why else would they have slashed Maggie's dresses? They must have thought she might have sewn it into the lining of her bodice.

God help her if tonight's booty proved worthless.

He went to his desk and dashed off notes to Aynsley and Cook. Damn, but he was tired! He glanced at the clock on the mantel. It was half past three. Another night of impaired sleep. He might as well go to bed.

Cummings awaited in Edward's chambers. "See that these are delivered in the morning," Edward told him, handing him the notes to Aynsley and Cook. He was so beastly tired it was all he could do to lift his arms to remove the shirt.

"I shan't wake you in the morning, my lord. What you need is a good night's sleep."

"A very good plan, Cummings."

As he lay in his bed he pictured Maggie's face when she had entered her chambers earlier that night. Pure, red-hot fear stamped itself across that lovely face. Was that fear because she knew firsthand how vile her husband's accomplices were?

If Andrew Bibble turned out to be genuine, Maggie's trustworthiness would be confirmed.

Heaven help him, he was beginning to trust her. And wished like the devil he didn't.

Chapter 5

"You bloody, lucky dog," Harry greeted Edward, narrowing his eyes in an exaggerated scowl.

"There's nothing bloody lucky about having one's home broken into because the Incomparable's there."

Harry's brows plunged as he slammed some maps onto his desk and spun toward Edward. "Is she, has she—"

"She's fine," Edward assured his concerned friend, "except for being scared out of her wits."

"When did it happen?"

"Sometime between the servants' bedtime and our arrival home from the theatre last night."

"So you didn't actually see the culprit, then?" Harry said, relief in his voice.

"No, damn it." Edward thanked God the break-in occurred when they were away from home. He hated to think what might have happened to Maggie had she been in the room when the intruder entered.

"What was taken?"

"A case with Henshaw's few belongings."

"The lady's chambers were the only ones disturbed?"

"The only ones," Edward said with a frown.

Harry grumbled a curse. "You know what this means?"

"I bloody well do. It means no one knew of the lady's existence until I shared the information yesterday."

"How many people did you tell?"

"Only you, Lord Carrington, and Kingsbury."

Harry's eyes narrowed. "Do you think one of us is responsible?"

"That's a distinct possibility." Edward lowered himself into his own chair some four feet away from Harry's desk and began to rifle through some correspondence that had been placed on his desk. He did not like a disorderly desk. "Did you mention the widow to anyone?"

"No," Harry said in a somber voice. "And I didn't do it."

"I know, old fellow."

"It must be Kingsbury. Goodness knows the man could use some extra income."

"Not all men are as fond of horses, women, and spirits as you," Edward said.

"Surely he'd like a mount of his own. What man wouldn't?"

"Let's not rush to conclusions. Perhaps Kingsbury or Lord Carrington told someone about Maggie's existence. Someone who's the actual thief."

"God help us if they didn't," Harry mumbled. "You haven't left the countess on Curzon Street unwatched, have you?"

"She's not a countess."

"I know. I'm merely staying in character like any good spy."

"You're not a spy."

"Can't one demonstrate one's natural aptitude for spying?"

Edward chuckled.

"Lord Carrington told me that in the event you could not keep watch over Lady Warwick, the 'chore' would fall to me, that she wasn't ever to be left alone."

"My valet's under orders not to let her out of his

sight. I'll be away only long enough to apprise Lord Carrington of last night's occurrence."

"He's in this morning."

In his superior's office, Edward narrated the events of the previous evening. "Did you, my lord, perchance mention the widow to anyone?" Edward asked.

Lord Carrington thought a moment before shaking his head firmly. "Who else did you tell about her?"

"Only Lyle and Kingsbury, and Lyle says he didn't tell anyone."

The marquis rang for his secretary and when the gaunt man entered the room, asked, "Did you discuss Henshaw's widow with anyone?"

Who would Kingsbury tell, Edward wondered. It wasn't as if the man had any friends.

"Of course not! Information I glean in a professional capacity is of the most confidential nature."

Kingsbury's response was in keeping with the man's obsession over his work. He was the first to arrive every morning and the last to leave, allegiance Edward attributed to the fact that Kingsbury's work was his whole life.

Lord Carrington nodded. "That will be all, Kingsbury."

Once Kingsbury had closed the door, Carrington spoke in a grave voice. "Either one of my most trusted men is a traitor, or the enemy has extraordinary means of surveillance."

"I hope it's the latter, but I'm not confident."

Carrington raked his hand through his graying hair, his face grimaced. "Nor am I."

"The widow was most forthcoming in disclosing what was in her husband's case."

"Any prospects?"

"Perhaps. There was a map of Hertfordshire, a Fielding novel, and a brief letter from a man in Greenwich."

"Did she know the man's name?"

"Andrew Bibble. Ever hear of him?"

Carrington shook his head. "I'll see what I can learn. What did the letter say?"

"Something about going into mourning for their mutual—unnamed—friend.

"That's all?"

Edward nodded.

"Was there anything else in Henshaw's possession when he died?"

"Only a pair of diamond spurs and a ring."

"If the widow is to be believed."

Edward's first instinct was to defend her. Instead, he said, "Yes, *if.* "

"Go back to Curzon Street and don't let her out of your sight."

Edward had never heard Carrington's voice so harsh before.

When he returned to the townhouse, his valet informed Edward that Maggie had not gone belowstairs during his master's absence. Edward sniffed. His home damn near smelled like a perfumery. "What the deuce is that smell? The whole floor reeks."

"That would be the mistress's flowers, my lord."

"What flowers?"

"She has received no less than five bouquets this morning."

"Anysley and Cook," Edward muttered.

"And Mr. Lyle."

"Who do they think they are? Turning my house into a damned orangery?" Edward growled. "I'll be in my library."

He really did need to send off a letter to dearest Fiona.

Before he had completed one sentence of that letter, a light knock sounded at the door.

"Yes?"

The dark wood door eased open, and Maggie poked her head in. "Am I disturbing you, my lord?"

"No. Please come in," he said. He had all day to write his letter since he had nothing else to do, owing to the lady standing before him—standing before him in a sumptuous aqua gown that dipped low at the neckline. He hated to stare at her as she gracefully moved toward him, but the disparity between her left breast (the high one) and the right one stole his attention. He was beginning to know those breasts fairly well—at least by sight—and was certain the nipples had been in perfect horizontal alignment last night.

She dropped onto the chair in front of his desk. "I'm perfectly aware that you're perfectly aware that my breasts are somewhat lopsided."

In the span of an eye blink he forced his gaze back to her face. How was he to reply? *Oh no, madame, your breasts are not lopsided* or *No, I hadn't noticed* when his eyes had been upon her bosom like ink on paper. He cleared his throat and willed himself to look no farther south than her chin. He seemed to be willing himself to do that a lot lately. "Is that what you wished to speak to me about?" he asked.

"Dear no! I've come to offer you my help."

"How, madame, do you think you can help me?" *For one, she could wear a high-necked dress.*

"I wish to assist you in apprehending the person responsible for last night's theft."

"I hardly think such a skill within your capabilities, madame."

"I don't mean I could *personally* apprehend the vile creature. What I meant was that I wish to help you learn the culprit's identity. I'm determined to make up for all the annoyances my stay in your home is costing you. You are stuck here with nothing but wretched females for companionship because you feel compelled to guard me. And you fear that your horse-faced fiancée—" She suddenly stopped, her face flaming.

"My what?"

"Forgive me, my lord. I should never have voiced my unfounded thoughts."

"Why, pray tell, would you think my affianced horse-faced?"

"Have you known her all your life?"

"Most of my life, but what does that have to do with her being horse-faced—not that she is, of course."

"I fancied that marriages among the aristocrats are rather arranged by families. From the time you were quite small, I daresay it was understood you'd marry a woman of Lady Fiona's class."

"Of course."

"You would not have been permitted to marry someone from a diverse background."

"Diversity does not make for good bedfellows."

"You see, the necessity of marrying within classes has been ingrained into you."

"Am I missing the horse connection or were you planning to get to it?"

"I don't know why you're talking about horses, my lord."

"I'm not talking about horses! You brought up their faces in connection with my lovely intended."

"So I did."

"Well?"

"Well what, my lord?"

"Explain, if you will, why you say my betrothed has a horse face."

"How should I know what Lady Fiona looks like? I've never seen her. Have you a likeness of her?"

"No." He could see the irrelevance of continuing in this vein.

"Oh, dear, where were we when all this started? Oh, yes, I was saying my presence in your home is causing you considerable worry over how your *lovely* intended will view it. In short, my lord, nothing about my presence has given you anything but grief. Now, I mean to make up for it."

She really was quite childlike. "How do you intend to do that?" he asked.

"By helping you learn the perpetrator's identity, of course. We shall be a team. You and I." She leaned toward him and lowered her voice. His traitorous eyes dipped to the valley between her ivory breasts. Then he jerked his gaze away. "I felt compelled to warn you, my lord. I believe someone you know is responsible for stealing into my rooms last night. Someone whom you told of my presence in your house."

"That, madame, has already occurred to me."

"See, we do make a team! Have you given any thought to Andrew Bibble?"

"I have."

"And still the name means nothing to you?"

"Nothing."

"Then I suggest you and I travel to Greenwich and locate the man. Perhaps he knows something that will be of help."

"If I *did* wish to travel to Greenwich I would not need you to accompany me."

"You're still worried about me? I'm confident that last night's intruder wishes me no harm now that he's got The Scoundrel's things."

Her logic made some sense. Perhaps she was not in danger, after all. And Edward had to admit he was itching to go to Greenwich—but not with Maggie. However, under Carrington's orders Edward was not allowed to leave her. Therefore . . . if he did go to Greenwich, she would have to accompany him.

But not her sister.

"Pray, madame, why would your presence be needed in Greenwich?"

She shrugged. "If I could meet this Mr. Bibble and talk to him, perhaps something The Scoundrel told me might resurface. I shan't know it until it hits me in the face."

Was her optimism contagious? Her speaking with Andrew Bibble *did* suddenly seem promising. "I'm willing to give it a try. Tomorrow?"

"That would be lovely," she said.

"My gig only holds two."

"That is most comforting. I daresay I could not pry Rebecca away from the current book—which she vows the most interesting ever—and since reading in a moving vehicle makes her dreadfully sick, she'll be only too happy to stay home. And there's no need to protect my virtue, given that I've been a married woman."

His rampant gaze trailed down her graceful white neck. And fixated on those lopsided breasts. "About your breasts . . ." he said, thinking aloud. Good Lord! What was he doing asking a single woman—a gentlewoman—about her bosom? His gaze jerked back to her face.

"Oh, yes, I meant to explain."

Explain how breasts that were perfect last night could have altered today? He carefully watched her eyes, afraid to blink for fear of raking his gaze once again over her "interesting" bosom.

"It's because Sarah's eyes aren't what they used to be."

"I fail to see what your maid has to do with your . . ."

"Breasts," she finished. "Actually she doesn't have a thing to do with my breasts. It's the bodices. The ones that were slashed last night. She repaired this one . . ." Her gaze lowered. "And as you can see the left side is quite tight and uplifting while I'm sorry to say the right is much lower. Not that they're that way normally. The breasts, I mean." Her face turned scarlet. "Oh dear, I can't believe I'm discussing such an indelicate subject with you, my lord. It's just that I wished to explain so that you would not think me deformed—for I know that you noticed my . . ."

"That will do, madame. I can see that your maid's eyesight prevents her from being a proper seamstress."

"And I'm no better. My needlework is abominable—as is Rebecca's."

"Due to her obsession with books."

"Yes, my lord."

"Has Miss Peabody no other interests?"

"Only reading. She's passionate about books."

"Romances?"

"All books. She's even read *Plato's Dialogues*—a most disappointing book, I thought. By the time I'd read seventy-two pages I had quite decided I much preferred Shakespeare's dialogues. They're much more interesting."

He smiled. "Plato writes about ideas, Shakespeare about people."

"And people are so much more interesting than, say, classification."

Her attempts to discredit her own intelligence failed miserably. He knew no women who had even a passing knowledge of classification. "I shall instruct your maid to gather up all your dresses, and we'll have a mantua maker put them to rights."

"I shouldn't want to be an expense on you."

"You came to my house with a perfectly serviceable wardrobe which was damaged under my roof. Whatever happens under my roof is my responsibility."

"Yes, my lord," she said meekly. She went to get up.

"Oblige me by wearing a pelisse or some such overgarment tomorrow when we travel to Greenwich."

"If the weather's as dank as it is today, I daresay I'll be wrapped in my heaviest wool cloak."

Good.

Chapter 6

"Do put that book down!" Maggie said to Rebecca as she closed her sister's door and came to throw herself on Rebecca's bed. "Your poor sister needs a sympathetic ear."

Rebecca shut her book and peered at Maggie through her spectacles. "You're still upset over last night?"

"Of course I'm upset over last night, but right now I'm even more upset over my idiotic practice of thinking aloud. In Lord Warwick's presence."

"Oh, dear. You didn't tell him he was built like a Greek god, did you?"

"That would have been preferable to what I did babble."

A lively flash lit Rebecca's eyes. "Pray, what *did* you babble?"

"That his betrothed is horse-faced!"

Rebecca's mouth dropped open. "What could have possessed you to say that?"

"Don't you remember me telling you his forthcoming marriage was likely arranged by their families years ago? That his affianced was probably some horse-faced peeress?"

"Oh, dear. You didn't say that in front of Lord Warwick?"

Maggie sighed. "I did indeed."

Rebecca giggled. "What did his lordship say?"

"He was outraged. He wanted to know why I would describe his *lovely Fiona* in such a manner. Then I'm afraid I really began to babble, and I'm sure he had no idea why I was trying to justify calling that blasted Fiona horse-faced."

"I've told you a thousand times," Rebecca scolded, "to think before you speak."

"Yes, but owing to the fact you're seven years my junior, by the time you were able to coach me to mend my ways, I was much too set them in."

"If you could just speak more slowly. That would give you time to phrase your thoughts."

"That's easy for you to say, you of little social intercourse."

Rebecca leaned back to one side of the window seat she had adopted as her prime reading ground. "Is Lord Warwick angry with you?"

Maggie thought about it a moment. "Oddly, I don't think he is."

"He was probably too distracted over your bosom."

A smile lifted the corners of Maggie's lips. "Do you think so?"

"I don't mean *good* distracted. He most likely thought you deformed."

"Oh, I explained that to him."

"Surely you didn't call his attention to your breasts!"

"I couldn't have him thinking I was deformed."

"I vow I could never discuss my breasts in the presence of a man."

"After you've been married you can."

A deep blush settled into Rebecca's cheeks.

"He's going to have a mantua maker repair all my gowns," Maggie continued.

"You're not accepting more of Lord Warwick's charity?"

"I told him I did not wish to, but he said he's responsible for anything that occurs under his roof."

"I suppose that does make sense. It wasn't your fault a madman ruined all your clothing. Lord Warwick should have his house better guarded."

"Yes, but the intruder would not have done his nasty work had I not been here."

"It's not your fault your husband was so vile a creature."

"Oh, pet," Maggie said with a sigh, "I feel so wretched that my disastrous marriage—along with that man-hating Miss Broom—has soured you on men and on love. I could positively box that governess's ears for scaring you away from men, telling you that all men want to steal your virtue. Not all men are vile, you know." Lord Warwick could never be wicked. Maggie fleetingly thought of how kind and gentle he had been to her last night when she had been so horridly upset. And he had no desire to get beneath her skirts. He had told her so. Besides, she couldn't imagine him doing something improper. She pictured his embarrassed face this morning when he had inadvertently mentioned her breasts.

"I'm glad you've brought that up," Rebecca said, "for I have quite decided that not all men are dastardly."

Maggie gave her sister an amused glance. "To what do we owe your change of heart?"

Rebecca held her book to her breast, a dreamy look in her eyes. "To Mr. Darcy."

"Who is Mr. Darcy?"

"The hero of *Pride and Prejudice.*"

"I take it *Pride and Prejudice* is the name of the current tome?"

"It's not precisely a tome. It's a novel. The most wonderful novel I've ever read, actually."

"That's heady praise, indeed, given your vast reading experience. I shall have to read it when you finish."

"You may have it in the morning, for I shan't be able to sleep until I've read the last word."

"I do wish you wouldn't read the night through.

You'll ruin your already-deficient eyes, and where would you be if you were blind?"

"I should die if I couldn't read," Rebecca said in a mournful voice.

Maggie sighed. "Don't fret, pet. If you go blind I vow I'll read to you." She looked around the room. "Is Tubby here? I've looked everywhere for him."

"I haven't seen him this morning. He's probably hiding after being petrified last night."

"A pity he's not a dog. If he were a dog, he could have attacked the wretched intruder."

Just to be sure the cat wasn't in the room, Maggie looked under Rebecca's bed, but he wasn't there. "I shan't be able to read about your Mr. Darcy tomorrow. I'll be going to Greenwich with his lordship," Maggie said when she straightened up.

Rebecca gaped at Maggie over the rims of her spectacles. "Unchaperoned?"

"Now you sound like Miss Broom. I have no innocent reputation to protect. I've been a married woman."

"Think you Lord Warwick wishes to get beneath your skirts?"

"Do quit talking like Miss Broom! I'm certain the only skirts Lord Warwick wishes to get beneath are Lady Fiona's." *More's the pity.*

"Then why does he wish to take you to Greenwich?"

"Actually, he doesn't wish to take me. I asked him to take me."

Rebecca pushed her spectacles back up to the bridge of her nose. "Why?"

"Because The Scoundrel was in possession of a letter from a man in Greenwich—a letter that was stolen last night."

"I still don't understand why you wish to go to Greenwich."

"I'm not precisely sure myself," Maggie said, biting

at her lip. "I only know that if I can talk to this man, perhaps I can remember something The Scoundrel may have mentioned—something that might help Lord Warwick sort out why someone's so mad to get ahold of The Scoundrel's things."

"I don't know which is worse. The Scoundrel's propensity to cavort with lewd women—excluding yourself, of course—or his being a traitor to his country."

"Being a traitor, for certain! His betrayal cost many English lives. Besides, many worthy men, I am told, associate with prostitutes."

"Mr. Darcy wouldn't."

Maggie found herself wondering if Lord Warwick would. He seemed much too straight-laced to sully himself with that sort of woman. But, of course, he *was* a man. Unsummoned, she pictured him as he had looked two nights ago, standing shirtless near the top of the stairs, his physique tall and athletic, his countenance reeking of power. The sudden vision of him lying against her naked flesh ignited a searing heat that rose up from her torso and settled in pebbles of perspiration on her brow. She was possessed of the oddest feeling that little puffs of clouds floated within her.

She moved toward Rebecca's door and spoke breathlessly. "I'll see you at dinner."

"Be sure to drape a shawl around your bosom so that Lord Warwick doesn't choke on his food while gaping at your breasts."

Lord Warwick was not in good humor at dinner. "Madame," he said to Maggie in a sharp tone as soon as she sat at his table, "can you tell me why that cat of yours has claimed *my* library as his . . . his throne room."

Maggie did not like anyone to malign her cat. Her spine went taut. "He has a name."

"Tubby," Lord Warwick spat out. "Every piece of

furniture designed for sitting in my library is covered with gray cat hair, and the beast has now claimed the windowsill beside my desk for his principal throne."

Maggie knotted the Kashmir shawl at her neck and spoke stiffly. "Tubby is not a beast."

"By some definitions," Rebecca interjected, "cats most certainly are beasts."

"Thank you," Edward said, nodding to Rebecca.

Maggie's eyes shot daggers at her sister. "Beast, you must admit, has decidedly negative connotations."

Rebecca shrugged.

"I don't need a lesson on word etymology," Lord Warwick said. "I want to know why your . . . ahem, animal, chooses to spend his days lounging in my sacred library."

Maggie bristled. "Pardon me, my lord, I did not know your wretched library was *sacred*. Do you have a shrine there I perhaps neglected to see?"

"You know what I mean!" he said in a harsh voice.

"My lord," Rebecca said calmly, "my sister is unusually sensitive to any censure of her cat." She scowled at Maggie. "Her misplaced anger has overruled her deep indebtedness to you for your kind hospitality."

Of course her sister was right. "I'm sorry, my lord," Maggie said meekly.

"I daresay it's not your fault that animal of yours has taken to destroying my library," he conceded.

Maggie's eyes widened. "I assure you, my lord, that cat hair can easily be removed from your furnishings."

He stared down his aristocratic nose at her. "What about the torn draperies?"

"What torn draperies?"

"Your . . . Tubby took a running leap, launched himself on my silken draperies and attempted to climb them."

"Oh, dear," Maggie said, then she stiffened and

glared at him. "I shall see to it that my maid repairs the damage tomorrow."

To which Lord Warwick burst out laughing.

When Maggie realized what the draperies would look like if Sarah attempted the repair, she too began to laugh.

Then Rebecca joined in.

The rest of the dinner went more smoothly than the beginning. They spoke amiably. He told them the vouchers had come for Almack's but because of his fears for Maggie's safety they would wait until next week to attend. He explained the strict decorum that was observed at Almack's. He and Rebecca discussed her favorite authors and he told the ladies they had barely escaped one of the coldest Januaries Londoners had ever experienced.

"Then I am most happy we did not come in January," Maggie said, "for February is quite cold enough for me."

When they were finished eating, Lord Warwick asked the ladies to join him in a card game. "Or do you not play cards, Miss Peabody?"

"Despite what my sister says, I do have other interests besides reading, but as it happens tonight I shall have to bow out."

"You will see that my sister has brought the current book to the dinner table," Maggie said. "She tells me she won't sleep tonight until she's completed it."

"Pray, what is the title of the book that demands such attention?" he asked.

"*Pride and Prejudice*," Rebecca answered.

He nodded. "By 'A Lady.' An excellent book." He rose from the table and eyed Maggie. "I hope you will do me the goodness of playing backgammon or chess with me, madame."

"I dislike backgammon," Maggie said, setting her

hand on his proffered arm. "I dislike all games whose outcome is ruled only by chance."

"Then we are in agreement on something," he said, steering her toward the saloon. "I daresay your opinions are not shared by others of your sex. It's been my observation that most women dislike chess." He looked over his shoulder at Rebecca, who followed behind them, her nose in the book.

In the saloon, Rebecca and her book plopped on the sofa while Maggie sat at the game table where Lord Warwick was setting up the chess pieces.

Out of the corner of her eye Maggie saw Tubby come waddling into the room on soft paws. He walked around the room, investigating its every nook and came to leap on the silken sofa where Rebecca sat with the book on her lap. Tubby proceeded to try to sit on the open pages of the book.

Rebecca tossed him on the carpet. "You really are the most maddening creature."

Lord Warwick whirled around. When he saw Tubby, his eyes narrowed, an act that did not escape Maggie's notice.

"Does my cat's presence in your *sacred* saloon offend you, my lord?"

"The saloon is not my sacred chamber. My library is. And, no, your cat's presence does not offend me so long as he keeps his distance."

Once he had the board set up they began to play. At first they both were intent upon the game, but as Maggie sat there watching his brooding face, something touched her heart. He might dislike having her and Rebecca—and Tubby—under his roof, but he was being quite a gentleman about the whole thing. She felt guilty that Lord Warwick must share so dull an evening with a woman he could barely tolerate when he would most likely prefer to be at his club with other young bucks. The man's immunity to her

charms was really most vexing, and it was all because
of Lady Fiona—a woman Maggie was envying more
with each passing hour.

"My lord?" she said.

His amber eyes locked with hers.

"I'm really very sorry that Tubby has so vexed you.
I'll see that he stays out of your library." It was the least
she could do since he had been so kind to them.

"Now you're making me feel like an ogre."

"You're not an ogre," she said in a whispery voice.
"You're . . ." She did not finish.

His glance trailed from her face to her bosom,
which was thankfully covered by the shawl. He swallowed, then moved his pawn.

She admired his play and knew she was outmatched
though she managed to hold her own. After two and
a half hours Lord Warwick realized they would be unable to finish the game that night. "We need to rise
early," he said, "if we're to go to Greenwich. I suggest
we resume play another night."

His eyes, indeed his whole face, looked tired. "Yes,
my lord, I think we both could benefit from a good
night's sleep."

They rose from the table, and Maggie called for Rebecca to come to bed. Lord Warwick offered his arm
to Maggie as they began to mount the stairs, Rebecca
behind them. "Your sister never stumbles while walking and reading at the same time?" he asked Maggie.

Maggie turned around and saw Rebecca's bent
head scanning the pages of the book she held with
both hands. "I beg that you don't read while climbing
stairs! You'll—"

"Break into a thousand pieces," Rebecca finished,
closing her book, holding her place with a thumb.

As they neared the top of the stairs, Edward said, "I
wish to compliment you on your play."

"Thank you, my lord. Unfortunately, you are even better."

"The game's outcome is still unknown." They exchanged good nights as Rebecca entered her chamber.

They nodded to the footman who guarded Maggie's door, then she lifted her face to Lord Warwick. "I do hope you finally get a good night's sleep, my lord."

"We shall both need it, for tomorrow's journey will be most tiring." Even his voice sounded weary, she noted as her gaze whisked over the fine lines that crinkled around his eyes.

In her room Tubby, his feet daintily tucked beneath him, sat in the middle of her bed grooming himself. "You naughty boy," she scolded as she went to undress. She put on her nightshift and came to remove the cat from her bed in order to pull back the coverings. Then she held the cat close and kissed the padded back of his neck. "Come, fur ball, let us sleep," she said as she extinguished the candle and laid down. Tubby put his head on the pillow beside hers.

"Oh, Tubby," she sighed, "I do detest that horse-faced Lady Fiona."

Tubby purred in perfect agreement.

Chapter 7

"It will be damp, and it will be cold," Edward said, looking up into gray skies the next morning, "but I give you my word it won't rain."

She regarded him with amusement as he handed her up into the gig. "Pray, my lord, are you in direct communication with the Almighty?"

He came around and climbed up to sit beside her. "My weather predictions are based on years of studied observation," he said as he took the ribbons.

"For whatever purpose?" she asked, smiling up at him. "It's not as if you're a farmer."

She looked especially fetching today in her scarlet cloak trimmed in ermine. Her cheeks were flushed—with cold, not rouge. Which was reassuring since he disliked artifice in women. It suddenly occurred to him that there was nothing artificial about Maggie. Not in her extraordinary appearance, not in her sleekly rounded body, not in her demeanor. If she had a fault, it was that she was too forthcoming. "I used to be mad for angling and shooting, if you must know," he said. "That's why I educated myself on clouds."

"And you're not mad for those pursuits anymore?"

"Ever since English troops landed in Portugal, I haven't had the time."

"You should allow yourself a holiday."

"Every time I think I'll go to the country, something important comes up—something much more important than shooting grouse."

"Something like saving lives, bringing this war—and its bloodshed—to an end?"

She understands. "I don't mean to exaggerate my own importance," he said.

"There's nothing conceited about being conscientious in your duties. A man of honor puts duty first."

Her praise made him feel deuced awkward. He had best change the subject. "Did your sister finish her book last night?"

"Not quite. She succumbed to fatigue at four this morning. When I left she had just awakened and planned to read the last fifty pages before dressing."

When they crossed Westminster Bridge, Maggie watched with interest the barges and sailing vessels upon the murky Thames, then turned to him. "I would have thought the fastest way to Greenwich would be along the River Thames."

"You're correct. Unlike most of your sex, you must be able to read a map."

She put hands to hips and gave him a mock scowl. "You, my lord, have a low opinion of women's intelligence. 'Women can't read maps. Women can't play chess,'" she mimicked. "If you think us so mentally deficient, it's a wonder you're pledged to spend the rest of your life living with one of us!"

Fiona. Fiona did not play chess. Fiona did not read maps. Fiona, he'd swear, did not know what classification was. Yet he was prepared to grow old beside her, despite that they had little in common. "Lady Fiona is possessed of many fine attributes."

"Attributes, I take it, but not intelligence."

He whirled toward her, his brows lowered. "Why do you keep maligning the woman I intend to marry?

"See! You didn't defend her. She's an empty-headed beauty, I daresay."

"She is not empty-headed! She writes the cleverest letters imaginable."

"I'm sure she does," Maggie said in a humble voice. "I don't mean to speak harshly about Lady Fiona. I have no right to speak of her at all since we've never met. Your affection for her speaks to her worthiness."

He hoped that meant Maggie realized he would be loathe to spend the rest of his life with an empty-headed beauty. Surprisingly, he had at first thought that description aptly applied to Maggie. After all, it was Maggie who turned into a watering pot not once, but twice the first night he met her. It was Maggie who said the most outrageous things about his beautiful Fiona being horse-faced. It was Maggie who had been taken in by the charlatan Henshaw. But with the clarity of spring water he suddenly realized that Maggie was *not* empty-headed.

She might disparage herself for not liking to read the great thinkers, but she was possessed of a keen mind. If she knew the Thames was the fastest way to Greenwich, she knew her geography. Even if she did get Hampshire and Hertfordshire mixed up. Which was of no great significance since she had never stepped foot on English soil until this week.

"So why, my lord, are we not traveling to Greenwich by water?"

He would rather not tell her the real reason. "My horse needs the exercise."

She gave him a quizzing look. "So you're willing to increase your travel time by three hundred percent in order to exercise your horse?"

Damn. She knew her arithmetic, too. "If you must know," he said through gritted teeth, "traveling on water makes me ill."

She had the audacity to laugh at him!

"What do you find so amusing, madame?"

"Forgive me, my lord," she said, sobering. "It was just

such an incongruous image picturing a big, strapping man like you weakened by a perfectly placid waterway."

"There's nothing funny about being seasick."

"No, there isn't. I'm sorry."

Now she made him feel the ogre again. "Were you ill during your crossing of the Atlantic?" he asked.

"No, but Rebecca was. Dreadfully ill. And you're right, it's nothing to laugh about."

As they traveled Maggie turned her head this way and that, eager to take in the sights of the city coming awake: the milk carts and hay carts and street urchins and plump matrons hanging out their wash. All of it held her childlike interest. Then he remembered this was all new to her. She had never before been in a city nearly as populated as London, the capital of the world.

When their surroundings turned more rural, the skies darkened, and she turned to him. "You're wrong about the rain."

"I'm never wrong about rain."

"You are this time."

He glanced at the menacing sky. "What makes you think it will rain?"

"I can feel it in the air."

"Madame, if you will but look at the clouds. The clouds never lie. Those are cirrus clouds. They're not given to producing rain."

She gazed up, and the hood of her cloak dropped from her head. He thought she looked like an angel, the ermine circling her dark hair like a halo. "I don't care what kind of clouds they are," she said. "It's going to rain."

His lips thinned as he flicked the ribbons. "You'd best put your hood back. You'll take an earache from the cold." He patted his pocket where the pistol was concealed. He might not be able to protect her from the cold, but he could fight off anyone who threatened her.

"It's beastly cold," she said. "Perhaps it will even snow."

"It's not going to snow."

She began to laugh.

"Oblige me by telling me what you find so amusing."

"You. You're so absolutely pig-headed."

No woman had ever spoken to him in such a manner. "Precisely what do you mean by 'pig-headed?'"

"Stubborn. Unyielding. Cocky. Arrogant. Take your pick."

Oil and vinegar. That's what they were, he and Maggie. Whenever he would be on the verge of thinking that perhaps she wasn't so objectionable, she would begin to say the most outrageous things about him. Or about Fiona.

He chose not to reply. His glance fell to her ermine muff. "Cold?"

"Terribly."

"I shouldn't have brought you," he said.

"I don't mind the cold, and an outing in dreary weather is preferable to sitting around your townhouse. My sister's no company whatsoever."

"I daresay your admirers would have endeavored to entertain you." The only three men who had met Maggie all seemed to have been completely captivated by her, but none of them would do. Perhaps at Almack's she would find a more suitable man.

"That might have been true—had you allowed me out of doors—but I would not think any of the men particularly interesting in a drawing room."

Her assumptions were on target, except for Harry, but Harry was never his jolly self around women. How had a woman of such sound judgment been hoodwinked by Henshaw? *The title.* Edward himself, having come into his title just eighteen months ago, well understood how differently a titled man was treated than a man who had no title. Fortunately, Lady Fiona was not marrying him for that. She had been attracted to him when a baronetcy had been his only prospect.

"Perhaps you'll meet the right sort of man at Almack's." As he flicked the ribbons along the country lane Edward found himself wondering what kind of man Maggie would be attracted to, putting titles aside.

"Does Aynsley's title not attract you?" he asked.

"I would hope I've learned my lesson regarding men bearing titles—yourself excluded, my lord. If I'm fortunate enough to marry again, you can be assured it's the man, not the title, who has won my affection."

Edward cleared his throat. "What . . . sort of man appeals to you?" Then, he hastened to add, "If I know, perhaps I can be of some service in locating such a man."

"An honest man!" she said with a laugh.

"I assure you, madame, I would not have you making the acquaintance of dishonest men."

He still had a keen desire to know more about what kind of man would win Maggie's heart. Surely she required more than honesty. She had previously told him the man did not have to be rich. All she required as far as that was a comfortable home for herself, Rebecca, and the maid. He cleared his throat again. "Other than honesty, there must be something else you seek in a potential mate."

"I'll know when I meet him." She flicked a glance at him and frowned. "I could enumerate the attributes I seek, but I could still reject a man who's in possession of all of them if the spark isn't there."

"The spark?"

"What you feel for Lady Fiona."

"Oh, yes." He slowed as a post chaise loaded with baggage and swarthy men sitting on top came whirling past them. "Then none of the three men from the theatre meet your criteria?"

"First, I really have no specific criteria. And as to those three worthy gentlemen, it would be most uncharitable of me to dismiss any of them after one partial evening together. They all seemed very fine men. In fact I found nothing objectionable in any of them."

"Then you wouldn't be adverse to marrying a man with a large brood of children?" *Lord Aynsley.*

"Of course not. I love children."

Edward frowned, squinting against the straining sun. Aynsley was sure to offer for her. The very thought had Edward's chest tightening. Not that Aynsley wasn't a fine man. It was just that the stiff fellow and the vivacious Maggie would not suit. Aynsley would likely keep her in Shropshire tending his progeny and keeping her breeding. The thought of Maggie carrying Aynsley's seed produced a profound physical reaction in Edward. His stomach felt as if he had fallen from a great height, and his breath quickened, his pulse pounded. The possibility of Aynsley's intimacy with Maggie ignited a strange jealousy within Edward.

He could not allow himself to think of Maggie in any intimate way. He tried to picture Fiona's blond beauty, tried to recall the sound of her silken voice, but he was unable to. He kept hearing Maggie's voice, picturing her lovely face, the auburn glints in her dark hair, the creamy neck and full breasts.

"I dislike my own shallowness in saying this," she said, "but I've never been attracted to portly men."

"Therefore poor Cook is not in the running." Edward easily recalled Henshaw's looks, which had attracted many women even though he had no title. "But your mate doesn't have to be tall. Henshaw certainly wasn't."

"You must admit he looked especially fine in his clothing with his broad chest and slender waist. And he had an eye for fine tailoring."

"He had an eye for the ladies, too," Edward grumbled.

"Pray, my lord, I do not wish to discuss him. Would that I'd never met him."

"Discuss, then, what attributes your dream husband must possess." What was the matter with him? He was obsessing over the woman's mythical husband. Why should it even matter to him?

Her rosy little mouth lifted into a smile and she sighed. "A perfect mate would be kind above all else. Intelligent. Honorable. Compassionate." She bit at her lip. "Physically, the perfect man would be tall. And handsome. And rich." She stopped for a moment, then added. "And titled. Remember, you asked for the *perfect* mate. I don't expect to find half these attributes in one single man."

"That's reassuring since you've already conceded on the title, wealth, and height."

"I daresay I'll concede on other attributes before I'm finished."

"You're that desperate?"

She nodded gravely and spoke in a somber voice. "Would that I had time on my side, time to be sure, time to know, time to find true love, but sadly I don't."

He wished he could just give her a tidy enough sum for her and Miss Peabody to live comfortably until Maggie could find the right man. But of course he could not do that. There was Fiona to consider. "You mustn't worry about haste. You're free to live at Warwick House for as long as it takes."

"When will you be marrying, my lord?"

No date had been set. He had assumed they would marry before the year was out, but since this was only February, his nuptials could be nearly a year off.

Surely that would give Maggie enough time to find someone suitable.

The sooner she found someone, the better, as far as his relationship with Fiona was concerned. As dear as Fiona was, he doubted she would understand her affianced residing with two unmarried females. "Before the year is out," he answered.

"Lady Fiona is most fortunate."

"Why do you say that?"

She gave an insincere laugh. "Has it not occurred to you that you possess all the attributes I just described in the perfect mate?"

Chapter 8

His hands stilled as if frozen. The most beautiful woman he had ever seen had just told him he was her perfect mate. He should be ecstatic with pleasure, but the emotions that surged through him were the complete opposite. He felt as if a horrible grief had descended upon him.

He belonged to Fiona. No other woman had ever received a second look from him since Lady Fiona had acknowledged her affection for him. Fiona was the woman he would spend the rest of his life with. He had known their lives were intrinsically woven together since he'd been a young man at university with her brother.

That a lady who had rejected dukes and earls had bestowed her love on a mere mister had brought him incredible happiness. Until this week he had been unable to even think about her without swelling with most pleasant surge of emotions. He'd often tried to analyze the deep affection he held for her. It wasn't merely her blond beauty that had attracted him, or her title, or her sweet, unaffected nature. Her possession of his heart went so much deeper than those things. He could not be with her, could not remember her honeyed voice without experiencing a profound feeling of well-being.

And she loved him. The moment she had confirmed

it was he—and none of the bevy of her admirers—who held her heart was his life's defining moment. He had been teasing her that day—they had always taken great pleasure in laughing and teasing one another—about her perpetual flock of admirers when she had met his gaze and—for once—spoken somberly. "A pity the one who matters most is not one of those men." In that instant he knew she spoke of him, and the most magical feeling of jubilation washed over him.

So why did he now feel as if someone he loved had just died?

Since Maggie had invaded his home Monday night, nothing was the same. It was as if all the components of his predictable, well-ordered life had been tossed into a jar and shaken at high speed.

And his opinion of Maggie continued to be shaken. Now he was certain she must be the most honest woman who had ever walked the earth. Did she not know about feminine coquetry? Whoever heard of a woman babbling about a man's perfection to the very man she spoke of? A man who was pledged to another. A decidedly honest woman, to be sure.

He did not trust himself to look at her. There was something absolutely provocative about the way she lowered those long lashes. And in his shaken state of mind the last thing he needed was to lust after the woman who sat beside him.

Gathering his wits about him, he realized the lady's statement demanded a reply. "I daresay it's the title," he finally managed. "Had you known me eighteen months ago I would have been just another mister with very little fortune."

"With your abundant physical attributes, you would never have been just another mister."

Why did the woman always blatantly state what was on her mind? Were he a woman, he would be blushing at the moment. "I cannot deny being tall is a distinct advantage. I daresay it's my height which has you thinking me some kind of prize." Good Lord, he sounded like some conceited fop!

"Oh, it's not just me thinking it. You are a prize. Lady Fiona is a most fortunate woman."

"It is I who am fortunate to have won her hand."

She went silent for a moment, then said, "I should very much like to meet her."

When pigs fly. If Fiona ever saw how achingly beautiful Maggie was, she would never believe he could be immune to Maggie's incredible charms.

Which, of course, he was.

They did not speak until they were on the outskirts of Greenwich.

When it began to rain.

They were drenched by the time he found the Spotted Hound and Hare Inn where they could take shelter from the deluge. "Come, Maggie, sit in front of the fire," he said in a gently apologetic voice. "It will dry your clothing." He led her to the hearth of their private parlor.

She had begun to shiver. He felt deuced responsible for her discomfort, first for bringing her out on a day like this and second for not taking a barge. Had they come by water, they would have arrived, conducted their business, and returned to London by the time the skies burst. Lastly, he regretted that he'd been guilty of what she had called him. What was it? Oh, yes, he'd been damned pig-headed.

He assisted her in removing her cloak and was pleased to see her dress beneath it was dry. The dress she had worn yesterday. The one with the low neckline. And lopsided breasts. He jerked his gaze back to her moist face and without thinking what he was doing, he gently brushed away droplets from her brow. "Forgive me for being so bloody pig-headed," he said.

Her warm brown eyes softened. "It's not your fault it's raining, silly!" Her teeth rattled, and she was turning blue. Which made him feel even more wretched.

When the innkeeper's wife entered the chamber he offered to pay her handsomely if she could procure a dry wrap for his "wife."

A few minutes later the woman returned with a knitted shawl which Edward was only too happy to place around Maggie's trembling shoulders.

She looked up at him gratefully. "Thank you, my lord. No garment has ever been so treasured."

Once they had drunk hot cider Maggie stopped shaking.

Then the thunder struck.

And Maggie screamed.

He whirled toward her and saw sheer fear on her face. It took him a moment to realize thunderstorms terrified her. He moved to stand behind her, placing firm hands on her trembling shoulders. "You've nothing to fear," he said in a soft voice. He had never seen a grown person more frightened, yet oddly, no tears gathered in her eyes. *Just like the night of the theft.* Was this stoic creature the real Maggie? He was coming to believe her hysterics that first night and the following morning had been a ploy to gain his sympathy. Which meant she was not possessed of the truthfulness he was beginning to credit her with.

She gave a long, bitter laugh.

"What's so amusing?" he asked.

"You have your aversion to travel by water; my aversion's to thunder."

"Aren't we a pair?" he said with a chuckle, shaking his head. He came to sit on the bench next to her and took her hand in his.

She gave him a puzzled look.

"We must convince the innkeeper we're husband and wife."

"A good thing we're not traveling in your crested coach."

"Yes, isn't it?" He hated to think what sordid tales would get back to Fiona.

The skies flashed white again and thunder rumbled in the distance, then grew to a roar. The very bench they sat on shook. And Maggie nearly jumped out of her skin.

"Don't be afraid." Like the circling motion of his hand over hers, his voice was gentle.

"I know better," she said in a painfully fragile voice. "I try to tell myself I'm indoors. I'm safe from danger, but still I can't dispel my unreasonable fear."

"Do you know why you're so afraid?"

She nodded solemnly. "For years I didn't, but now that I'm an adult I've been able to comprehend the source of this vexing fear."

"Which is?"

"There was a terrible thunderstorm the night Rebecca was born. I was only seven and not permitted in Mama's chamber." She sighed. "It was a difficult birthing, and Mama screamed throughout the night. I wanted to go to her, but they wouldn't let me."

"Your mother died?" he asked in a concerned voice.

She shook her head. "Not until many years after that, but every time there's a thunderstorm I am possessed of the keenest sense that something horrible will happen to my mother—or to someone I love. I still feel it though I know how ridiculous my fear is."

"At least you're intelligent enough to have traced the fear to its source."

The thunder cracked again, and Maggie went dead still—except for the trembling and the frightened pucker around her mouth.

"It's not going to hurt you—or anyone you love," he assured.

She frowned. "I know the wisdom in what you're

saying, my lord. But I cannot seem to govern my own wretched fears."

He scooted closer to her and settled an arm around her quivering shoulders. "Don't think about it. Let's talk of something else. Do you play whist?"

"I enjoy the game very much," she said in a flat voice, her gaze riveted to the flames in the fireplace.

"I would imagine you're good at it."

"You will have to judge for yourself," she said lifelessly. "Perhaps we can play tonight. That is, if you're not engaged for the evening."

A pity he couldn't tell her the truth, that Lord Carrington had ordered him not to allow her out of his sight. Edward did not wish for Maggie to think he was forming an attachment to her, nor did he wish for her to believe he was gallant. "I'm not engaged this evening. Perhaps Mr. Lyle will be able to make a fourth."

"He's such a nice man. He sent me the most beautiful flowers."

Nothing nice about that, Edward thought. *Stinking up my home.* "He's a tolerable whist player."

The innkeeper's wife returned with a tray heaping with hot food. The way she stole a glance at them as they huddled together in front of the fire told Edward she thought the two newly married. "Madame," he said to the woman, "could you direct us to the lodgings of Mr. Andrew Bibble?"

"Well if it were night 'e'd be right here in our tap room," she said with a laugh, "though, come to think of it 'e weren't here last night. Might be that 'e be out of town. 'e leaves town on important business from time to time."

"To London, I suppose," Edward said.

She shrugged. "I couldn't say. Mr. Bibble don't speak much about 'imself."

"Where are his lodgings?" Edward asked again.

"If ye stays on this street till ye pass the docks, ye'll turn right at the next street. His house is down on the right. Got a bright green door."

"I thank you," Edward said, rising and offering Maggie a hand. "Come, my dear, we've hot food to eat."

Thankfully, the lightning and thunder had moved to the west.

After they ate and settled with the innkeepers, they started for Andrew Bibble's. A light mist had replaced the rain, but it was still beastly cold. His glance slid to the muff Maggie seemed only too eager to slide her hands into.

He quickly turned the gig onto the first street past the docks, and saw a house with a bright green door.

"I daresay, my lord, you're surprised a mere woman could give accurate directions," Maggie said factitiously.

"One wouldn't have to read a map in order to find Mr. Bibble's home," he countered, drawing his gig in front of the house.

After he helped Maggie down from the box they walked together to the door, and Edward rapped sharply. They waited a moment, but no one answered.

"I supposed we should have asked if Mr. Bibble has a wife," Maggie said.

"He certainly has a dog," Edward grumbled.

The bark of what sounded like a big dog continued unrelentlessly.

"If Mr. Bibble were out of town," Maggie said, "it's unlikely he would leave his dog indoors while he was gone."

"If he's not married, surely he has a housekeeper," Edward mused.

He had been rapping soundly on the door for a good two minutes when he stopped and tried the knob.

"My lord!" Maggie shrieked in a scolding voice.

He paid her no heed as the door glided open and he stepped into the untidy house. Then he halted in midstride as he realized the house was not merely untidy. It had been ransacked. That would explain the opened books fanned out on the wood floor and the gaping cabinet doors where pots and utensils and linens spilled out. Edward's heart thumped. He shouldn't have brought Maggie.

Her mouth clamped shut as she followed toward the sound of the yapping hound.

He saw the blood first.

Then he saw the body of the man he presumed to be Andrew Bibble.

Chapter 9

Maggie screamed.

"Go back!" he ordered as he surged toward the body. "Whoever did this might still be here."

Instead of obeying him, the maddening wench pushed past his outstretched arm. "We're safe," she said in a shaky voice. "This must have occurred last night."

He remembered the innkeeper's wife saying Bibble had not been to the taproom the night before. An unusual occurrence, she had said. Edward dropped to one knee and lifted the man's lifeless arm to feel for a pulse. The arm was stiff. Cold. Taking the pulse was useless, but Edward still tried.

"Look! There's blood beneath him," she said.

Edward rolled the rigid corpse over. The handle of a long knife protruded from the victim's belly, red staining his shirt and coat liked spilled ink on parchment. Edward fought back nausea.

Drawing in her breath, Maggie spun her head away from the morbid sight.

"A pity we don't actually know what this Bibble looks like," he said, studying the dead man's fair face and blond hair. Edward would guess the man was the same age as he.

"It's got to be him, I'll vow." Her voice grew even more solemn as she bent over to stroke the mongrel lapping at her skirts. "You poor pooch," she said sweetly. "I feel so responsible. Your owner had been perfectly safe these two years past, but once I arrived in England—and The Scoundrel's things stolen from me—Mr. Bibble's killed." She straightened and faced Edward. "This is no mere coincidence."

"I'll own it's not," Edward said as he stood and put both hands on her shoulders, peering into her wide chocolate-colored eyes. "Don't waste your remorse on him. If he was important to Henshaw, he was up to no good."

Her gaze scanned from the sad eyes of the dog beside her to encompass the disorderly room. "I'm certain the same person who went through my possessions was at work here."

Edward chuckled. "How can you make that assumption with such conviction?"

"Quite easily. Just look at the method behind this search. It's identical to the method used in my chambers. The storage pieces have been completely emptied of their contents, then the contents thoroughly searched." She gazed pensively up into his face. "Will you think me correct if the deceased man's clothing has been slashed?"

A grin tweaked at the corner of his mouth. "Shall we go see?"

They mounted the narrow stairway, first Maggie, then Edward. Despite that she wore several layers of clothing—including the soggy red cloak—his gaze fastened on the sweet movement of her hips. Until he yanked his gaze back to safer territory.

Both of the upstairs bedchambers had been completely ransacked. The coverings were stripped from the beds and feathers from the slashed pillows littered the rooms. Other things had been dumped willy-nilly. In the second room, Edward's eyes locked on the dead man's clothing strewn on top of the bed, the shoulders of every coat slashed.

The dog went straight to his master's clothing and whimpered.

"Oh you poor thing," Maggie uttered, petting the long, beige hair of its back.

"It seems you're right, madame." It chilled him to his very bones to think this murderer had rummaged through Maggie's things. Thank God she had been away from home for Edward had no doubt the murderer would have killed her too. "Your pillows weren't slashed, though."

"I had been in my chambers less than a day. The . . . killer knew I wouldn't have had time to conceal something in the former countess's pillows—if I had something to conceal—which I assure you I do not."

He nodded as he swept a protective arm around her trembling shoulders. "I'd better get you out of here."

She stiffened. "We can't go until we conduct a search of our own. The killer obviously seeks something he didn't get from me."

Damn! Of course she was right. That the killer was still so wildly searching meant that the elusive something he sought—which Edward suspected was a document—was still missing. Which could mean that Maggie might be in danger. Until that document was found, the killer would assume she knew something that might lead to the document. Edward's gut clenched. "What if he comes back?"

"He won't," she said in an assured voice.

"What makes you so confident?"

"He must have done this last night. I'm also extremely confident the murderer is *not* from Greenwich. Therefore, he left Greenwich after his dirty deeds were done and planned to be far away when the body was found this morning."

She made perfect sense. "All right. Will you be all right searching the upstairs while I search down?"

She nodded.

Given that the house was so small, it would not take them long to conduct a search. There was no desk, but Edward deduced that the dead man must have kept his papers in a wooden box because the emptied box reposed on a slender table above a heap of papers strewn on the floor. He stooped down and began to go through them. There was a letter from a solicitor in Bloomsbury regarding the disposal of Bibble's mother's estate, a receipt for stocks in a Birmingham factory, a poem written in a feminine hand, and a lease agreement for the house in Greenwich.

He heard Maggie's light footstep hurrying down the stairs. "Look at these!" she exclaimed, extending her palm, which held men's rings and studs made of precious jewels. "This shows the murderer was disinterested in riches."

It also showed Maggie's honesty. As desperate as she was for money, she could easily have slipped the jewels into her reticule and sold them for a substantial amount when she returned to London.

"Which is really quite chilling," she continued. "It would be much less frightening were we up against a mere thief."

"Indeed."

She eyed the papers in his hand. "Have you found something?"

"Nothing important."

"Does it not strike you as incongruous that a man who lived so modestly was in possession of such expensive jewels?" She asked. "And his clothing was rather well made—before it was slashed, of course."

"I was wondering the same thing. We neglected to ask if Bibble had a livelihood here in Greenwich. He appears to have come into some small sum from his mother and owned stocks which I assume paid quarterly dividends."

She was standing some ten feet away from the

corpse, looking askance as it. "What age would you say he was?"

"Bibble?"

"Yes."

"I suppose he's the same age as I."

"Which is the same age as The Scoundrel. I wonder how many years he was associated with my late husband."

Was she wondering if perhaps Henshaw and Bibble might have been at school together? Edward began to examine the books lying on the floor. He stacked them, thirteen volumes in all, on the table where the wood box stood. The dead man read Sir Walter Scott, Oliver Goldsmith, Thomas Paine, and Fielding. *Fielding?* Was it a bit too ironic that the only book Henshaw brought to Virginia a Fielding novel? Edward turned back to Maggie. "Which Fielding book was stolen with Henshaw's things?"

She bit at her lip as she thought for a moment. "My first instinct was that it was *Tom Jones,* then I wondered if it was *Moll Flanders,* but I must go with my first instinct. I'm almost one hundred percent certain it was *Tom Jones.*"

Edward looked at the book in his hands. *Tom Jones.* The cryptographer in him had him wondering if the two men somehow communicated through the pages of this novel. He started to thumb through its pages, looking for any kind of marking.

There was none.

"I see where your mind's taking you," she said, moving toward him, "but you must own the book was exceedingly popular. My father had a copy."

He laughed. "So did mine."

She shrugged. "Anything else?"

"If there was something here, it's gone now."

"I agree. What are we going to do about the body?"

"I suggest we return to the Spotted Hound and

Hare," he said, his hand dropping to her waist, steering her toward the door.

It was only then he realized the skies had turned black again. As they reached the door, the sound of distant thunder rumbled. Maggie went stiff. The thunder grew louder. And, like a rag doll, she collapsed against him. His protective arms swooped around her and he murmured, "We can't stay here."

"I know," she said morosely.

"If you could just make it back to the Spotted Hound and Hare. It's not very far." He looked down into those frightened eyes and without being aware that he was doing so, he cupped a gentle hand to her face.

And felt a violent quivering.

As if she were awash at sea and he her rescuer, her arms reached around him and held firm. Then she nodded.

She seemed so frail he did not trust her not to swoon and spill into the lakes of mud that had puddled on the streets outside. In a gallant gesture, he scooped her up, carried her into the blinding rain, and set her on the seat atop his gig. Leaping up beside her, he took the reins, then gathered her close and swept half of his great coat around her. Not that it did any good. She was already as drenched as if she had taken a swim fully dressed.

A moment later he was disembarking at the inn, giving orders to the ostler to see after his horse and scooping up the terrified Maggie.

Now lightning whitened the skies and the roar of the thunder cracked directly overhead.

She screamed and buried her face into his chest as his arms tightened around her. Ten strides brought them back into the warmth of the inn. He carried her directly to the flaming hearth and set her on the same bench that she had sat on earlier, but she continued to cling to him.

He sat beside her and held her close, his hands weaving sultry circles on her trembling back.

When their hostess entered the chamber and took in the tender scene in front of the fire, she said, "The poor lady! She's as wet as a 'erring! What she needs is dry clothes."

"My thoughts exactly," Edward said, sending the innkeeper a grateful half-smile.

"Ye've paid for chambers, and ye'll not be returning to London today on these muddy roads," the woman said.

Edward nodded as he gathered Maggie up and took her to the adjoining bedchamber. "A candle, if you please," he said to the innkeeper when he realized the room was as dark as night.

With the door still open, he set Maggie upon the bed. "Better?" he asked in a tender voice.

Then a bolt of lightning walloped the inn as the thunder made everything in the room vibrate.

She grasped for his hand and spoke in a frightened, surprisingly weak voice. "Not really."

The innkeeper returned with a fresh candle, lighted it, and turned to Maggie. "Once you're out of them wet clothes, ye can dry them in front of the fire." Then she left the room, closing the door behind her.

Edward sank onto the feather mattress beside Maggie and began to tug on her drenched red cloak. She allowed him to remove it.

When he saw that her dress was also soggy, he mumbled a curse. The cloak must have been so wet already that it offered no protection under the second deluge.

The room shook again and went white, and Maggie hurled herself into his arms. They sat there quietly for a moment, listening to the rain pelting against the windows, his arms caving around her. "You'll take a chill if you don't get out of those clothes," he finally murmured.

She seemed not to have heard him. Her desperate grip around his back tightened.

Caught up in the overwhelming desire to protect her, his lips brushed over hers. It had been meant as an innocent kiss. But he had not reckoned on her frenzied response.

Her lips crushed against his, her mouth open and warm. Something snapped inside him as the kiss deepened and a searing heat bolted through him. He kissed her face. He kissed her graceful neck. His hands cupped her breasts, and she began to make soft, whimpering sounds. He freed her breasts and bent to taste them as she arched into him, tossing her head back, her smoldering eyes those of a woman drugged.

Then her lids lowered, her long lashes feathering against her cheeks. A gentle peace had settled over her.

There was nothing gentle about the desire for her that strummed through every cell in his body. God in heaven, but she was exquisite! His heated gaze dipped to those perfect, pink-tipped breasts and he began in earnest to remove her dress.

When he unlaced her stays and dipped his head to kiss a rigid nipple, she offered no resistance.

More sounds of thunder roared into the room and lightning sizzled through their very window. And Maggie melted into him. He gently eased her down until they were lying beside one another, his own need throbbing through him louder than any thunder. As his hungry gaze caressed every inch of her perfect body, he saw the simmering desire firing her dark eyes.

"You can stop me now," he whispered throatily.

She fiercely shook her head and pulled his face down to hers. When their lips met, a ravenous need consumed them both.

Somehow he managed to disengage their lips and swiftly peel off his clothing, then stretched out beside her, their bodies tangling until the smooth curves of her body were beneath him.

He parted her legs and entered her in one sleek, sure move. The raging storm outside their window was nothing compared to the shattering heat that consumed them. Pure, intense pleasure engulfed him, sweeping him up in its roaring, leaping, flooding tide.

Her movements pulsed against the plunging and retreating of his hardened, throbbing shaft as wave after wave of flaming, liquid heat slammed into them. He lost all sense of time, all sense of place. The only reality was Maggie and the intense pleasure she was giving him. It was as he'd never lived until this moment, as if this union would reverberate into infinity.

She trembled violently, then stilled. He gazed down into her smoky eyes and saw the simmering passion as she collapsed back into the soft sheets.

Smoothing away the wet hair from her delicate brow, he lowered his face to hers and dropped soft kisses on her brow, her cheeks, her nose, then at last their mouths touched as gently as a feather falls to the ground. He held her close for a very long time. Finally he became aware that her lids had lowered, and he realized she slept.

A profound feeling of contentment washed over him as they lay together in the dusky room. He had not realized that the severe weather had passed, replaced by a lulling tap of rain upon the window.

As she slept he tried to analyze what had just occurred between them. Of course he would have to offer for her. His stomach sank. What of Fiona? How could he have been so insensitive? How could he have allowed himself to wound the sweet woman who had pledged her life to his?

He eased the counterpane over Maggie and managed to slip from the bed without waking her. For a long moment he stood over her, drinking in her incredible beauty, then his gaze dropped to the heap of wet clothing on the floor, and he absently began to drape her dress and cloak over chairs he had scooted up to the fire.

Then he re-dressed in his damp clothes and went to report a murder.

Chapter 10

A soft rain fell against the windows. Her eyes slowly opened, and she saw the room was in complete darkness, save for the circle of yellow glow around the candle beside the bed. At first she did not realize where she was. She was suffused in a fuzzy warmth of well-being. Her breasts felt heavy. A spiraling tingle settled low in her torso. She stretched out languidly and only then came to realize she was completely naked.

With that thought, she bolted up, clutching the thick counterpane over her bared breasts.

And the stark memory of making love to Lord Warwick slammed into her with the force of an angry ocean. Her face flamed and she cursed herself as she sprang from the bed and began to madly throw on her now-dry clothing. How could she have allowed herself to behave as a strumpet? Oddly, she was more angry with herself for having lost his respect than she was over her wanton actions. Actions that had been too pleasurable, by far.

Once she was dressed, she began to pace in front of the fire, trying to predict how Lord Warwick would view the lascivious act that had taken place in this very room earlier. Would he dismiss her as a gentleman would dismiss a trollop? Or would he offer for her? Her stomach clenched.

Visions of the gallant Mr. Darcy paraded through

her muddled mind. What would Mr. Darcy do? *He would offer for me,* she reflected sadly.

Her heart softened. Though her acquaintance with Lord Warwick was not of long standing, she believed she could accurately gauge his character. A man of noble sentiments, he would most definitely offer for her.

The very thought of belonging to the man who had so thoroughly made love to her filled her with a satisfied glow. The sweet memory of his hands gliding over every curve of her body had her breath coming in quick, labored gasps.

There was also the fact that she had been fiercely attracted to him since that first night she looked up and saw him on the stairway, and even more so now that she could visualize the length of his sleek, hard body pressed against her, his rock-hard shaft pulsing within her. She gulped a deep breath and shook her head to dispel such a torturing memory.

Marriage to him would solve all of her problems.

Then she cursed herself for thinking so. Marriage to him would only bring on more crippling problems. She had no desire to marry a man who was in love with another woman. And Lord Warwick made no secret of his devotion to that wretched Fiona Hollingsworth.

With a bitter, morose sense of doom, Maggie knew she would have to turn him down.

A soft knock sounded at her door.

"Please come in," she said, drawing in her breath, steeling herself to face the man who had come to know her body so intimately.

Her heart melted as she watched the darkly brooding Lord Warwick walk into the room, tray in hand.

"I've brought you dinner, my dear," he said before kicking the door shut. He set the tray on the bed and faced her. "You're dry."

"Yes."

"And rested?"

"Yes."

"Good."

"And now that the storm has cleared out," she said with false brightness, "I'm sure you'll be happy to learn I'm perfectly back to my old self." She moved to the bed and picked up a slab of bread and began to nibble upon it, hoping to dispel the trembling that had begun to assail her.

"I'm happy to learn that," he said, taking a seat on the chair in front of the fire.

Maggie brought her plate and sat beside him. "You've eaten?" she asked.

He nodded.

She ate her turnips first. Bite after bite, she expected him to say something about their passionate encounter. Would he apologize? Would he, indeed, offer for her? But he only stared into the flames and said nothing.

She started on her meat pie, and still he did not speak. Should she broach the subject? Her cheeks grew hot at the thought.

She took another bite of bread.

Then he turned to her. His eyes were gentle, his voice low when he spoke. "I'll marry you, of course."

The arrogant, maddening, broodingly handsome, *noble* man! A pity he didn't love her. She cleared her throat. "You most certainly *will not!*"

He gaped at her. "I most certainly will! I took advantage of your weakened state. I compromised a well-born lady."

Her appetite deserted her, and she set the half-eaten plate on the hearth. "You only took what I too gladly offered." Her lids dropped and she spoke in a husky whisper. "Forgive me for being such an absolute idiot."

"I beg that you forgive me, madame. It was I who acted without regard to propriety."

She spun around to face him. "You acted as any man would, given the situation." She could scarcely believe she had so completely humiliated herself.

"I mean to marry you," he said again.

"Well, I don't mean to marry you!"

His glittering eyes sought hers. "Why?"

"Because I'm determined to marry for love. I don't love you, and you don't love me."

She felt uncomfortable as his stunned gaze locked with hers. "We may not love each other, yet," he said, "but what occurred in this room today between you and me is something I'll vow not many married couples will know in lifetime."

Her insides sank. The pity of it was that what he said was true. Even in the early days of her marriage when she thought she was madly in love with her sensuous husband, their lovemaking had never been as passionate or as glorious as what she and Lord Warwick had shared in this very room.

She gathered her courage for it would take every ounce of courage she possessed to deny herself more nights in this man's arms. "I beg that you speak no more of what happened between us today. I mean to forget it."

His mouth dropped open. "You may forget it, but I assure you I won't!" The fire captured his attention again. She could tell he was collecting his thoughts. Finally, not removing his gaze from the fire, he said, "What if . . . what if you find you are with child?"

Her heart stampeded. Her stomach flipped. Her voice trembled when she replied. "Then, and only then, would I consent to marry you." She gave up a silent prayer that it would never come to that. Lord Warwick belonged with his precious Fiona—damn her!—and Maggie was loathe to come between them.

Even if they had made such sublime love, Maggie thought with a deep, gnawing pain.

His hard eyes still on the fire, he nodded thoughtfully. "As you wish, madame." Then he got to his feet and moved toward the door. "I shall return to the tap room. It looks as if we're stuck here for the night." His hand moved to the handle. "Because our hosts believe us married, I will return once you're asleep." His glance flicked to the homespun rug. "I'll sleep on the floor."

"You'll do no such thing! You'll sleep in the bed you're paying for. I'll sleep on the floor."

"You will not!"

Her chin lifted defiantly. "Then we'll sleep together." Her voice dropped. "I promise not to ravage you, my lord."

He mumbled a curse and swept from the room.

"I'm sure you're relieved the magistrate identified the dead man as Andrew Bibble," Maggie said on the journey back to London the following day.

Not nearly as relieved as he was that she did not mention the intimacy they had shared the previous afternoon. He thanked God she had been sound asleep and he so drunk he went immediately to sleep when he had slipped into bed beside her late last night. Now they were some forty minutes out of Greenwich and there was no sign that yesterday's rains would return. The ride had thus far been somber with neither of them speaking. He wondered if her thoughts drifted to the sultry, dusky bedchamber at the inn, then he tried to push thoughts of Maggie from his mind.

If he could not allow himself to remember the feel of her, the smell of her, or their shattering sexual encounter, he could allow himself to worry about her.

Ever since he'd found Bibble's body he had worried about her. It was obvious the thief and murderer had not gotten what he wanted from Maggie's chambers. If he did not get what he was looking for at Bibble's, Maggie's very life was in danger. Edward's grip tightened around the reins. A frown sent his brows plunging, and he vowed to keep watch over her day and night for as long as it would take.

That was the least he could do for her.

Her remarks about Bibble's identity were on target. How well she was coming to know him. Despite all the evidence that the dead man was Andrew Bibble, Edward would never have been satisfied over the corpse's identity without a positive identification. Such thoroughness had been ingrained into him over a decade of life-and-death work in the Foreign Office. "Hypotheses serve their purpose but cannot be substituted for fact," he said. He wondered if she even knew what a hypothesis was. Women studied French and drawing but definitely not scientific method. He'd vow Fiona had never heard of a hypothesis.

"Men are so empirical!"

He laughed. *Maggie did know.*

"It's my opinion a peer of the realm can easily get away with murder," she said. "Did you notice how that blathering magistrate was intimidated by your title? He treated you as if you were royalty."

Edward could not argue with her. Far too many people were easily impressed by titles. "Such unfounded respect must be alien to a colonial."

"Not really," she said. "Even though we don't have aristocrats, we have the very wealthy, and they command unwarranted respect."

Human nature, he had learned, was the same across all nations.

As they continued along the still muddy road, he scanned the clouds. Cumulus today. Which reminded him of his arrogance the day before. "I shouldn't have brought you," he said, flicking his gaze to her wind-flushed cheeks.

"I don't mind the cold. It's only the thunderstorms that terrify me. Besides, it's good that someone was with you when you discovered Mr. Bibble's body."

Did she have no memory of lying in his arms, of taking him inside her?

He gaped at her. "What's good about stumbling upon a gory corpse?"

"Not good precisely, but intriguing. I would never have been satisfied there were no clues had I not conducted a search myself."

His thoughts drifted back to that day in his library when she had offered to help him track the thief. She had said, "We'll be a team. You and I." How could they have known then just how close they would become? He was unable to purge the memory of her sweet lovemaking from his mind. The very thought of it sent the blood thundering through his veins, caused his breath to grow short.

He must not allow himself to remember. Maggie would not have him. She'd told him so. Besides, there was sweet Fiona to consider. To destroy the precious gift of Fiona's love would destroy something in him.

"I was wondering," Maggie began, casting a glance at him, "if you'll be dining at home tonight."

"I'm not leaving you. At the present time. That the killer conducted so thorough a search of Bibble's things tells me he did not get what he wanted from you the other night."

"Yes, I thought the same thing." She tugged the hood of her cloak closely about her face. "Dare we hope the killer did find what he was looking for at Mr. Bibble's?"

"We can hope, but it's best to be prepared for the worst."

She turned to look at him with those huge, solemn eyes. "How, my lord, does one prepare for the worst?"

"By being bloody careful. The killer may come back for you—thinking you know something."

She shivered. "Oh, dear. Perhaps my confinement won't be so intolerable, after all."

He kept picturing Bibble's body, grotesque in death and soaked in blood. His hands tightened around the reins and he vowed to guard Maggie with his life. "I must insist on your confinement." How long before the killer struck again? As maddening as Maggie was, Edward would not like her harmed, especially while she was under his protection. The very thought of it was like a blow to his gut.

"Surely you won't have to be confined also. You've important work that demands your attention."

"While you're under my roof, you're my responsibility," he said in a grave voice.

"But how shall I find a husband if I can't mingle in society? I'm well aware that my presence in your home is most repugnant to you, so I really must meet a man who will take me off your hands."

Even in a fit of raging lunacy, he could never find Maggie repugnant. Irritating. Maddening. Honest to a fault. But not repugnant. Her cat, however, was a completely different matter. "You are in no way repugnant to me, madame, but you must admit the impropriety of us living under the same roof will be sure to raise some eyebrows." *I hope Fiona will understand.*

"You have written her about me?" She asked.

Dear God, could Maggie read his mind? "I posted it the day before yesterday."

"Did you tell her I had been your uncle's secret wife?"

His lips thinned, his jaw tightened. "I had to. For now."

"If she's the sweet, gentle creature you keep assuring me she is, she will be most understanding."

"As long as she doesn't see how beautiful you are." He hadn't meant to say it. Was Maggie's propensity to tell the truth contagious?

A wistful look washed across her lovely face, and her eyes danced. She started to say something, then she stopped and grew solemn.

Fighting against the damned wind slowed their progress. It would be almost dark before they would reach Curzon Street. He had been a fool to ride out in a gig on a blustery day like yesterday. Especially since he possessed a very fine enclosed carriage and a coachman who would have been only too happy to make the trip to Greenwich. An overwhelming, illogical desire to take the damned gig had taken possession of him. Could he have wished unawares to exclude Miss Peabody, to have Maggie all to himself? Even his mind was muddled by Maggie's presence.

He found himself regretting the bleakness of the day with its somber gray skies and chilled air. Showing an American the verdant English countryside would have given him much pleasure. In another month the meadows would change color, the trees would transform from naked brown to lush green, thick with leaves. The daffodils would poke their yellow noses along every byway from here to Scotland. Where would Maggie be when spring replaced winter's dormancy? Would she share the Englishman's passion for pastoral valleys, ivy-clad cottages, and neat little gardens?

Would she be the wife of another man?

She remained solemn. Quiet. Had his warning terrified her? Eventually, she broke the silence. "You must have Mr. Lyle come tonight. We could play whist after dinner. I think you would like that."

Did she now? There was nothing likeable about

watching Harry make a cake of himself over Maggie. Even worse, watching Maggie lower her lashes seductively at Harry. Not that she realized how seductive it was when she lowered those extraordinary lashes. "Yes, I'll send a note around when we get back to Curzon Street," he said.

Chapter 11

In response to Edward's note requesting Lyle to dine with them and to make a fourth for whist afterward, Harry Lyle met Edward in his library shortly before dinner. "You've got that brooding look on your face," Harry began as he sank into a club chair near Edward's desk. "That brooding look women seem to adore."

"I've reason to brood."

Harry hitched a brow.

"I discovered the dead body of Henshaw's accomplice yesterday. It was ghastly, and unfortunately, I could do nothing to shield Maggie from witnessing the bloody scene."

"Where was this bloody scene?" Harry demanded.

Edward swallowed. "In Greenwich."

Harry's green eyes flared in anger. "How could you endanger Lady Warwick when you've been charged with keeping her safe?"

"I wasn't precisely charged with keeping her safe. I was instructed not to let her from my sight—an order I upheld. And it's not as if I set off unarmed."

"You took a pistol?"

"I did."

Harry glared at him. "You've known since Tuesday night's unpleasantness that she was in danger. How could you expose her to possible harm?"

Lyle was right to be angry. Edward had no business dragging an endangered lady all over the countryside. "We foolishly thought that after getting Henshaw's things from her, the thief would have no further use for Maggie. We also thought that if she could speak with the man in Greenwich she might remember something The Scoundrel may have told her, something which might help us find the thief." He added solemnly, "The thief who now appears to be a murderer."

"The Scoundrel? I take it you're referring to Henshaw."

"As his widow refers to him."

Harry nodded, leaning back in his chair. "Tell me about the man in Greenwich."

Edward told him everything, dating back to Henshaw's stolen letter from Bibble.

"It sounds to me as if the killer's desperate to get the document, for I too believe he seeks a document. Why slash the clothing? What else could be so unobtrusively concealed beneath the folds of fabric?"

"If the document wasn't at Bibble's," Edward said in a grave voice, "my fear is he'll return to Maggie."

"The hell if I'll allow that!" Harry thundered. "I'd lay down my very life for her."

"I'll do the protecting!" Edward said with outrage. "After all, she's my family. Or she's pretending to be my family. My uncle's widow. And I'll bloody well look after my own family."

"Do you realize how ridiculous you sound? I think the beauty has affected your ability to think rationally."

She had certainly affected everything else in Edward's life. Negatively. "I'll do whatever's necessary to ensure the lady's safety," Edward said, standing up. "We need to go in to dinner. Do me the goodness of imparting all we have just discussed to Lord Carrington tomorrow."

* * *

As Maggie sat before her dressing table while Sarah arranged her hair, she coached herself to think carefully before she spoke at tonight's dinner table. Her habit of blurting out her every thought had been the source of great humiliation during the journey to Greenwich. For as long as she lived she would never forget how painfully still Lord Warwick had become when she had confessed she thought him in possession of all the qualities she sought in a husband. The poor man was stunned and, no doubt, repulsed by her admission, but being a gentleman he was attempting to extricate himself from an awkward situation without insulting her.

Despite his carefully phrased rebuttal, Maggie had been completely and utterly humiliated. And to compound her humiliation, she had blathered on endlessly. It was bad enough she had confessed that he was the most perfect man in the kingdom, but when he had given her a perfectly good excuse for the source of her admiration, she had insisted that he was inordinately handsome!

"The devil take him!"

"I beg your pardon?" Sarah asked.

"Oh, dear, I was thinking aloud again. I pray that I don't do so tonight." *Think before you talk.* Perhaps if she told herself that every waking moment she could shed her horrid habit. Rebecca knocked on Maggie's door and entered while Maggie watched her through the looking glass. "You look lovely in yellow, pet," Maggie said as Rebecca came to stand beside her.

"Not as lovely as you. And I see your bosoms have been repaired. I daresay Lord Warwick will still gape at your breasts all night. It's really not fair, you know."

Maggie turned to face her sister. "I'm afraid you've lost me. What's not fair?"

"You have the good eyes *and* the womanly breasts."

"Yours will grow. I vow my breasts were no bigger than yours when I was seventeen."

"But I shall be eighteen in a few weeks!"

Maggie giggled. "Perhaps you'll get breasts for a birthday present!" She thanked Sarah and stood up, linking her arm through Rebecca's.

"By the way," Rebecca said, "I've thought of something you can do to prevent your babbling."

Upon her return from Greenwich Maggie had evaded most of her sister's questions. Especially the one when Rebecca asked if Lord Warwick had tried to get beneath her skirts. "Of course, not!" Maggie had responded. She also failed to inform her sister of the dead body. "Pray, do tell me."

"You must resolve to put a bite of food in your mouth as soon as you decide to speak. While you're chewing, you can mentally phrase your words." She handed Maggie a tin. "Here are some comfits. For after dinner. Whenever you wish to speak to Lord Warwick, you must pop a comfit in your mouth first."

"A brilliant plan," Maggie said, tucking the tin into her left glove.

Lord Warwick and Mr. Lyle awaited them downstairs, and Lord Warwick escorted Maggie into the dining room, where she was seated at his right. She vaguely recalled some rule of etiquette that the highest ranking person should be seated next to the host. She almost laughed, then decided to pinch a prawn from the center of the table and pop it into her mouth. Rebecca's approving nod did not escape her notice.

"A pity the weather was dreary for your outing to Greenwich," Harry said to her as they filled their plates.

Maggie looked at Lord Warwick, who had agreed to keep Bibble's death from Rebecca.

He nodded.

Maggie popped another prawn into her mouth. Once she was finished chewing, she said, "It wouldn't have been so dreadful had we not met with a thunderstorm."

"Oh dear." Rebecca cast a worried glance at Lord Warwick. "My sympathies to you, Lord Warwick, for being exposed to my sister's irrational fear of thunderstorms. Pray, I hope she wasn't too hysterical for I know how vexed you are by hysterical females."

Maggie popped another prawn into her mouth.

Lord Warwick's voice softened. "There's nothing irrational about your sister's severe aversion to thunderstorms."

"I comported myself as any irrational six-year-old would have," Maggie said with a laugh. *Except a six-year-old would not allow a man to strip her bare or . . .* She felt her cheeks burning.

"I should never have exposed you to the storm," Lord Warwick said. "I should at least have taken the carriage. The gig offered little shelter from the rain. I'll feel wretchedly responsible if you take a lung infection."

"Pray, don't give it another thought," Maggie said. "I'm not prone to lung infections."

The footmen cleared the seafood and set out the second course. Maggie eyed the peas. They would be her babble preventer during this course.

"You shouldn't have taken the lady out in weather that would frighten her delicate sensibilities," Mr. Lyle said to Edward.

Maggie scooped a spoonful of peas and inserted them in her mouth.

"At the time," Lord Warwick answered, "I was not aware of the countess's fear of thunder."

"And lightning," she added.

Lord Warwick's amused eyes locked with hers for the briefest second.

"Did you know, Mr. Lyle," she said, "that Lord Warwick fancies himself an expert on weather?" Oh dear, she should have filled her mouth with peas.

Instead of being angry over her chastisement, Lord Warwick flicked her an amused glance.

"I had some idea," Harry said. "He's always talking about clouds. Daresay he's wrong about them as often as he's right."

"Her ladyship is humbling me," Lord Warwick said. "She told me I was pig-headed."

Rebecca's mouth dropped open, her stunned gaze shifting to Maggie.

Maggie stuffed a spoonful of peas into her mouth. After she had chewed and swallowed, she said, "It was most uncharitable of me to speak in that manner to Lord Warwick." There, she was perfectly contrite. If only she could take back the other blathering statements about his lordship's perfection.

"Uncharitable but true," he said before turning his attention to Rebecca, querying her about *Pride and Prejudice* while Harry Lyle discussed *The Tempest* with Maggie.

Throughout the night as Mr. Lyle engaged Maggie in conversation (or, to be more accurate, hoarded her attention), she observed him closely. Were he not so close to Lord Warwick, he would be considered rather handsome. He was as tall as his lordship but thinner. Where Lord Warwick was dark, Mr. Lyle was fair with light brown hair, but the two men had much in common besides their privileged backgrounds and the shared nature of their work. Both were men of fashion, both struck her as being exceedingly kind, and both men were arrogant. Only a confident man could dress down a peer as Mr. Lyle had done to Lord Warwick on more than one occasion.

Mr. Lyle's kindness to her, Maggie realized, was fueled by his obvious ardor, ardor he had eloquently expressed in a poem he had written in praise of her beauty and delivered with a lovely bouquet that afternoon.

After dinner Mr. Lyle begged Maggie to be his partner at whist. They made a good team. She was a better player than Rebecca, and Lord Warwick was better than Mr. Lyle—which made for balanced teams.

She set her tin of comfits upon the playing table and continued to pop them into her mouth to prevent her from saying something blathering.

"I didn't know Lady Warwick was so fond of comfits," Lord Warwick said.

Maggie could feel his eyes on her, had ever since they'd sat down. She had even observed his gaze flicking to her bosom, a bosom that looked perfectly fine in the newly mended emerald dress.

"My sister is using the comfits—"

"And prawns and peas," Maggie added.

"To keep her from speaking before she thinks," Rebecca said.

Maggie's lashes lifted, and her eyes met his lordship's and locked. In that brief second she would vow they both remembered her blathering declaration on the journey to Greenwich.

As the color rose to her cheeks, neither could break the gaze. He may have rejected her outright that afternoon, but there was an intimacy between them now that hadn't been there earlier. She finally looked away, instantly opening the tin to procure a comfit. It wouldn't do at all for her to start blabbering about how a sultry glance from him sent liquid heat rushing to her core.

"Will Warwick take you ladies to Almack's?" Harry asked Maggie.

Maggie tossed Edward a quizzing glance.

"Hopefully next Wednesday," Edward said.

Harry directed his attention on Maggie. "I beg that

you allow me to be your partner for the first set, my lady."

"It will be my pleasure, Mr. Lyle." Her gaze flicked to Edward.

He was brooding again.

Chapter 12

The following afternoon when Harry Lyle brought documents for Edward to work on he also presented Maggie with another bouquet. "How very thoughtful of you, Mr. Lyle," she said as she requested a maid to put the flowers in water. "I shall put these on the demilune table in Lord Warwick's entry hall so that everyone can enjoy them." The scent from the many bouquets she had already received permeated her chambers, making the addition of one more intolerable, but she would not share that information with Mr. Lyle. "Do you have time for tea?" she asked him.

"I always have time for you," he said, his tender gaze whisking over her.

Pulling her shawl over her breasts, she summoned her sister to join them, then she and Harry went to the saloon. Its asparagus-green draperies swung away from the tall casements, exposing another gray day.

"A pity the weather prohibits an excursion in the city," he said as he sat on a satin settee that matched the one upon which Maggie sat across from him.

She met his gaze and spoke frankly. "I think we both know the real reason why I'm not permitted out. Does Lord Warwick not share everything with you?"

A contrite look on his thin face, he nodded. "On the matter of your confinement I'm in complete agreement with Warwick. Beastly about the man in Greenwich."

"I beg that you not mention that in my sister's presence."

At that moment Rebecca entered the saloon and courteously greeted Mr. Lyle before sitting beside her sister. Maggie approved of Rebecca's mint-green dress. For the first time ever, her sister was taking pains to present herself attractively. Maggie wondered if the fictional Mr. Darcy was responsible for this improvement and vowed to finish reading the book.

"Will you be presented this year?" Harry asked Rebecca.

"My sister had wished that I could attract a well-to-do husband, but I prefer to wait until next year to be presented."

"Rebecca's hoping by then—" Oh dear, she couldn't continue. She withdrew the tin from a pocket in her morning dress—she wished to be prepared in case his lordship engaged her in conversation—and inserted a comfit into her mouth. Oh! She had almost said that Rebecca hoped to grow breasts by next year, and such a topic was sure to mortify her timid sister. "By then Rebecca's aversion to matrimony might not be so keen," she finished. "My disastrous marriage to The Scoundrel has rather soured poor Becky against men—despite my assurances that not all men are like him."

"Permit me to say I am pleased you don't hold all men in dislike because of the vile actions of one man," Harry said to Maggie.

Wiggins brought in the tea tray and placed it on the table in front of Maggie, who served.

"I've been reading in the newspapers," she said, handing Harry a delicate cup and saucer, "that Lord Carrington is the Foreign Secretary. He was kind enough to secure vouchers for my sister and me to attend Almack's."

"Lord Carrington is a very important man whose favor is courted everywhere."

"I shall look forward to meeting him," Maggie said.

"I should not be surprised if he doesn't pop in to see Warwick," Harry said.

Maggie sighed. Poor Lord Warwick was neglecting his duties because of her. She exceedingly disliked being responsible for rearranging his lordship's well-ordered life, particularly since the disruptions plunged him into such ill temper. If only she and Rebecca had some other place to go. If only she could find a nice man to court her.

A nice man to court her. It suddenly occurred to her the man sitting in front of her fit the requirements. She had not heretofore considered him eligible, most likely due to how poorly he compared to Lord Warwick, but Lord Warwick was the ineligible one! She must school herself not to remember what Lord Warwick looked like without a shirt, not to think about the way her heart melted when she studied his broodingly handsome face, not to recall his heated gaze, and especially not to recall how exquisitely he made love to her. Lord Warwick had no serious interest in her. He loved Fiona. End of story. End of secret longings.

She drew in her breath to redirect her attention to Harry Lyle as Tubby came prancing into the room. The cat circled the tea table and came to stand in front of Mr. Lyle's boots. After a quick lick at his shiny Hessians, Tubby leaped upon Mr. Lyle's lap.

To Maggie's stunned approval, Mr. Lyle began to stroke Tubby's gray fur and speak to the cat as if he were cooing a baby. "Well now, my pretty girl, what's your name?"

"She's a he," Rebecca corrected.

"His name is Tubby," Maggie said.

A huge grin spread across Harry's face. "So you like to eat, do you?" he cooed to the cat. "A most fitting

name for a most friendly cat." He ignored the cat hair
which carpeted his charcoal breeches and cradled the
animal to his breast, continuing to speak tenderly.

Maggie was delighted. "It's so refreshing to see a
man show affection for felines," she said, "a partiality
to dogs seems a more manly preference. In fact the
only man I've ever known to adore cats was—" Oh
dear, she had as good as told him his affection for cats
made him effeminate. Which she'd vow he wasn't.
She quickly popped a comfit in her mouth. "Was
quite highly regarded by me," she finished after chewing her candy. Thank goodness she had changed her
original sentence in which she had planned to say
"was a fop."

"Personally," she continued, "I don't see how anyone could prefer dogs over cats. Especially big dogs
that can't cuddle on one's lap."

"Not all cats are as cuddly as Tubby," Rebecca
pointed out.

Mr. Lyle tickled under Tubby's chin and spoke affectionately. "As it happens, I love dogs too. In fact, I
love all animals. Daresay it comes from not having any
brothers or sisters. Pets were my playmates when I was
a child."

"So you're an only child," Maggie said. "You must
tell me all about yourself, Mr. Lyle." Her eyes dancing,
she folded her hands in her lap and leaned against
the back of the settee, eager to learn more of this
prospective suitor.

Before any words left Mr. Lyle's mouth, Wiggins announced Lord Aynsley was calling upon Maggie.

"Do show him in," Maggie said, noting that Mr. Lyle
had stiffened. "And please bring more tea."

When Lord Aynsley strolled into the room carrying
more flowers for Maggie, Mr. Lyle set Tubby on the
Turkey carpet and stood to greet the peer. That the

two men obviously resented the other's presence reminded Maggie of two circling cocks about to fight.

She gushed over the flowers, smelling them before setting them on the tea table. The viscount came to sit on the end of the settee Harry occupied and addressed his attentions to Maggie. "I've been concerned about your ladyship's health."

"Why so?" Maggie asked, taking in the peer's satisfactory appearance. His slight build, trim waist, and natty style of dress belied his forty years of age. Were it not for his thinning brownish gray hair, he could pass for thirty. His face was genial, not at all unattractive, and he was in the habit of perpetually smiling. *Perhaps he was more eligible than Mr. Lyle.* Now she was in a quandary as to which man she should endeavor to form an attachment to.

"Because of Lord Warwick's note informing me that your propensity to colds excluded you from outdoor pursuits until the weather warms," Lord Aynsley said.

She did wish Lord Warwick would first apprise her of his silly excuses. "The weather, I must admit, has been abominable since I've been in London."

"But you have stayed well?"

She gathered her shawl around her. It was the knitted shawl Lord Warwick had procured for her in Greenwich at great cost, the one she had told him she treasured. She had taken to wearing it throughout the day and night. It served as a reminder that Lord Warwick was not always an ill-tempered ogre. She tortured herself remembering how solicitous he was of her when she was damp and frightened in the inn's dimly lit parlor, remembering what a tender lover he had been. "Though it's very dank, I've managed to keep warm," she said. "Lord Warwick has promised an outing to Almack's next Wednesday, provided the weather isn't too inclement—and provided my . . . delicate health holds up."

Maggie ignored the fact Rebecca was glaring at her.

"I beg that you dance the first set with me," Lord Aynsley said.

Mr. Lyle's cold gaze shot daggers at the viscount. "I'm afraid the lady cannot do that. She has promised the first set to me."

Lord Aynsley's posture went stiff, then his eyes softened and he spoke to Maggie. "Then oblige me by saving the second for me."

"I will be happy to do so, my lord."

She found herself looking from one man to the other, mentally comparing them. They were both so terribly amiable. They both were above average in appearance. Both men had apparently met with Lord Warwick's approval—even if Lord Warwick had eschewed the fact that Lord Aynsley's progeny included seven children and his country seat was in Shropshire—neither of which seemed a hindrance to Maggie. Both men seemed genuinely fond of her. Not like . . . oh, she could not allow her vexing thoughts to turn to the utterly ineligible Lord Warwick.

It was as if her thinking of Lord Warwick summoned him for he and another man—a distinguished looking man in his fifties—presently strolled into the room. Lord Warwick's gaze skimmed from one man to the other, then stopped with a frown at the lush bouquet that tumbled on the tea table.

"Lord Carrington," he said, "allow me to present you to the Countess Warwick."

Lord Carrington swept into a gallant bow. "May I say, my lady, you're even more beautiful than Warwick said?"

Her insides fluttered and she willed herself to not meet Lord Warwick's gaze. "You're very kind, my lord, and may I say you're every bit as distinguished as I've been told you were?" Her gaze skipped from his gray hair to his blue eyes and aristocratically handsome face, then along his lean body clothed in exceeding good taste.

"Please join us for tea, my lord," she said to him.

Lord Warwick nodded his mumbled greetings to the two men then came to sit on a chair a few feet away from Maggie while Lord Carrington sat in a chair close to Lord Warwick.

"I thought you had work to do," Mr. Lyle said to Lord Warwick.

Lord Warwick glared at his coworker. "I could say the same to you."

Oh dear, Lord Warwick was in one of his sulking moods, she could see.

To compound his ill temper, Tubby decided to pay him a visit. Not *just* pay him a visit. The cat launched itself upon the earl's lap and was settling in when Lord Warwick picked up his boneless body and tossed him to the carpet. "It's bad enough that my house is turned into an orangery, that men come and go as if it were a livery stable, but to make matters worse, an exceedingly overfed feline has determined that my lap is his bed." He directed an icy glance at Maggie. "I thought you were going to keep your cat from my library."

"Oh dear, has Tubby been disturbing your work?" Maggie asked.

"As a matter of fact, he has!"

"I'm very sorry indeed," she said. "I won't let him bother you again."

"Let up, Warwick," Mr. Lyle said. "You should be honored that Tubby likes you." He reached down and scooped up the cat. "You're a sweetheart, aren't you, Tubby?" Mr. Lyle said in a tender voice.

"Mr. Lyle and Mr. Tubs get along beautifully," Maggie said, scowling at Lord Warwick. "*He* appreciates Tubby's affectionate nature."

"Daresay it would be different were he a dog," Lord Warwick grumbled. "A big dog."

"I think you're being very pig—" Maggie reached for the comfits. After she had chewed one, she amended her statement. "Very big-hearted to allow my sister and me to cause such upheaval in your home."

She redirected her attention to Lord Carrington, whom she feared she was neglecting. "Tell me, Lord Carrington, about your family. Have you children?"

"I've not had that pleasure since I've never been married."

How did such a prize escape the marriage mart all these years, she wondered. She could easily imagine how handsome he must have been thirty years ago, for he was still handsome today. And how should she respond to his comment? She could not very well lament the waste of his title and his lack of heirs. Nor could she express her sadness that his line would pass to extinction. She opened the tin of comfits and ate one. "Let us hope, my lord, the perfect marchioness for you is just around the next corner."

The way his gaze slithered along her body made her unaccountably uncomfortable.

"Sorry, Warwick, if my presence has disturbed you," Lord Aynsley said, "but I haven't come to see you. I wished to assure myself as to the countess's good health."

"You can see she's perfectly healthy," Lord Warwick snapped.

"But that's not how I perceived things from the note you sent around to Cavendish Square."

"Oh, yes," Lord Warwick said, as if he were reminding himself of the missive. "Daresay her staying indoors has . . . protected her delicate lungs." His gaze lit on her blue shawl.

She could have sworn his eyes softened.

Yet a few seconds later he was scowling at Lord Aynsley. "How are your children, Aynsley?"

"I'm presuming they all are well. They're at Dunton Hall at present."

"Still having trouble keeping a governess?" Lord Warwick asked. "As I recall, your sons' penchant for putting crawling creatures into the ladies' beds has made keeping a governess rather difficult."

Lord Aynsley squirmed uncomfortably on the settee. "As it happens I am currently seeking a new governess."

Maggie's heart went out to Lord Aynsley and his motherless children. "It sounds to me as if your dear children only lack for a loving mother."

His face brightened. "I agree, my lady. The lads are really good boys."

"I should like to meet them," Maggie said.

"I would be honored to have you make their aquaintance."

Lord Warwick cleared his throat. "It's unlikely Lady Warwick would wish to brave the dank weather in Shropshire—because of her delicate lungs."

Really, Lord Warwick was being a positive ogre! She looked from one uncomfortable visitor to the other. How could two such amiable men have turned into stone statues in the span of a few minutes? Only Lord Carrington maintained his composure.

"Well," Lord Aynsley said, getting to his feet. "I'd best be on my way." He bowed to Maggie. "May I call on you tomorrow?"

"I should be delighted," she answered.

Mr. Lyle scowled at Lord Warwick, then got to his feet. "I had best return to my work."

"I'll go with you," Lord Carrington said. He turned to Maggie. "It's been a pleasure to meet you, my lady. May I call on you again?"

"Yes, of course," she replied.

Once the gentlemen were gone, she snatched up

the tin of comfits and ate one. Had she not, she would have unleashed her temper on his lordship for his rudeness to *her* guests. But she had no right to chastise him since she was a guest in his house. She picked up Tubby and stroked his soft fur. A pity her visitors, her cat, and herself so ignited Lord Warwick's wrath. "I'm only trying to be agreeable to the men," she told the earl, "to attract a husband in order to allow you to be rid of my repugnant presence."

His goldish brown eyes held hers. And softened. "I told you before. You could never be repugnant." Then, breaking the gaze, he got up and left the room.

Chapter 13

Lord Warwick had no guests for dinner that night. She had thought he'd rather enjoyed playing whist the previous night, but he seemed to enjoy nothing tonight. He was out of charity with poor Mr. Lyle, with Tubby—and with her.

He avoided looking at her. He avoided speaking to her. And that brooding look was back on his darkly handsome face.

During dinner, she put her mind to devising ways to please her host. If only there was some service she could render him in payment for his hospitality—as grudgingly as he had bestowed it. Even if she had money to purchase something for him, what did one give to a man whose pockets were so deep? Were she a needlewoman, she could sew him a fine linen shirt, but everyone knew she was no needlewoman. Since she was a rather well-organized person, she had thought to tidy his library for him, but had discovered he was even more well-organized than she. No matter how many papers were piled on his desk, he never left the library without completely cleaning its surface. She remembered his interest in shooting and angling but was powerless to help him in that quarter also. Mental challenges appealed to him, as they did to her. She would have to content herself by being his formidable opponent at chess.

During dinner he directed most of his comments to Rebecca. *What was Miss Peabody reading now? Had she read "Childe Harold's Pilgrimage?" Who were her favorite poets?*

Maggie did not like being ignored. "I've been reading *Pride and Prejudice,*" she informed her dinner companions.

"And do you like it as much as Miss Peabody did?" he asked, studying the sturgeon he was putting on his fork and avoiding eye contact with her.

"Since I've read only half of the book, I cannot say it's the best novel I've ever read, but I am enjoying it excessively." She turned her attention to Rebecca. "Do you think the author means for the book to be humorous?"

Rebecca smiled. "The author is very talented, and I don't doubt that she intended Mr. Bingsley and Mr. Collins be portrayed in a humorous light."

Lord Warwick began to chuckle. "I'll own Mr. Collins is devilishly funny—for being so utterly self-absorbed and shallow."

Thank goodness Lord Warwick had laughed. The tenseness in her body uncurled as she joined him in laughter. If only she could think of another humorous character to lighten their banter. "I vow I've not enjoyed any characters—except Shakespeare's—so much," she said. "I think *Taming of the Shrew* is my favorite of Shakespeare's plays because it's so light." Turning to his lordship, she added, "I expect being a man, you prefer the tragedies or histories."

"The histories," he said.

"And which is your favorite?"

He thought for a moment. "It's difficult to choose between *Richard the Third* and *Julius Caesar.*"

"I would think English history much more interesting to an Englishman," Maggie said.

"But Caesar is intrinsically tied to the history of

Britain. We would not be the country we are had his troops not settled here."

"It's quite incredible to think Roman soldiers who lived here eighteen hundred years ago left a legacy that's still evident today," she said.

He set down his wine glass. "Nowhere is the Roman occupation more apparent than in Bath," he said. "You must go there sometime."

"There are many things I wish to see in England, provided I'm ever free of my chains," she said lightly.

He gave her an apologetic glance. Her stomach tumbled as her gaze flicked from his compelling eyes and over that handsome face that spoke of power and ageless strength. "It shouldn't be for long," he said. "It appears Lyle and Aynsley would be only too happy to offer for you, but I would advise you to wait and see how you take at Almack's."

"I daresay no man there can be more agreeable than Mr. Lyle or Lord Aynsley," she said.

Lord Warwick's brows lowered as he mumbled, "Don't know what's gotten into Aynsley. Though he's two and forty, he appears to be under the illusion he's twenty years old again."

"Don't be so harsh on him, my lord," Maggie said without malice. "I daresay he's not courted a woman since he was twenty. It's only natural that he revert to those youthful ways."

He gave her a puzzled look but said nothing.

As the dinner came to an end, Maggie addressed her sister. "Would you mind terribly, pet, if Lord Warwick and I resume our chess game tonight?" Maggie was determined to engage her host in an activity that would bring him pleasure.

"I should be delighted to return to my present book," Rebecca assured her.

"It's not possible to resume the game," Lord

Warwick said with a frown. "My servants put up all the pieces."

"But I remember exactly where they all were," Maggie protested.

A smile curved his lips. "How can I trust you not to set up the board to your own advantage?"

"Very well, my lord," she said with a mock scowl, "we'll start a new game—if that is agreeable to you."

As he set up the chess pieces he allowed himself to admire her keen memory. It was really quite incredible that she could remember where every piece had stood three nights ago. Were he pressed to do so, or had he studied the configuration before they retired that night, he could be assured of remembering only ninety-five percent of the positions.

Better to admire her memory than to actually glance at her. When she had sat down beside him at the dinner table, he had to force his gaze away from her. Her stunning beauty in the ruby-red gown that swept low at the neckline had sent his pulse surging. He told himself it was only that the red was extremely becoming with her rich, dark hair for she was more beautiful this night than he had ever seen her before. Yes, he decided, it had to be the red.

As he spooned the soup into his bowl, he had willed himself to picture Fiona's loveliness, but only a vague, distant picture of her fair blond beauty arose. Damn! It had been too long since he'd seen her. Before Maggie came he had ached to see Fiona, to hear her sweet voice, to enfold her slim body in his embrace, and to marry her and love her to completion. The very thought of his precious Lady Fiona often sent the blood rushing to his groin. But no more.

Now, it was Maggie who summoned vibrant life below his waist. It was Maggie who had invaded his erotic dreams the night before, even though it was Fiona—and only Fiona—whom he loved and always had. Fiona was the only woman he wanted.

Until this week. *Damn it.*

During the first course of dinner, he alternated between being angry at himself for his carnal weakness and angry with Maggie for giving herself to him. Then he would chastise himself for blaming her. She hadn't tried to seduce him. Looking back on it, there were so many ways she had innocently ignited his passion leading up to that stormy day in Greenwich. First, she had spoken of her breasts in his presence. But not in a seductive manner. She had discussed them as if she were commenting on the weather. And when she had told him he was some kind of prize, he would vow she said it as innocently as she would comment on the color of his hair.

To give her her due, the woman had not actually tried to ensnare his affections. Not that she *had* ensnared his affections, of course. In fact, the maddening woman did not even *want* his affections. He would vow she had not knowingly stirred his lust. Which she most certainly had done and continued doing at this very moment. It wasn't her fault she was so deuced beautiful. Nor was it her fault thunderstorms reduced her to an amorous heap of raw emotions. He would endeavor to get through the rest of the night without allowing himself to drink in her beauty. Or remember the feel of her beneath him.

A pity he could not play chess blindfolded.

Maggie made the first move in the game; his followed quickly. "Who taught you to play?" he asked.

"My father. He must have had the patience of a saint for I was but eight years old when we started."

"Your early start explains why you're so good."

She smiled up at him. "Do you really think so? Or am I only good for a woman?"

She had him there. "I've played with but a few men who were better than you. Your play is vastly superior to any woman I've ever known."

She quickly moved again, and he countered. "What of your brother? Did your father play chess with him also?"

"I suppose Papa and James must have played chess when James was younger, but my brother was a grown man when I was born. We had never lived under the same roof until last year."

She must have been desperate to get away from Henshaw if she had to beggar herself to that insensitive brother of hers. *Damn Henshaw.*

Edward found himself wondering about her relationship with the charlatan she had married. "Did you play chess with your husband?"

Her spine went ramrod straight. "A few times."

"And was he a worthy opponent?"

She gave a bitter laugh. "It was my opinion that The Scoundrel was far too impatient a person to develop any kind of skill at any kind of endeavor." Her gaze dropped to the board and she murmured, "Would that I'd the good sense to have played chess with the man before marrying him."

"If it's any consolation," he said in a low voice, "I was fooled by him, too. I spent a good bit of time with him and found him the jolliest of fellows."

"That would be Lawrence," she said with a distasteful frown. "Always living for a lark. I daresay that's why chess bored him so much. His life was nothing but the pursuit of fun. A pity his idea of fun centered around liquor and lewd women."

Edward coughed. Lewd women was definitely not a topic he wished to touch. Especially since it would do nothing to reduce the throbbing between his legs. "That's the Lawrence Henshaw I knew."

The more Edward was with Maggie, the more certain

he was that she could not be feigning such intense dislike of Henshaw. Edward would wager his estates that she had been completely duped by her scoundrel husband, and he planned to convey his opinions to Lord Carrington at the earliest opportunity.

"Please, can we speak of something else?" she asked. "Anything else."

His glance jerked away from those huge, solemn eyes. He wished to comply with her request at the same time he wished to learn more about the early affection in her marriage. "As you wish, madame."

His gaze flicked to Miss Peabody, who sat twenty feet away, reading beside a brace of candles. He could not look at the young lady and not be struck over how closely she resembled Maggie, yet her beauty in no way compared to her sister's—even if she were to remove those spectacles she always wore. The deep brown of their hair and eyes was identical, as was the creaminess of their complexion. Both were fine boned and graceful. Perhaps it was Miss Peabody's absence of breasts—or absence of sizeable breasts—that made Miss Peabody less attractive. His glance leaped to Maggie's lily bosom before he forced his gaze back to the chessboard, wishing for a blindfold.

"And who taught you to play, my lord?"

He did not trust himself to look at her. There was something utterly seductive about the way the candlelight played on that incredible face, in the way it cast deep shadows beneath those extraordinary lashes. "Actually, my elder brother," he said before thinking.

She went silent for a moment. "Pray, how is it you succeeded the earldom if you have an elder brother?"

He stiffened. The air seemed to swish from his lungs. He fleetingly thought of her comfits and vowed to carefully form his response before replying. "My brother is dead," he said gravely.

"I'm very sorry for you, then," she said in a kindly voice, "for I perceive that you were close."

He winced. "Yes."

"How old was your brother when he died?" she asked, her brow pleating, her voice as soft as a feather's touch.

He waited a moment before replying. "Quite young." *Let her leave it at that.*

She flicked him a querying glance but made no further comment. A few minutes later she asked if he had any sisters.

"None."

"That explains it."

Knight in hand, he looked up at her. "That explains what?"

"Your aversion to having females underfoot. I daresay you would not be nearly so vexed with Rebecca and me were you used to having sisters."

In his wildest imaginings he could not picture Maggie as a sister. "I don't believe I ever said your presence vexed me."

"No, not in so many words."

"What do you mean by that?"

"Forgive me," she said. "I had no right to say that."

He saw that she eyed the tin of comfits that rested on the table.

"You've been exceedingly well mannered," she added.

Because he had the decency to offer for her after losing himself in her arms . . . and body? "I'm sorry if I've been discourteous to you in any way."

She laughed.

What was so deuced funny? "I daresay it's my cat who vexes you," she said, "and I'm heartily sorry for that, my lord. I shall endeavor to keep Tubby out of your sanctuary, or should I say your shrine?" She met his gaze with laughing eyes, and he was powerless not to laugh with her.

Even when that blasted Tubby came rubbing up against his ankles, he refrained from complaint.

"Should you like me to remove Tubby from the room?" she asked.

"Only if he's stupid enough to get on my lap."

Miss Peabody put down her book and called to the cat. He did not come at first, but after realizing he was getting no attention from Edward, Tubby waddled over to Miss Peabody and climbed onto her lap. The chit actually seemed to enjoy petting the creature.

Edward returned his attention to the game, not that the game garnered his full attention when Maggie herself was such a distraction.

After they had been playing for an hour and a half, he realized he was enjoying himself. Really enjoying himself. Not only did he relish a challenging game with an intelligent opponent, but he realized he was growing comfortable with Maggie. Like with a sister. But altogether different.

After the second hour Maggie started to yawn, and he could see the impossibility of finishing the game that night. "You did not sleep well last night, did you?"

"How did you know?"

"You're yawning."

She shrugged. "It's difficult to fall asleep when I feel as if I've the woes of the world on my shoulders—even though I know my worries are quite trivial compared to so many other less fortunates."

"What woes rob you of sleep?" he asked, feeling wretchedly guilty that he contributed to them.

"The necessity of finding a husband, the fear of the workhouse—or poorhouse, being forced to leave Rebecca." Her solemn gaze met his.

He swallowed hard. "I would be most happy, in light of a certain recent occurrence, to wed you myself." He spoke in a low voice so Miss Peabody would not hear.

"That's very kind of you, but I have no wish to be your wife."

But because of her pressing circumstances she would jump into marriage with another man—a man who would not value her as he did? His heart constricted. "Oblige me by not rushing into marriage with a man who's not worthy of you." Neither Harry Lyle nor Lord Aynsley would do. "I'm a wealthy man. I'll see to your needs until such time as you do find a worthy husband. No strings attached."

The soulful look she gave him wrenched at his heart. "Do you know," she asked, "how difficult it is for me to accept your charity? Especially when I have no hope of repaying you?"

"It's no more difficult than having to remove to your brother's, and I assure you I'm much more sympathetic to your failed marriage than he was." He could see from her somber reaction that his words had not quelled her anxieties. "And I do wish you'd stop thanking me and apologizing to me. I've done nothing to merit your gratitude. You're a guest at my house because my suspicious superior ordered me to keep an eye on you."

Damn it—he hadn't meant to tell her that. If she were a pawn in some traitorous scheme—which he was convinced she was not—what he had just told her amounted to treason. In his ten years with the Foreign Office, he had never once betrayed a professional confidence. Until now. Until Maggie had invaded his domain. And his dreams. And his every waking thought.

He saw the look of contempt on her face. "So it seems it's Lord Carrington to whom I owe my thanks. For thinking me a spy to my parents' mother country," she said bitterly, stumbling to her feet and rushing from the room.

Chapter 14

In the days that followed, Maggie confined herself to her own or her sister's chambers. She had no wish to either see Lord Warwick or to speak to him. The only time she came downstairs was to greet her callers: Mr. Lyle, Mr. Cook, Lord Aynsley, and Lord Carrington, all of whom continued to send flowers that permeated the house with scent. The meals that she scarcely touched were taken in her private chambers.

With one simple statement Lord Warwick had pulled the carpet from under her, showing her how glaringly she had misjudged him. She was furious with herself for the way she had so persistently praised him for his kindness to her. *Kindness indeed!* What a fool she had been. Her initial instinct that her presence was repugnant to him had been confirmed. The only reason he allowed her to be a guest in his home was because he had been ordered to do so.

To compound her disillusionment, she was outraged that both Lord Warwick and Lord Carrington suspected her of so odious an offense as spying.

In those first hours of humiliating disappointment, she had vowed to leave his lordship's house immediately. And if she had only herself to consider, she would have left that very night. But it would not be fair to Rebecca to deprive her of food and a warm bed in exchange for . . . a life on the streets, hungry and cold and so desperate for a livelihood that she might be forced to . . . It was unthinkable.

So, with a heavy heart and grim determination, she vowed to pledge herself to one of the men vying for her affections. She desperately needed to be free of the odious Lord Warwick. Even if it meant marrying where there was no love. At least the men who were her suitors were good men. Except for Lord Carrington, whose only interest in her was that he thought her a spy.

But which of the others would she choose? It was easier to eliminate, so she eliminated Mr. Cook by informing him that she had formed an attachment to someone else. But choosing between Lord Aynsley and Mr. Lyle was six of one and half a dozen of the other.

During the hours she sat at her desk in the countess's study, she drew up lists comparing the two men's assets and detractions. Both men were amiable. Both men were gentlemen, though Lord Aynsley's title gave him the edge there. Both men were fine looking. She had paused and pictured each man in her mind's eye. Then in the column of attributes beside Mr. Lyle's name, she credited him with being the better looking. After all, he was ten years Lord Aynsley's junior. And he was taller. There was something about his lanky form she found most attractive. Mr. Lyle also got credit for being the more youthful. That Lord Aynsley was fifteen years older than she posed the distinct possibility that she could be widowed again at an early age, and she wouldn't like that. Lord Aynsley, however, was wealthier than Mr. Lyle. Another plus in his column.

When it came to the detractions column, she listed his lordship's age. She fleetingly thought of the seven motherless children. While some women might see that as a distraction, Maggie did not. The prospect of nurturing them tugged at her heart, and she could not deny that her organizational skills would be put to use running so vibrant a household.

In the end, she did not score his lordship's children in either the attributes or the detractions column.

She did score Mr. Lyle down for his lack of wealth, which Lord Warwick had quickly pointed out to her early in their acquaintance, but she credited Mr. Lyle for his intelligence. Not that Lord Anysley was not intelligent. It was just that Mr. Lyle was possessed of a quicker wit and a broader scope of interests. Lord Aynsley was too enamored of the sporting pursuits, to her way of thinking.

Lord Aynsley was marked down for his idleness, even though she knew most men of his class *were* idle. She liked that Mr. Lyle was conscientious in his work at the Foreign Office.

His poor lordship was also marked down for his lack of humor. In comparison to Mr. Lyle, Lord Aynsley's personality was sadly flat.

Another mark on the detractions column went to Lord Aynsley for his meekness. She did not like meek men at all. She smiled when she remembered how Mr. Lyle never failed to stand up to the smug Lord Warwick. *Damn his lordship!*

When she finished, she realized if she had to spend the rest of her life with one of the men, it must be with Mr. Lyle. She might even be able to grow to love him. In time.

Now all she lacked was his offer.

Lord Aynsley's offer came first. She suspected he had been wanting to offer for several days but was unable to do so because every time he came to Warwick House, Mr. Lyle was there.

On the day of Lord Aynsley's offer he came earlier and did nothing to hide his glee that Mr. Lyle was not there. His gaze flicked to Rebecca, who sat reading by the window of the saloon. "If I might have a private word with you, my lady," he said to Maggie.

Her breath grew ragged and she began to tremble. She tentatively thought of denying his request in order to spare herself from the onerous duty of turning him down. Instead she said, "Shall we go out in the garden, my lord?"

After she donned a pelisse, the two proceeded to enter the walled garden behind Warwick House. Despite the cold, the sun shone. Her heart pounding, she bent down to scoop up a feather and began to twirl it in her gloved hands.

"You must be wondering why I wished to speak privately to you, my lady," he began.

Her gaze lifted from the feather to his fine gray eyes. "If you wish to offer for me, my lord, I must tell you my affections are engaged elsewhere."

His face fell, all hope that had been in his eyes a moment ago gone, his brows forming a deep V. "Lyle?"

She nodded gravely.

His lips thinned. "He has no fortune, you know?"

"I hope I'm not so shallow that a fortune would be a man's main attraction." She lifted her gaze to him. "I'm extremely flattered over your interest in me. You're a very fine man, and I sincerely hope you find a woman who will return your regard in a way I cannot." Maggie was exceedingly sorry she had ever led him on, exceedingly low that she had to reject so worthy a suitor.

"Has Lyle offered for you?"

"No," she whispered.

"He will." Then Lord Aynsley took his leave of her.

Edward rued the night that maddening woman had invaded his home. Had someone told him a week ago he would betray his duties in a fit of babbling anger he would never have believed it. But that's just what he had done. That night he had told her the true reason he allowed her to stay, Edward had despised himself afterward. If she *were* involved in some evil plot, he had just foiled any chance they had of entrapping her. But after he'd had a couple of days to ponder his treachery, he realized his betrayal could do no real harm. It would only make her—and her possible accomplices'—work harder for they would loose their foothold in the enemy camp.

Then there was the matter of her silly obtuseness in evading any possible contact with him. He may have told her he had not wanted her, but that same night he had also told her she could stay as long as she needed, for he had no wish for her to enter into another bad marriage. Quite a concession on his part, he thought, considering dear Fiona.

As angry as he was over Maggie's avoidance of him, he could not blame her. That she was proud, he did not doubt; that he had humiliated her, he was certain.

He consoled himself her estrangement was a good thing. Not being exposed to her disquieting charms was a good thing. He had not dreamed of her last night. Which was a good thing. He had grown to hate himself for his weakness in desiring her. Now he could redirect all those lusty thoughts to the woman who would share his bed for the rest of his life, his dearest Fiona.

Why, then, he asked himself, was he so bloody low? Why did he feel as if he were the bloodiest, lowest creature on earth? Of course, he had betrayed Fiona. Even if Fiona never learned of it, he would know. Not only that, he had taken advantage of Maggie's fragile emotional state.

If he had been in ill humor last week, his grumpiness was compounded tenfold now. He still felt compelled to stay home to guard Maggie's safety. Despite her excessive dislike of him, he wished her no harm. But Lord Carrington compelled him to watch her for suspicious activities, even though Edward had pleaded with Lord Carrington to believe her innocent of any ill intentions. Edward was deuced sick of never leaving his house. He was deuced sick of eating alone. And he was bloody resentful that his evenings were so damned lonely.

He was loathe to admit he actually missed Maggie. Not in the way he missed Fiona, of course. Not at all. Yet he remembered fondly their quiet evenings in front of the fire playing chess. His mood gentled when he recalled her inordinate fear of thunderstorms and how his efforts to protect her and soothe her fears had filled him with a most satisfying sense of purpose. Until those feelings went too far.

Even now he wished to go to her, to allay her feelings of humiliation, to assure her of his affection for her. Of course, it was not the same kind of affection he held for Fiona.

But it was decidedly different from the affection Lyle, his best friend, elicited in him.

Yes, he consoled himself, this estrangement between himself and Maggie was for the best, after all.

A pity he felt lower than an adder's belly.

The door to his library began to ease open. His pulse accelerated as he anticipated seeing Maggie's lovely face peek around the slightly opened door.

But it was not she who entered the room. It was Wiggins. "The post has come," the butler informed him, crossing the room to deliver the mail.

Edward thumbed through the letters until he recognized Fiona's lovely penmanship and tore the letter open.

My Dearest Lord,

   My own inadequate words cannot express what a buoying effect a letter from your dear self has on the lowness of my spirits since my dearest mother's death. It was with all-too-infrequent pleasure that I read Wednesday's letter from you, but seeing that hand of the one I hold in such high esteem only makes me long to see that beloved face again.

   My heart goes out to your poor uncle's widow. It is so very good of you to extend your hospitality to one who has lost so much. Having no sisters of my own, I wish to extend my heartfelt affection to the dear countess as I would to a sister for I think I'm not premature in believing we will soon be related. Please impart to your aunt that she will always be welcome at Windmere Abbey.

   The abbey is a most grim place at the present, due to our great loss. The only thing that could bring me pleasure would be to see your sorely missed countenance, to hear your voice after so long a silence.

   Forgive the maudlin tone of this letter, my dearest Lord Warwick. It is just that I am possessed of such low spirits, spirts than can be lifted only by the presence of one person.

   Yours affectionately,
   Lady Fiona

Were it not for having to guard Maggie, he would fly to Fiona this very day. How low she must be. How dearly he wished to brighten her dark spirits.

He was ready to be rid of Maggie, to resume his old life, to marry sweet Fiona. Bloody hell, he wished for Maggie to show her hand or for Carrington to call off the dogs—though he knew the latter far more likely.

Was there anything he could do to speed along a resolution? *Take her to Almack's.* She had spent an inordinate amount of time with those bloody suitors—neither of which would do at all. Edward's need to be rid of her was not as great as his desire that she fall into good hands. And soon. Today was Wednesday; tonight most of the *ton* would descend upon Almack's. Neither he nor Maggie nor Miss Peabody had left the house since last Friday.

He rang for Wiggins.

A moment later the reliable butler stood in the library's doorway. "Yes, my lord?"

"Please instruct Miss Peabody and the countess that we go to Almack's tonight."

"Very good, my lord."

Edward's voice stern, he added, "And assure them their compliance is mandatory."

"Yes, my lord."

Chapter 15

After so many days of confinement Maggie was looking forward to getting out—even if it meant she would have to ride in a carriage with the odious Lord Warwick. The prospect of seeing England's *beau monde* in their elegant finery and of dancing with well-bred gentlemen filled Maggie with excited anticipation. Most especially, she hoped Rebecca would take. Even if her sister was not ready to marry, Maggie wished to expand Rebecca's limited interests, wished her sister to know life by living it, not through the pages of a book.

Indeed, Maggie had taken more pains with her sister's toilette than she had with her own. Her efforts were rewarded when she noted her sister's elegance in the soft ivory gown that gently draped off her shoulders and puddled into a train in the back. With her dark hair swept back in the Grecian mode and adorned with ivory satin rosebuds, Rebecca—sans glasses—was stunning.

"Oh, Becky, you're beautiful!" Maggie said as she watched Rebecca fasten her gloves.

Rebecca kept pausing to stare into the looking glass. "I'll own I never thought I could look this becoming. I only hope that I don't stumble all night. Without my glasses I'm quite blind."

"I wouldn't worry about that, pet. I perceive that you'll not lack for men's arms to cling to." Maggie glanced into the mirror, pleased over her own appearance in a snow-white gown threaded with silver. "I daresay we'd best not keep the ogre waiting."

"How can you refer to his lordship as an ogre when he's been so very kind to us?" Rebecca asked.

"He's only being kind because he was told to do so by the equally odious Lord Carrington. The pair of them believe I'm a spy."

Rebecca's eyes widened. "Whoever do they think you'd be spying for?"

Maggie shrugged. "The French, I daresay."

Even though Maggie intensely disliked Lord Warwick and told herself she did not care what he thought of her, it did matter what he thought. As she came down the stairs with Rebecca, her pulse accelerated. And when she saw him standing there looking up at her with those brooding eyes, her heartbeat hammered.

"You look lovely tonight, Miss Peabody," he said.

And me? Had the man even given a thought to Maggie? Would he deign to speak to her? "If she doesn't dance every set," Maggie said with a sigh, "I shall declare London men most deficient in their vision." There. She had broken the ice. Now would he address her?

"I agree," he said. "There can't be a prettier girl in all of London." Then, to Maggie's humiliated consternation, he offered his arm to her little sister.

In the carriage, Lord Warwick sat beside Rebecca. Which meant that he and Maggie faced each other. Uncomfortably. He still had not remarked on her appearance, which she thought quite acceptable and which she knew other men would find exceedingly agreeable. *Odious man!*

Still, she was happy that Lord Warwick was endeavoring to put Rebecca at ease on the night of her first London ball. If Almack's could be called a ball. Were his lordship to actually lead Rebecca out for the first dance, her sister's acceptance would be assured. He was wealthy. He was handsome. Incredibly so. And he was an earl. Everyone at the assembly would have to take notice of the extraordinarily handsome couple.

Maggie tried not to look at him, for he was disgustingly handsome in his well-tailored black tailcoat and striking white shirt points framing an elaborately tied cravat. Then her eyes fell to his black pumps and up along the breeches that stretched tautly over muscled calves. No doubt all the ladies would be whispering about him behind their fans. Unaccountably, the thought of other women vying for his attentions made her stomach roil. They could have him! Fiona could have him. Please, take him.

At Almack's Assembly Rooms, Maggie smiled and spoke cordially when Lord Warwick introduced her to the patronesses, though her insides trembled as she faced the formidable matrons. To her great relief Mr. Lyle rushed across the lofty chamber and asked her to dance the first set, a lively quadrille.

During the dance she was able to observe Lord Warwick trotting Becky about the room, introducing her to young fellows who had probably not yet started shaving, then he himself swept her onto the dance floor for the first set.

It did not escape Maggie's notice that practically every female eye in the room was on him. She frowned. *Odious man!*

She flicked her gaze back to her partner. At least Mr. Lyle was tall. She rather liked dancing with men who were tall.

When their hands touched he spoke in a husky voice, "I vow, my lady, your beauty has robbed me of my breath tonight."

Maggie tossed back her head. "Oh, la, Mr. Lyle. Were you truly robbed of breath you wouldn't be able to speak to me now."

"Ah, but when I first saw you walk in with Warwick I was forced to gasp for air."

The next time they came together, Maggie asked, "How think you my sister looks tonight?"

"Ravishing! Her resemblance to you is uncanny now that her spectacles have been removed."

"We are related," she said with a laugh.

"Warwick's an attentive host, given that he has no love for dancing," Mr. Lyle said the next time they came together.

"But he dances so well," she said. Of course she would never admit that to his odious lordship.

"Truth be told, he hates Almack's."

"Then his consideration of my sister at her London debut is commendable." Lord Warwick *was* lavishing his attentions upon Rebecca out of a fatherly sense of charity, wasn't he? Surely he did not have designs on a mere seventeen-year-old. Maggie's shoulders slumped. Of course he had no amorous desire for Rebecca! The man was positively reeking of his devotion to Fiona Hollingsworth.

By now Maggie'd had the opportunity to study the assemblage of the most elegantly dressed people she had ever seen. The young dancers all seemed so amiable, it quite made her fret. They had the advantage over her in that they had many acquaintances among the English high born. A pity she had turned down Lord Aynsley for she had at one time promised him the second set. She consoled herself that if her popularity at assemblies in Virginia was anything to go by, she would not lack for dance partners tonight.

And she didn't. Without question, she and Rebecca were the most sought-after ladies in attendance. If Maggie could only remember the names of half the gentlemen who had asked permission to call upon her at Warwick House the following day. There was a rather dandified Sir Percival in kelly green, a Mr.

Brighton of too tender years, the promising Lord Heffington, a Mr. Campbell from Scotland . . . oh dear, she had forgotten the names of a half dozen others. She must make careful mental note of them when they called tomorrow.

An hour after the festivities started, Lord Carrington swept into the room amidst a great hum of whispers. As she was dancing a second set with Mr. Lyle, Maggie asked, "Pray, why does his lordship attract such notice?"

"Because he never comes to Almack's. Misses just out of the schoolroom ain't his style."

"Yes, I can see where they wouldn't be." She wondered if he had a voluptuous mistress. Weren't mistresses supposed to be voluptuous?

As Mr. Lyle led Maggie off the dance floor, Lord Carrington strode forward, his steely blue eyes never leaving hers. "Ah, Lady Warwick, permit me to say how lovely you are tonight."

She offered her hand, and he duly brushed his lips over it. "Thank you, my lord."

"I beg that you do me the goodness of partnering me for the next dance," he said.

Seeing that Lord Warwick was coming toward them, she turned a bright smile onto Lord Carrington and said, "The pleasure, my lord, would be entirely mine."

When the violins began to play, she realized the next dance was a waltz and gave her sister a meaningful look to make sure Rebecca remembered that maidens were not permitted to waltz without permission of one of the patronesses. Maggie was satisfied when she saw Rebecca stroll to the refreshments room with a gentleman at each side of her.

Lord Carrington was an outstanding dancer, graceful with regal posture and a fluid step. "You are aware of the nature of Lord Warwick's work?" Lord Carrington asked.

"I have some idea, though his lordship does not share any information with me, considering that I'm a suspected spy," she said.

"Oh, my dear woman, you're no longer a suspected spy. In fact . . ." His voice lowered, "I should like for you to perform a service for our government."

"Pray, my lord," she said with some astonishment, "what kind of service could a colonial like me perform?"

"There is a traitor in the Foreign Office," he whispered close to her ear.

"So it would seem."

"Four men in our office—myself, Lord Warwick, Lyle, and Kingsbury—knew of your arrival in London. One of those four is the traitor."

She nodded.

His voice lowered. "I wish for you to monitor all of Warwick's activities."

It was as if Lord Carrington had thrust a dagger into her windpipe. The traitor couldn't be Lord Warwick! Despite her recent dislike of him, she knew the worthiness of the man's character. He would never betray his country.

She could not respond. She could not find her voice. She could scarcely breathe. Surely Lord Carrington was going to laugh and tell her his accusations were nothing more than a joke. She kept watching the man's narrow face with its sapphire eyes, kept seeing his lips moving, but felt as if she had stumbled into a bad dream. He couldn't be saying these things about Lord Warwick. It couldn't be true.

"I understand you're in dire need of funds," he said. "I will pay handsomely for any information you uncover that might reveal Warwick's—or your late husband's—accomplices, or uncover any documents they might possess. With two hundred a year for the rest of your life, you won't have to speedily marry, I think."

Now she understood. Lord Carrington still thought she was a spy, but he was willing to pay her to reveal what she knew. To Lord Carrington's way of thinking, she might as well take her money from the English as from the French. That's why the marquis was talking utter nonsense. The accusations against Lord Warwick must merely be a ploy.

Lord Carrington's mouth was moving again. Her thoughts splintered. What he said next affected her even more profoundly than his initial accusation against Lord Warwick. "I have only just come to learn that the man we know as Warwick is indeed an imposter."

Her face turned to his, mere inches separating them. "What do you mean?"

"The Earl of Warwick's title became extinct eighteen months ago. He had no heirs."

"That cannot be! He was Lord Warwick's uncle."

"That's what the man we know as Lord Warwick said. Due to the fact the old earl was a recluse, no one knew anything about him. When Edward claimed the man as a distant uncle, quite naturally, everyone believed him."

The disillusionment and hurt she had suffered a few nights ago when she learned why Lord Warwick allowed her to stay was nothing compared to this. She could not have been more stunned, more unhappy, had one of her departed parents dropped into the room and told her Rebecca was not her sister.

Nor was it possible to feel more shattered. For despite her anger with Lord Warwick—or whatever his name was—she had admired him. Even loved him, she realized. He had to be honorable! Hadn't he offered to marry her out of honor? And hadn't he

murmured, "You can stop me now," as she felt his engorged flesh throbbing against her naked body?

She would have wagered her very life on his honor.
How could she have been so wrong?

"If you please, my lord," she said breathlessly, "may
we go for lemonade?" She had to get off the dance
floor, had to gather her thoughts, restore the rhythm
of her breathing, stop this wretched trembling.

As Lord Carrington placed a glass of lemonade in
her trembling hand, Lord Warwick came strolling up.
As soon as he saw Maggie's face, his composure
shifted, his face fell. "Are you all right, my lady?"

No doubt she looked as frightened as she had the
day of the thunderstorms. "Yes, quite. I'm just tired."

"Still not sleeping?" he asked, his brooding eyes
locking with hers.

"My sleeping habits are really none of your concern, my lord." *If he is my lord.*

An unreadable emotion flashed in his inscrutable
eyes. "I had hoped you were not so angry with me that
you would deny me the honor of dancing with you
the next set," he said.

She saw that Lord Carrington inclined his head, a
silent order for her to be agreeable to Lord Warwick.

"How could I deny a man who's been so gracious a
host?" she said with sarcasm, offering him her hand.

Once they were dancing—another waltz—he spoke
in a gentle voice. "What's the matter, Maggie?"

Her heartbeat stomped. "What makes you think
something's the matter?"

"I don't think it. I know it. You have the same look
you had during the thunderstorm."

He knew her too well. "I assure you I'm not gripped
with terror tonight. I daresay my discomfort is because the room's so exceedingly hot."

His step slowed and he solemnly gazed down into her face. "Would you like another glass of lemonade? We could stand before one of the open windows while you drink it."

She shook her head. "I'll be fine. I daresay it's just been too long since I've been in a ballroom."

Like that day at the inn, the man was treating her with extreme courtesy. *Damn him. Damn all men.* Either they were all scoundrels, or she was the poorest judge of character in the entire universe! How could she have bestowed her affection twice on completely unworthy men? Was another woman on earth as cursed as she?

For his part, Edward found Maggie the most obstinate, vexatious woman he had ever known. His life had been a dizzying hell since she had stormed into it, his feelings for her quite the opposite of those he felt for sweet Fiona. Fiona who had evoked in him nothing more than a lulling desire. Maggie, on the other hand, elicited a profound passion that settled deep in his loins. It was Maggie whose face he seemed to see the first thing every morning and the last thing every night. It was Maggie whose absence left him feeling only half alive these past several days.

Other than dancing with Miss Peabody to ensure her success, he had danced with no other woman tonight. He tortured himself by glaring at Maggie throughout the evening as she held court for a dozen men who were agog with worship of her striking beauty. Did she have to lower those lashes so seductively when she spoke to them? Must she dance so close to Lord Heffington? Did her neckline have to plunge so very low?

Edward's throat felt parched as he watched her glide along the dance floor in a fetching white gown that fell softly against the sweet curves of her luscious body, the body he had known so intimately.

As his body responded to her, he cursed himself. It was Fiona—not Maggie—who held his heart.

His grip on Maggie's hand tightened and he brought her slightly closer. He could not make himself forget the intoxicating blending of their bodies.

"I've been deeply disturbed since the night you fled from the chess table," he said. "I've been trying to apologize to you for days, but you wouldn't see me."

"Apology accepted. Now can we speak of it no more?"

"Yes, damn it, we will speak of it! I don't believe you a spy. I haven't believed you a spy since the first night I met you, and I've expressed my opinions on the matter to Lord Carrington."

"How kind of you, my lord. Now are you happy? I've regressed back to my former, disgustingly grateful self."

"Please, Maggie," he said, his hand tightening at her waist, yanking her closer. But he did not finish whatever he had intended to say.

Furious with himself for groveling to her, he spoke no more during the remainder of the waltz, then stiffly led her off the dance floor as a half dozen men collapsed around her.

When the evening drew to a close he found Maggie and Rebecca as they were securing their wraps. He glowered at Maggie as she looked up at him, then he silently offered his arm and led them outdoors beneath the canopy to await their carriage.

It was a half hour before they were in the carriage and he turned to Rebecca and said, "You were a great success tonight. No doubt Warwick House will be filled with flowers tomorrow from all of your admirers."

"And Maggie's, too," she said, her voice lively.

"Did you enjoy Almack's, pet?" Maggie asked.

"I hadn't expected to, but I did. It's really most gratifying to have men swooning about one, is it not, Maggie?"

Maggie shrugged. "I am no authority on such matters," she said with feigned modesty.

To which Edward burst out laughing.

"What, my lord, is so amusing?" Maggie demanded.

"You, madame, could give every woman in that ballroom lessons on how to beguile men."

Suddenly the coach lurched to a stop. They heard the voices of men surrounding the carriage, then the door was yanked open by a large, swarthy-looking fellow sporting a black patch over one eye and missing a front tooth. He was flanked by two men armed with long, shiny daggers who ordered them out.

"Don't move," Edward told the ladies through gritted teeth. "I'll not have you order these women around," he said to the man with the eye patch.

The man laughed a deep, bellowing laugh that displayed his missing front tooth. His gaze shifted from Maggie to Rebecca. "Which of ye ladies is Maggie, the Countess Warwick?"

Edward's heart stilled. "You've got the wrong carriage," he snapped, not giving Maggie a chance to answer. "Neither of these women is Lady Warwick."

Then the other door swung open and a smaller man lunged into the carriage and tried to pull Maggie out. "This 'ere's the countess—there's silver in her dress."

Chapter 16

Edward's fist connected with the man's jaw, but as the man fell backward he grabbed Edward's sleeve and pulled him down to the pavement, Edward's full weight on top of him. The man's desperate effort to roll away failed. With a few brisk jabs to the man's whiskered face, Edward easily disabled him.

Then Edward heard Maggie scream his name and whirled to face the other three reprobates who had circled the carriage to pounce on him, two of them flashing daggers. His pulse pounding, he knew he would have been no match against three men even had he been armed. He sprang to his feet, taunting them. "Are you such cowards that you send three men against one?"

His words had no effect on their consciences. Like a vicious wave, they came forward. As the closest man reached him, a fleet kick from Edward sent the man's knife flying. Edward lunged for it and managed to pick it up just as the biggest of the three swooped down on him, pinning him to the ground and trying to dislodge the knife from Edward's tight grasp.

The man was possessed of incredible strength, and Edward knew he would not be able to hold out for long. He squirmed from side to side beneath the man's weight, hoping his up-tilted knife would nick his opponent, but he could budge only a few inches due to the other man's heftiness.

As his strength began to wane, Edward feigned capitulation by closing his eyes, turning his face away and sighing. "You've got the better of me."

Then when the brute relaxed, Edward heaved the knife into the flesh between the man's arm and shoulder. He cried out and fell back, clutching his wound as the blood seeped through his thick fingers.

Edward leaped to his feet, knife in hand, facing the other two as they powered toward him.

Then he heard his coachman shout, and a shot rang out. One of the men cursed and fell to the ground. The other began to run. Edward swung around and saw that the coachman had found the rifle that was stored beneath his seat. "Quick!" Edward shouted, "Let's get these women out of here!" He hurled himself up on the box with Rufus and grabbed the rifle while the coachmen took the reins.

Breathless, Edward stood on the box as the coach lurched forward, his weapon aimed at the remaining cutthroats as the coach-and-four pounded off toward Curzon Street.

As they neared his house, he cursed himself for a fool. Because no one had tried to get to Maggie in the days of their confinement, he had become complacent. He had even given in to the optimistic hope that the murderer had gotten what he sought at Bibble's. And he'd idiotically let down his guard.

He wondered if one of tonight's abductors had killed Bibble. The vision of Bibble's dead body arose powerfully and he closed his eyes against it. *It could have been Maggie.*

God help her if he had not been on hand tonight to thwart the abduction.

As they drew up in front of his house, he came to a decision. He told the coachman to get anything he would need for a journey and to await them in one hour—armed.

Edward himself swung open the coach door and let down the steps for the shaken ladies. "Are you ladies unhurt?" he asked.

"Thanks to you, my lord," Rebecca said.

His gaze locked with Maggie's. Her eyes were bigger than ever and so woeful it tugged at his heart. She nodded and he took her trembling hand as she stepped down. Then he assisted Miss Peabody.

Once they were inside the house he asked them to come to his library.

There was no fire in the drafty, chilled room. Never mind. They would only be there for a few minutes. He closed the door behind them, set the candle upon his desk, and faced them. "I wish for you ladies to pack a valise for a stay in the country." His lips thinned. "We leave tonight, and we will tell no one— not even our most trusted servants—where we are going." He had to get Maggie away, to protect her from almost certain death.

And, he thought grimly, he could trust no one.

Hadn't one of the abductors known her dress was flashed with silver? That could mean that someone who knew Maggie had betrayed her. Harry Lyle's and Lord Carrington's presence at Almack's instantly came to mind. One of those men could be the traitor, could wish to harm Maggie.

His mouth formed a grim line. Neither of those men would learn Maggie's whereabouts. When it was discovered she was gone, the assumption would be they had gone to one of Edward's country holdings. And that wild goose chase would give him time.

"Pray, my lord, where do we go?" Maggie asked.

"I'll tell you when we get in the carriage."

"May I bring Sarah?" she asked.

"Unfortunately not." Knowing Maggie was inordinately attached to the woman, he added, "I'll instruct my servants to show her the utmost kindness if that will ease your mind about leaving her."

"It will, but I'd also ask that you release her from any responsibilities while we are gone. She has earned a well-deserved rest."

"I'll make sure my servants understand."

"My lord?" she said.

"Yes?"

"Can I bring Tubby?"

He frowned. "I'm afraid you'll have to leave him with Sarah."

Thank God Maggie accepted his orders with a silent nod.

In less than an hour, a saber at his side, Edward led the ladies to the coach. Before getting in himself, he spoke to Rufus. "Anything suspicious?"

"No, my lord," the coachman said. "Not a soul has come down the street since I've been here."

"Good." Edward climbed into the coach, taking a seat beside Maggie, who had changed into a wool traveling dress topped by her red cloak. "You ladies are comfortable? Will you require another rug?"

"We're fine," Maggie said, "though still unhinged."

"I have no doubts as to that," he said.

"I shudder to think what those wretched beasts would have done to Maggie," Rebecca said. "I am ever so grateful to you, my lord, for your gallantry."

"Yes, my lord," Maggie concurred, "I am wholly indebted to you."

"It was only right that I save you since it was my foolish complacency that put you in jeopardy."

"It was obvious to me," Rebecca said, "that armed or not you could have beat all four of them. I think you had the advantage over them in your knowledge of pugilism."

He laughed. "Three mornings a week at Jackson's

salon now seems to have been well worth the time and money expended. But I don't share your optimism that I could have handled all four of them without a weapon."

They went some little ways further before Rebecca asked, "Pray, my lord, where are we going?"

"To Yorkshire."

"Is that where your seat is?" Maggie asked.

"No. The . . . people we're up against will know where all my holdings are and are sure to look for us there first."

"I . . . I am most cognizant of why you didn't wait until morning," Maggie said, "and I thank you for losing still another night's sleep on my account."

He gave a little laugh. "Oh, I plan to doze, and I hope you ladies will do so, too. Once we clear all the London tolls and reach a dark country road where progress will be slow, we can stop at a posting inn for a few hours of sleep."

From there he would write to Fiona to announce his impending visit. Hadn't Fiona's recent letter begged that he come to her, hinted at her desire to meet the countess? He had thought of writing to Fiona from Warwick House and having a servant post the letter in the morning but decided against that plan. If the letter fell into the wrong hands . . . he hated to think what would happen to Maggie. And to him.

"Why don't you recline on the seat, pet?" Maggie said to her sister. "You've just experienced the most exhilarating evening of your life, and you need to rest."

Rebecca yawned. "I believe I will."

"I would be only too happy to lend you a shoulder, my lady," Edward said to Maggie.

"I shan't need your shoulder. I'm much too exhilarated to sleep."

Worried too, he would vow.

Few signs of life could be discerned on the streets

Take A Trip Into A Timeless World of Passion and Adventure with Kensington Choice Historical Romances!
—Absolutely FREE!

Enjoy the passion and adventure of another time with Kensington Choice Historical Romances. They are the finest novels of their kind, written by today's best-selling romance authors. Each Kensington Choice Historical Romance transports you to distant lands in a bygone age. Experience the adventure and share the delight as proud men and spirited women discover the wonder and passion of true love.

4 BOOKS WORTH UP TO $24.96— Absolutely FREE!

Get 4 FREE Books!

We created our convenient Home Subscription Service so you'll be sure to have the hottest new romances delivered each month right to your doorstep—usually before they are available in book stores. Just to show you how convenient the Zebra Home Subscription Service is, we would like to send you 4 FREE Kensington Choice Historical Romances. The books are worth up to $24.96, but you only pay $1.99 for shipping and handling. There's no obligation to buy additional books—ever!

Save Up To 30% With Home Delivery!

Accept your FREE books and each month we'll deliver 4 brand new titles as soon as they are published. They'll be yours to examine FREE for 10 days. Then if you decide to keep the books, you'll pay the preferred subscriber's price (up to 30% off the cover price!), plus shipping and handling. Remember, you are under no obligation to buy any of these books at any time! If you are not delighted with them, simply return them and owe nothing. But if you enjoy Kensington Choice Historical Romances as much as we think you will, pay the special preferred subscriber rate and save over $8.00 off the cover price!

We have 4 FREE BOOKS for you as your introduction to
KENSINGTON CHOICE!
To get your FREE BOOKS, worth up to $24.96, mail the card below or call TOLL-FREE 1-800-770-1963.
Visit our website at www.kensingtonbooks.com.

Get 4 FREE Kensington Choice Historical Romances!

♡ **YES!** Please send me my 4 FREE KENSINGTON CHOICE HISTORICAL ROMANCES (without obligation to purchase other books). I only pay $1.99 for shipping and handling. Unless you hear from me after I receive my 4 FREE BOOKS, you may send me 4 new novels—as soon as they are published—to preview each month FREE for 10 days. If I am not satisfied, I may return them and owe nothing. Otherwise, I will pay the money-saving preferred subscriber's price (over $8.00 off the cover price), plus shipping and handling. I may return any shipment within 10 days and owe nothing, and I may cancel any time I wish. In any case the 4 FREE books will be mine to keep.

Name_____

Address_____ Apt._____

City_____ State_____ Zip_____

Telephone (____)_____

Signature_____

(If under 18, parent or guardian must sign)

Offer limited to one per household and not to current subscribers. Terms, offer and prices subject to change. Orders subject to acceptance by Kensington Choice Book Club.
Offer Valid in the U.S. only.

KN015A

4 FREE

Kensington
Choice
Historical
Romances
(worth up to
$24.96)
are waiting
for you to
claim them!

See details
inside...

KENSINGTON CHOICE
Zebra Home Subscription Service, Inc.
P.O. Box 5214
Clifton NJ 07015-5214

of London at this hour. They passed only the occasional hack as their carriage wheels churned through the night. Row after row of narrow houses were dark as pitch, and the only sound they heard was the rhythmic clopping of their horses' hooves.

Then came the sound of Miss Peabody's steady breathing as she fell into slumber.

"I think," he said to Maggie in a low voice, "you'll have to tell your sister the truth about Andrew Bibble. She needs to be fully aware of what kind of peril you're in."

"Yes," Maggie agreed. "She does need to know. Have you considered that in their desperation to get me, they might abuse her?"

"I had not, but it's a distinct possibility."

Silence, like a steel barrier, rose up between them again. Edward surveyed the sleeping city through his window, his fears for Maggie mounting with each turn of the wheels.

"Do we go to Lady Fiona's?" Maggie finally asked.

"How did you know?"

"I believe you once mentioned that she was up in Yorkshire."

"You'll be safe there."

"I thought you did not wish me to meet her."

To be more precise, he had told Maggie he did not want Fiona to see how beautiful she was. "I've had a change of mind. My last letter from her spoke of you. She expressed a strong desire to meet 'the poor countess who has lost so much.'"

Maggie gave a bitter laugh. "And when she sees me?"

How could Fiona see Maggie and not be swamped with jealousy? Would Fiona see the hunger leap to his eyes whenever Maggie was near? More to the point, would his words and actions convince Fiona that he would honor his long-standing intentions toward her? He prayed that once he beheld Fiona's fair beauty all the powerful feelings he had once felt for her would overcome his debilitating desire for Maggie. "She will be all that is amiable, I assure you," he said. "Fiona is a true lady." He had no doubt he spoke the truth.

Maggie thought otherwise. Lady Fiona would likely wish to scratch out her eyes! Which Maggie could well understand since she herself had taken an extreme dislike to Fiona without ever having met her.

But she could not think of Fiona now. She was far too distressed. Her very life was in danger. The man Lord Carrington would have her believe a traitor had risked his own neck to save her tonight. She would never forget the fear that numbed her when she saw the three men moving toward Lord Warwick, their knives glittering in the pale moonlight. He had been magnificent! Like Rebecca, Maggie thought he could have single-handedly disarmed the whole trio.

How could so brave and selfless a man not be honorable? Despite Lord Carrington's accusations, Lord Warwick held Maggie's respect.

Yet Lord Carrington's charge that Lord Warwick was an impostor rang true. She had thought it odd that he had succeeded to the title when he was a mere second son, and when he told her his brother had died, she'd had the oddest feeling he was hiding something, that he had not told her the full truth. Now she knew why.

As the carriage chugged along the dusty country roads she pondered the horror of her predicament. What if Lord Warwick was luring her away from London for his own evil purpose? What if tonight's scene had been staged in order for him to win her confidence? Then she dismissed her own lunacy in even thinking of so ridiculous a scheme.

Which brought her back to her pre-Carrington-talk

state of mind. Though Lord Warwick was a most vexing man, he had never done anything that would cause him to lose her respect. She would trust him with her life.

In fact, that's what she was doing at this very minute, sitting beside him under the cover of night in the middle of nowhere, she'd vow. She had not put up the least resistance when he had informed her they would leave London within the hour.

She had almost fallen at his feet in gratitude, for after the terrifying abduction attempt she had been possessed of a frantic desperation to leave London, to go where those evil people could not find her. The gruesome memory of Andrew Bibble's dead body kept rising before her, and she was too keenly aware that in all likelihood, she would meet the same fate.

Yet as she sat so close to Lord Warwick she felt safe. His powerful presence dispelled her fears now as it had done the day of the thunderstorm. Once she was in his arms, all her fears had vanished.

He was her own personal dragon slayer—despite what Lord Carrington had said about him. The thought of Lord Carrington reminded her that one of the abductors knew the woman they sought wore a silver-threaded dress. The man responsible for the abduction—the one who paid the band of cutthroats—must have been at Almack's assembly rooms tonight. Either Harry Lyle or Lord Carrington. Of course, it could have been someone else, perhaps someone she had never met, someone who had Maggie pointed out to him. But she thought not. There was the previous disturbance in her chambers when only three men beside Lord Warwick knew she was in London: Mr. Lyle, Lord Carrington, and another man whose name she could not remember, a gentleman who had a position at the Foreign Office.

Because of Harry's amiability, she did not wish for her enemy to be him, but she did not want it to be Lord Carrington, either. He seemed so passionate about his precious Foreign Office she could not believe he would ever thwart his own efforts. Besides, a blueblood with generations of ties to England who had more money than he could ever spend had no reason to betray his country.

She yawned.

"Tired?" Lord Warwick asked in a voice one would use with a child. Or a sweetheart.

She nodded. "It's been quite a night." She regretted the pride and obstinacy that had compelled her to refuse the offer of his shoulder. She ached to melt into him, to shed her woes in his all-too-comforting embrace. Yet were he to ask again, her answer would not change. She would have to deny her need for his touch. Its potency could strip her of every ounce of pride, could rob her of rational thought. Worst of all, she could drop her guard.

And she could not allow herself to do that.

"We should be in St. Albans shortly," he said. "We'll stop there for a few hours' rest."

It took all her strength to nod as her head rested against the window. The inky black skies paled as they rode into the dawn and stopped at the posting inn in St. Albans.

Chapter 17

Before he could allow himself to sleep, he must dash off a letter to Fiona. He went to the window where a hazy light from the awakening dawn squeezed into his bedchamber and he took up his pen.

My Dearest Fiona,

The deep melancholy I perceived in your last letter has disturbed me greatly. I hope I am not amiss in thinking that a visit from the man you have so singularly honored might in some way brighten your grievous period of mourning.

Forgive me for the brevity of this letter, but I wish to inform you to expect a visit from me before the week is out. For reasons I will share when I see you, please do not tell anyone of the impending visit.

Yours,
Warwick

P.S. My uncle's widow and her younger sister shall accompany me, owing to your own gracious invitation.

Before franking it, he read it over once more, rather pleased with the offhand manner in which he had mentioned Maggie. As if she were an after-thought.

Would that she was.

He removed his boots—only now regretting he had not brought Cummings—untied his stiff cravat and took off his coat, then stretched across the clean feather bed.

Only then did he realize how sore he was. He must have pulled a muscle in his shoulder during the fight. It hurt like the blazes whenever he moved. And if he were to take off his shirt, he had no doubt there would also be an immense bruise on his left arm to go along with his bruised knuckles. He winced in pain as he attempted to roll over into a more comfortable position.

Though he was devilishly tired, he could not go to sleep. More than from the intense aching which throbbed to his bones, he was beset with fears for Maggie's safety. Even as he lay there, he worried that the band of cutthroats had crept up the stairs to her room.

He bolted up, then set about donning his boots and coat and whipping the cravat into a semblance of a tie. After he dressed, he crept from his room and along the hall to Maggie's and Miss Peabody's chamber at its far end. His step as light as a cat's, he paused outside their door, listening intently. All was quiet. He gave a grateful smile and vowed to protect the ladies with his life. He could not let down his guard until they got to Windmere Abbey.

Therefore, he trudged wearily down the stairs to the first floor where he heard muffled kitchen noises. When the innkeeper saw Edward, he crossed the parlor to greet him. "An early start for your party, my lord?"

"No. We'll wait until nine of the clock. The horses must be fully rested and harnessed again and my coachman needs his sleep if he's to drive throughout the day and into the night."

"Where are you headed?"

Edward's pause was indiscernible. What westward destination would be accessible from St. Albans? "Shropshire."

"A mighty long way indeed."

"That it is, and I'm unable to sleep. Can I trouble you for a cup of tea? Perhaps that will provide a jolt to this weary body."

After the first cup of tea Edward returned to his room for Fiona's letter, then requested the innkeeper send it by today's post. He took the second cup of tea to his chamber and drank while he attempted to shave himself, a skill he had never quite mastered. And he had the nicks to show for it. A pity he hadn't brought Cummings.

He put on a clean shirt and took his time tying the cravat—another task Cummings performed considerably better than his master, Edward lamented.

When he finished, it was nearly nine. He would rap at the ladies' door to rouse them for the day's long journey. He knocked once. Nothing. He knocked again, then heard women's indistinguishable voices, then the sound of a light footfall crossing the room, followed by Maggie saying, "Pray, who is it?"

"Warwick," he answered. "Can you ladies be down for breakfast in twenty minutes?"

"I daresay it won't take us twenty minutes to put on our traveling clothes, my lord. It's not as if we're dressing for a ball."

"Very good," he said. His presence obviously did not warrant careful attention to her grooming. The woman had no interest whatsoever in him. Hadn't she flatly turned down his offer of marriage?

* * *

"How many miles do you think we can go today?" she asked him over a breakfast of cream, toast, cold chicken, and ham.

"I'm hoping Rufus can manage a couple more hours at the end of the day since it gets dark so beastly early this time of year. If he does, we should be able to cover nearly sixty miles. If all goes well, we could be in northern Cambridgeshire tonight." His voice lowered. "Our destination, I don't need to tell you, is not to be revealed to anyone. I've told our host we're going to Shropshire."

"My sister knows everything," Maggie said, "and she realizes the importance of our journey."

"Good," he said.

With amusement in her voice, Maggie added, "I cannot think of Shropshire and not think of poor Lord Aynsley—and your disdain for the location of his seat."

Edward's brows lowered. "Speaking of Aynsley, I was shocked not to find him at Almack's last night. Was he suddenly called out of town, do you know? If the man were in London, nothing could have kept him from coming to dance with you last night—and attempting to keep as much distance possible between you and Harry Lyle!"

A contrite look on her face, Maggie said, "I'm afraid we won't be seeing his lordship any more."

The room went deadly silent for a moment, then Lord Warwick said, "Then you turned down his offer?"

"How did you know?"

"The man was an open book."

As Lord Warwick stared at her, Maggie felt like a horse being auctioned at Tattersall's. "Then a title, I take it," he said, "is no significant recommendation to you?"

"Apparently not," Maggie said, shrugging.

"Does that mean you've made a decision to bestow your affections elsewhere?"

That was certainly none of his concern. She squared her shoulders and spoke haughtily. "As a matter of fact, I have."

"Enlighten me, if you please," he said, never letting his gaze drop.

"I drew up a list of each man's attributes."

"Cook, Aynsley, and Lyle?" he asked.

"Oh no," she said with a shake of her head. "I had already told Mr. Cook not to court me."

"I see," his lordship said in that arrogant voice of his.

"So I had narrowed it down to Lord Aynsley and Mr. Lyle."

"Even before you set so many hearts aflutter at Almack's?"

"It seemed expedient that I remove myself from your home under the circumstances."

"I always told you that you could stay as long as needed."

"Be that as it may, I did not wish to stay there a day longer than necessary."

"So you determined that marriage was the easiest way out of my house?"

She nodded.

"I take it Harry Lyle had more attributes than Lord Aynsley?"

"He did."

"Enlighten me, if you will," Lord Warwick said, "on Lyle's attributes."

She gave him an exasperated glare. "I like that he is not an idle man and that he is possessed of a sense of humor. And he doesn't allow himself to be bullied by you, even if you are an earl!"

Why wouldn't Lord Warwick respond to what she had just said? The man sat there watching her with the most positively brooding scowl.

"Then it would seem my felicitations are in order," he finally said.

"As a matter of fact," she retorted. "Mr. Lyle has not offered for me. I don't even know if he's in a position to do so, but if he does, I shall accept." At least that is what she had planned to do before Mr. Lyle fell under her suspicion.

Lord Warwick nodded thoughtfully. "So you're willing to spend the rest of your life with a man whose strongest recommendation is the ability to stand up to the wicked Lord Warwick?"

She gave him another haughty stare. "I never said you were wicked." She glanced at Rebecca, who sat at the breakfast table reading the newest book. "I declare, Becky, you haven't touched your food!"

Without looking up from her book, Becky absently reached for a piece of toast and took a bite.

Then Maggie's attention returned to his lordship. "Pray, my lord, what have you done to your face? It's bleeding."

He drew in an angry breath. "I cut it shaving."

A smile leaped to her face. "You're not accustomed to shaving yourself, I perceive."

"No, I'm not," he hissed.

She flicked another glance at her sister. "I daresay my sister's endeavoring to cram in as much reading as she can before we climb into your carriage."

He nodded. "I suppose she feels queasy when she reads in a moving vehicle."

"Do you suffer the same malady, my lord?" Maggie asked.

"Why do you ask?"

"Because of your seasickness. Rebecca gets ill at sea, too." Maggie would have sworn there was an angry twitch in his sculpted cheek. No doubt he thought seasickness unmanly.

"I . . . I have no desire to read when I'm riding."

Her mischievous grin unfurled. "Your ailment is nothing to be embarrassed about, my lord."

"I never said I had an ailment!" he protested.

"Despite the brevity of our acquaintance, methinks I know you well." She felt the heat rising in her cheeks when she remembered just how "well" he knew her.

"As I know you, Maggie," he said in a hoarse whisper.

Oh dear, was he too remembering their damp, bare bodies tangled in the bed coverings at the Spotted Hound and Hare?

"I know, for instance," he said in a wickedly mischievous voice, "that when you're truly upset you don't cry. Your tears are only a ruse to coax men into doing your bidding."

She glared at him. "You odious man!"

He laughed, then continued cutting up his cold ham. Neither of them spoke for the next several minutes as they polished off their breakfast.

When he finished eating he instructed the innkeeper to pack food for the journey. "I intend to let Rufus sleep until the last minute for he'll need all the sleep he can get," he told Maggie. "He can breakfast while we ride. I'll drive until he's finished eating."

"So that we can make our sixty miles today?" Maggie asked. "How many days until we reach Yorkshire?"

"Four days if the weather doesn't become too troublesome."

She did not know if she wished to pray for rain or not. As much as she disliked the tediousness of riding for hours cooped up in an uncomfortable coach and staying in equally uncomfortable coaching inns, she disliked even more the prospect of coming face to face with Lady Fiona Hollingsworth.

Once they were an hour out of St. Albans, Edward returned to the coach's interior. This time he sat beside Miss Peabody. Maggie's nearness was far too provocative. However, he had not reckoned on how deuced difficult it would be to face her, peering at the porcelain perfection of her face, at the woefulness of those huge brown eyes, at the graceful curves of her beautiful body.

"You didn't sleep, did you?" she asked in a soft voice.

"How did you know?" God, but he felt wretchedly tired.

"I told you earlier. I've come to know you quite well."

Did every word she uttered have to sound so damned seductive? "So you have," he grumbled.

"Why don't you nap?" she suggested in a concerned voice.

A bone-tired nod was his only response. "I believe I will."

He removed his sword and propped it against Maggie's seat, then settled back, but when his shoulder touched the side of the carriage, he winced.

"You're hurt!" she said.

"It's nothing."

"I'll wager he hurt himself in the fight," Rebecca said.

"Ladies do not wager," Maggie scolded, then returned her attention to Edward. "You are too hurt!"

"Just a little soreness," he assured her.

Maggie's gaze flicked to his scuffed knuckles. "Oh, my lord, I feel so wretched that you wounded yourself protecting me."

"I told you, it's nothing."

"Where else are you hurt?" Maggie asked, her brows—like her voice—lowering.

He shrugged. "I've got nothing more than a bruised arm and tender shoulder."

"When we get to the inn tonight, you must allow me to dress your wound," Maggie said.

"Maggie's ever so skillful in her doctoring abilities," Rebecca assured him.

He was not about to have Maggie touch his bare flesh. Again. "That won't be necessary."

"Oh, I insist," she said with sweet arrogance.

Maddening woman!

He scowled at her, then braced his head against the window to sleep. Despite his extreme discomfort, he managed to drift in and out of sleep over the next three hours.

Though they had eaten the nuncheon the innkeeper's cook had packed, by the time the countryside had settled into darkness, Edward was ravenously hungry again. After consulting his map, he had told Rufus not to stop until they reached Market Deeping, but he wasn't sure now if he could stand to ride in this blasted carriage for another hour.

"You may as well tell the coachman to set us down in the next village large enough to have a posting inn," Maggie said.

"Why, madame, do you say that?" he asked.

"It's perfectly obvious to me that you're starving, my lord."

"Maddening woman!" he muttered—but he followed her suggestion.

Chapter 18

When Lord Warwick lifted his left arm to assist her from the carriage, Maggie saw that he winced, then offered instead his right arm.

"I don't care how trivial you say your wound is, my lord," she scolded, taking his right hand, "I know you're hurt."

"I'll be fine in a day or two," he said as he helped Rebecca down.

They had come to a small posting inn in Burymeade where the innkeeper was only too happy to show persons of quality to a small parlor warmed by a fire blazing in the hearth. Maggie rejected his lordship's offer to help her remove her cloak. "*I'm* not the one who's wounded and am perfectly capable of removing my own cloak—as is my sister."

After shedding her heavy merino cloak, Maggie walked over to stand by the fire. "I vow, it feels so good to stretch my legs I believe I could eat standing up tonight."

He came to stand beside her, and Rebecca dropped into a chair to read by the light of the fire. "A walk would really feel good right now," he said.

"But it wouldn't do you any good to walk in the dark," Maggie said, "for I'm persuaded you'd only fall down in some rut, and I'd have one more injury of yours to tend to."

"I never said I'd allow you to tend my wound."

"See! You're not denying you're wounded."

"As I said, it will heal. Without your assistance."

"Be that as it may, I will not take no for an answer."

"We'll see about that!" he growled.

"You're just being an ogre because you're so beastly hungry."

There was amusement on his face when he faced her. "I do not recommend close confinement with a 'pig-headed' wench."

She laughed and was pleased to see that he laughed with her. "Because this 'pig-headed' wench is getting to know you too thoroughly."

A moment later he pulled out his watch. "Since it's only six of the clock, we shall all finally be able to get a good night's sleep."

"What time will we leave in the morning?" she asked.

"I'd like to have breakfast at five. That way we could get in a good twelve hours' journey tomorrow."

"If the weather holds," she said, her chest tight. Was he that eager to see that blasted Fiona? "Pray, my lord, what does your expertise on the clouds tell you tomorrow's weather will be?" She forced a smile and met his smiling countenance.

"I do believe you're ridiculing me, madame."

"Never that, my lord," she said dramatically.

"I am unable to predict tomorrow's weather from today's clouds. Clouds are subject to changing during the course of a night."

She feigned interest. "I did not know that!"

The door banged open and an aproned matron came into the room with a heaping tray of hot food as the three of them removed to the nearby trestle table where light from a single taper pooled on its well-worn pine top.

Maggie watched her sister as she returned her attention to the current book. "I do wish you would not read in such dim light. It can do your poor eyes no good."

Rebecca reluctantly lifted her gaze from the half-read volume. "But I've done it my whole life."

"And see where it's gotten you! You're half blind."

"Let your sister be," Lord Warwick said.

"That's easy for you to say," Maggie said, "you're not the one who's going to have to read deadly dull tomes to her when she does go blind!"

He began to chuckle again.

It must be the food, she thought, that accounted for his lordship's good humor. She made note to ask for extra cheese in the basket the following day, to keep Lord Warwick's stomach full and keep his foul temper at bay. She watched her sister from beneath lowered lashes. "I promise you can read through the night if you wish, pet, but I do wish you'd honor us with your conversation during dinner. I shouldn't want Lord Warwick to think you've the table manners of a toad."

"I think no such thing, Miss Peabody."

Rebecca folded back a corner of the page she was reading, closed her book, and faced Maggie. "What should you like to talk about?"

Maggie bit at her lip for a moment. "The gentlemen at Almack's. Which of them did you find the most agreeable?"

"I think," Rebecca said after a moment of reflection, "the gentleman who was taking religious orders after studying at Oxford."

"Who was that?" Lord Warwick asked.

Rebecca shrugged. "I was inundated with so many new names that night, I can't remember any of them." She thought for a moment, then added. "He wasn't a lord. I'm sure of that."

"Then you share your sister's disdain for aristocrats?"

his lordship asked. "You are aware that she turned down a marriage offer from Lord Aynsley?"

"I had forgotten," Rebecca said, "but now that you mention it, I seem to recall something to that effect."

"You, Becky, are a most singular creature, indeed!" Maggie said. "Any other girl your age would be up to her ears in the latest *on dits* regarding amorous affairs."

"I find amorous affairs tediously dull," Rebecca said.

Maggie began to giggle, her glance shooting to Lord Warwick. "I daresay her tune will change in a year or so."

She allowed herself to look into his face, to see the dark line of stubble on his jaw, the sensual curve of his mouth, the firelight glancing off his warm amber eyes as they met hers. She remembered the whisper of his hands gliding along her naked skin, delighting every nerve in her body, and the very memory created a deep, molten ache. She must think of something else! "A pity none of those young men will find you when they come calling at Warwick House," Maggie said.

"Even more men will be disappointed not to find you there," Rebecca said.

Lord Warwick gave Maggie an icy glare. "Save your feigned humility, Maggie. I'm aware that you're aware of your effect on men."

Maggie affected a look of outrage. "I'm aware of no such thing, you odious man!"

Even after their dishes were cleared away Maggie had no desire to go to her lonely bedchamber. Rebecca would only bury her nose in that blasted book. Besides, it was not yet seven. Entirely too early for bed.

"Now that I've been an agreeable conversationalist at the dinner table," Rebecca said, "do I have your permission to retire to our room?"

"We don't mind if you read here," Lord Warwick said.

Rebecca directed a puzzled glance at him. "Why

would I wish to read here when I could cozy up in my quiet bedchamber with my book?"

"Point well taken," he said.

Maggie frowned. "I'll be up as soon as I dress his lordship's wounds."

Before he could protest, Rebecca swung around to face her sister, a look of bewilderment on her face. "You cannot go to his lordship's bedchamber without a chaperone! Miss Broom says even the finest of gentlemen turn into lechers when permitted to be alone with a lady." She nodded to Lord Warwick. "No offense intended, my lord, but you are a man. An unmarried man—though Miss Broom says—"

"We don't need to hear what that sanctimonious Miss Broom has been filling your head with," Maggie said. "Miss Broom was my sister's governess," she explained apologetically to Lord Warwick.

Rebecca stomped her foot and stiffened her slim shoulders. "I shall accompany you to his lordship's chambers."

Maggie put hands to her hips and scowled at her younger sister. "You'll do no such thing! Have you ever seen a man without his shirt?"

"As a matter of fact, I have!"

Maggie's brows lowered.

"I believe that was me," Lord Warwick said.

Maggie whirled at him.

"The night we met," he explained.

"Oh, that." Directing her gaze at Rebecca, Maggie said, "That doesn't count. You are not to see a man's bare chest again until you're married. I, on the other hand, have been married. It's permissible for me to see a man without his shirt—and I'm perfectly comfortable in the knowledge that Lord Warwick is a gentleman who will not try to take liberties."

Rebecca's gaze shifted from Maggie to his lordship.

"Miss Broom says all men will try to get beneath your skirts."

Maggie scowled at her sister. "We don't wish to hear one more word of what Miss Broom says. Run along. My virtue—if I still have any—will remain intact with Lord Warwick." *Tonight at least.* She could hardly tell her sister she had already lost her virtue to the sinfully handsome lord.

"I pledge to you it will," Lord Warwick said to Rebecca, "though I'd as lief talk your sister out of this ridiculous scheme of doctoring me. I'm perfectly fine."

"You're not perfectly fine!" Maggie countered. "The motion of your arm, I've noticed, is more restricted today than it was yesterday. Can you deny it?"

He shook his head in resignation.

So the three of them mounted the dark, narrow staircase together, its boards creaking under their weight. Maggie dashed into the chamber she shared with her sister to fetch her medicinals and some fine linen for a bandage—items she never traveled without—then continued on to his lordship's chamber at the other end of the hallway.

Inside his room Maggie adopted an authoritarian air. "You will need to strip bare to the waist, my lord." Moving to him, she added, "I'll help with the left sleeve, for I know how difficult it's become for you to move that arm."

Did nothing escape the maddening wench's observation? "You take entirely too careful notice of me," he grumbled.

She stopped in mid-stride, her brows lowering. "Have you any laudanum?"

"Never take the stuff. Too damned addictive."

"Perhaps I'd better fetch some brandy, then," she said, turning to go back downstairs.

"I'm perfectly capable of getting brandy myself!"

"I never said that you weren't," she said calmly as she left the room.

She returned a moment later with a bottle of brandy and two glasses.

"Why two glasses?" he asked.

"Because that's what I was given. Besides," she added with a pout, "I believe I'll partake of a glass with you."

"Then I suggest we drink before I disrobe—to give the brandy time to dull my senses."

"A very good idea," she said, opening the bottle and pouring the amber liquid into the glasses.

Edward went to move a chair in front of the fire, but she stopped him.

"I'll do that! You must take care with that arm. It will never heal if you don't rest it." She proceeded to bring the room's two wooden chairs in front of the hearth, then she handed him his brandy and they sat down.

He watched her from over the rim of his glass as her nose scrunched up when she drank the foul-tasting brandy. "Nasty stuff, is it not?" he asked.

"Not if it's used to remove paint!"

He realized he was chuckling again. He had grown entirely too comfortable with the vixen. The sooner they reached Windmere Abbey, the better. One look at his fair Fiona should purge Maggie from his mind.

Wouldn't it?

"They must have distilled the brandy themselves," she said.

He took another swig and grimaced. "They ought to stick to innkeeping." His gaze moved around the spotless room. Judging from the low, timbered ceilings, he would guess the inn dated to the Elizabethan period, an architectural style he found masculine yet cozy. "Not a bad inn, and the food was excellent."

Now she laughed. Her eyes sparkled. Her cheeks dimpled. Her even, stunningly white teeth nipped at her sensuous lower lip. And he thought he had never seen anything more exquisite. His breath caught. Just once he had beheld an even more exquisite creature. That day in Greenwich when his eyes had hungrily raked over the bare flesh of her silken body.

"You would say that," she said, mirth in her voice, "had you been served a stewed shoe, you were so ravenously hungry."

He gave a mock frown. "Woman, thou knowest me too well." He settled back and watched as she sipped the potent potable.

"Think you this . . . so-called brandy is exceedingly strong?" she asked.

Undoubtedly so. Already her words were ever so slightly slurred. "I think so."

"Then this is my last. I must not jeopardize my patient."

"I am not your patient! And where, pray tell, did you acquire this purported expertise in treating wounded men?"

"Not just men. Women and children, too. I learned from my mother. She tended to all our tenants. With successful results. When she died I found the journal where she logged her remedies and patient histories and decided to take up her work."

"How old were you?"

"Thirteen. Now, eleven years later, I no longer have to consult my mother's log book." She tapped her temple. "It's all up here."

He could see there was no stopping her. "How fortunate for me," he said dryly.

She took one final sip, then faced him. "You might as well take off your clothes now. Not your breeches, though." She giggled. "Since there are no thunderstorms tonight, you can be assured I'll not be begging you to make love to me."

He wanted to ask her if it was only the thunderstorms that had cast her into his arms, but he would not allow himself to do so. Better to let sleeping dogs lie. In a couple of days he would be with Fiona, and Maggie and one searing afternoon in a Greenwich inn would be only a distant memory, albeit a memory he would never forget.

He got up and went to remove his coat, but Maggie leaped to her feet. "Allow me to help."

As she helped him out of his coat, then his shirt, he stood frowning. One look at his festering bruise and she winced. "Oh my lord! We should have attended this right away. I believe it's become infected."

With a gentle touch of her hand against his chest, she eased him back to the chair.

"I'll just bring the candle closer," she said, "so that I can get a better look."

She held the candle up to study the wound, her breasts even with his eyes, her sweet rose scent at once transporting him back to that glorious afternoon in Greenwich. He forced his gaze away and availed himself of the opportunity to look at his wounds. Damned if he knew how it had gotten there, but there it was, running along his upper arm, the size of a small potato now. It hadn't been that big last night. Nor had it been such a disgusting yellow in color.

"It's a very good thing I've brought a decoction of pimpernel," she said as she asked him to hold the candle. Then she opened a jar and poured the liquid on a piece of clean linen which she pressed to the wound. Edward cursed as pain shot through him.

"I'm so very sorry, my lord," she said softly, "but you will have to be still. I promise I'll finish quickly."

He turned his head away, wincing as she probed the wound.

After a minute, she set the jar upon the chair next to him, then poured him another glass of brandy—or what passed for brandy at this inn. "Here, drink," she said. "Perhaps it will help dull the pain."

He gulped down the whole glass. "Are you quite finished, madame?"

"All except for bandaging." She tore more of the linen into narrow strips, then began to wrap them around his arm.

"Not too tight!" he warned.

"I'll be most careful," she assured.

"We'll need to re-dress the wound every day," she told him when she finished.

How was he to be this close to her—in a bedchamber, no less—and resist the urge to carry her to his bed and make love to her for the rest of the night? He would have to be possessed of the temperance of a monk. Which he most definitely was not. He shut his eyes. *No more nights like this.* "Now that I've watched you, I believe I'll be able to tend to the wound myself tomorrow."

"Oh, I don't mind doing it at all. I'm not squeamish like poor Rebecca." She gathered up her supplies, then turned to him. "Will you be able to undress by yourself?"

"I most certainly will," he said through gritted teeth.

"Then I bid you a good night. Perhaps a long sleep will promote recovery, my lord."

After she had gone he stripped off his breeches, cursing her. It bloody well did hurt to use that damned arm, but he would not have her undress him.

He collapsed onto his bed, went promptly to sleep, and dreamed of Maggie stripping away his garments one by one.

Chapter 19

"I daresay being jostled in a coach is the worst possible thing for your arm," Maggie said to him the following day as they continued north, staring at one another across the heaving carriage.

"Horseback riding, I believe, is worse," he said.

Rebecca offered her opinion. "I should think swinging an ax would be the worst."

"But earls don't swing axes," Maggie pointed out. "I would imagine Lord Warwick's never swung an ax in his entire life." Then she remembered what Lord Carrington said about Lord Warwick not really being a lord. She did wish she had thought to ask what Lord Warwick's real name was.

"Can't say that I have," he said.

As Maggie watched the stiff way he held his arm, her face softened. "Any more bleeding?"

He shrugged. "Enough to dampen your handiwork."

She had really been quite distressed over his wound. It bore too close a resemblance to their Virginia neighbor, Mr. Heart, who had been cut down when he was but twenty-five. And all because gangrene had set into his knee after it had become scuffed during a fall from his horse! His blood stream had carried the infection to his whole body, and he was dead within a week.

Of course, she would not tell Lord Warwick about Mr. Heart.

"Perhaps it will need dressing twice a day," she said.

He frowned. "It would only bleed more—from the jostling. We can wait until tonight."

"Where do we stop tonight?" Rebecca asked.

Lord Warwick pulled out his map and began to study it. Maggie had grown to hate the wretched piece of paper for stealing so much of his lordship's time. Truth be told, she had grown to hate the tediousness of being crammed into a carriage for hours a day with nothing to do and little conversation—due to the wretched map claiming his attention. The first day of the journey she had finished reading *Pride and Prejudice,* but felt especially guilty that she could sit there and partake of her sister's favorite activity with not the slightest bit of nausea. Not that she wished to be nauseated, of course.

Nor did she precisely wish to arrive at Windmere Abbey. If she never met Fiona Hollingsworth, it would be too soon. But upon thinking so wickedly of the lady, Maggie would suffer remorse. If Lord Warwick held his Fiona in such high esteem the lady must be possessed of many fine qualities.

So Maggie would settle back against the squabs and sigh. What was needed was something to break the tedium. She remembered the night before when he had expressed an interest in taking a walk. Perhaps they could stop and take a walk. "My lord?"

He looked up from the map, a single brow arched.

"If the weather stays fair and if we make good time, could we not stop this afternoon to stretch our legs and perhaps eat picnic style?"

"And I could read while you two walk," Rebecca added brightly.

"If the weather stays fair," he said in a stern voice,

"and if there are no impediments to our progress, we might be able to steal a half hour or so."

Maggie smiled and pushed back the curtain from her window in order to study the clouds. How was one to know cumulus from cirrus? Not that she believed in his lordship's foolish nonsense about the clouds portending the weather.

He watched her, a lopsided grin on his face. "Would you be studying the clouds?"

"I would if I knew what I was doing."

He set down the map and peered out his window. "Those are cumulus clouds. See, they're lower in the sky and plump. Their stark whiteness today tells me they bring no rain."

She nodded earnestly. "So if they're plump, there's no rain?"

"I didn't say that! Rain *does* come from plump clouds—just not starkly white ones."

Now Rebecca got into the discussion, lifting her curtain and staring at the clouds. "But my lord, if you will but look to the west, the clouds there aren't so white."

He grimaced and spoke with only barely controlled anger. "I cannot see to the west from my window."

Oh dear, he was getting grumpy again. Maggie ruffled through the basket and pulled out a chunk of freshly churned cheese. "Here, your lordship, eat."

"What makes you think I want cheese?" he demanded.

"I can always tell when you start getting hungry. You become a bear."

"I do not become a bear!"

"My sister's right, your lordship," Rebecca confirmed.

His narrow-eyed gaze shifted to Rebecca, then he snatched the cheese from Maggie's hand.

* * *

An hour later the carriage chugged up a hill, then rounded its smooth crest, causing Edward to lift the curtain and survey the sleepy little valley below that was dimpled with a deep blue lake. "We'll eat beside the water," he announced.

A few minutes afterward Edward strapped on the sword that rested against Maggie's seat, and they embarked from the coach to discover they were the valley's only occupants—save for a couple of hundred exceedingly lazy cows. Maggie busied herself spreading the food upon one of the rugs while Miss Peabody took the other rug and promptly sat down with her book.

"If you would like, your lordship," Maggie said, "we could nibble while we walk."

The cursed woman was beginning to read his very thoughts! He nodded as he bent to scoop up some cold mutton and bread.

But just as he and Maggie were about to begin their walk, Miss Peabody looked up from that damned book of hers, her bespectacled eyes narrowing. "If his lordship should attempt to take liberties with your person, you've only to scream. I'll come to your rescue." Then Miss Peabody had the audacity to say, "No personal offense intended, my lord, but your gender does not speak well to your trustworthiness. Miss Broom says all men turn into animals when permitted to be alone with a lady."

"Rebecca!" Maggie hissed. "Not another word about Miss Broom! And you most certainly owe Lord Warwick an apology."

"I never said Lord Warwick was actually an animal!"

Maggie's eyes narrowed. "Apologize!"

Miss Peabody fingered the pages of her book and without looking up at him said, "Forgive me, my lord."

He was too livid to be gracious. His head inclined slightly. "I'm possessed of a strong desire to strangle

Miss Broom, if ever I should meet her," he said, offering his arm to Maggie and strolling away.

It was still very cold and the wind was stronger than he would have liked, but it was a lovely day with the sun high in the bluest sky, its glints shimmering in the cobalt lake below. Damn but he'd been away from the country and its calming effect on him for too long. He stole a glance at Maggie as she nibbled a tiny bite of bread, her lovely face framed by the cloak's ermine hood. "Shall we circle the lake?" he asked.

She let out a little laugh.

"What's so amusing?"

"I, too, thought we'd circle the lake. Have you noticed that the longer we're with one another the more alike our thoughts seem to be?"

He had. But he wasn't about to acknowledge it. All morning in the carriage he had thought about how well Maggie had come to know him. She had learned things about him that no one else knew, some things he was still learning himself. Like the hunger business. He had never analyzed it before—the way his stomach ached and his head throbbed if he had gone without eating for more than a few hours. But Maggie knew. She knew when he needed to eat before he did.

And just as she knew things about him that no one else knew, he knew her in ways others did not. Like the crying—and lack of tears when she was truly distressed. He knew how emotionally wrought she became during thunderstorms. He knew that despite the setbacks in her life, Maggie remained upbeat and optimistic. He knew the taste of her lips . . . No, he could not allow himself to remember that. He must redirect his thoughts. "I know that you've been foolishly blaming yourself and your failed marriage for Miss Peabody's aversion to matrimony when the blame must be laid squarely at the feet of that bloody governess, Miss Bloom or Broom or some such."

"Miss Broom—whom I must say resembles that which is used to sweep with! She's tall and thin and possessed of the sourest disposition I've ever encountered."

"No doubt she was spurned by some man."

Maggie laughed. "By all men, I daresay."

He found much to admire in Maggie's sunny disposition. But, of course, there was much more to admire in Lady Fiona. Wasn't there?

After they had finished eating Maggie laced her arm through his as innocently as one might a kiss on an infant's downy head. Did she not know how profoundly such nearness could affect a man? Even a man who was in love with another woman? If she had been a maiden he could have understood her not knowing about the blood rushing to a certain part of a man's anatomy. But she was no virgin. She had to know what she was doing to him.

The tent effect in his crotch was most humiliating. He must sit down and elevate his knee to hide it. "Shall we sit beneath that tree over there?" he asked, striding in the direction of the ancient oak.

"But I thought you were as tired as I of sitting down?"

"The sun's very bright. A few minutes of shade will be welcome." Surely in a few minutes, his erection would go down.

They came to sit on the cool ground, putting their backs against the tree. One booted foot on the ground assured that his knee obstructed her view of his throbbing arousal.

She really wasn't a seductress, he told himself. He would vow that she was not aware of her inherent sexuality—though she had to be aware of her stunning beauty.

"I wonder if Mr. Lyle came to call on me Thursday?" she said.

Edward recalled that she had been about to bestow

her affections on his best friend. His mouth plunged into a frown. What if Harry was the one who had sent the henchmen for Maggie?

Obviously, she was thinking the same thing. "I was certain that—should he honor me with a proposal— I was going to accept, but now I'm not so certain."

"Good. It's best to wait until we know."

Know what? Know who sent the cutthroats, who ordered the search of her room, who killed Andrew Bibble? But the culprit might never be found out. Was there not something he could do to expedite an investigation? If he could trust Lord Carrington or Harry, they could employ all the resources of the Foreign Office, but he could not trust them until he learned the identity of the mole. And how was he to learn that when his chief concern now was keeping Maggie safe?

"I think you need to return to America," he finally said.

"But I haven't the money, nor do I have a home when I get there."

"I'll pay your fare—give you a settlement to live on until such time as you remarry."

Her face grew somber. "I cannot say that I'm not terrified for I most certainly am. For days now I've been obsessed with the idea that someone's following us, afraid to allow myself to go to sleep for fear I'll end up like Mr. Bibble. But I cannot accept your charity. If you're so hellbent on getting me out of your life so you can marry your precious Fiona, I vow to marry soon, to be out of your hair."

"Damn it, Maggie! That's not what I meant!" A strange rage blended with passion and fear and the deepest emotions he had ever experienced flooded him as he yanked her into his arms and crushed his lips against hers. Her hand flattened against his chest in fleeting protest, then her arms came around him, her lips opened beneath his. He was intoxicated by the feel of her, the taste of her, the sweet floral scent of her. His pulses pounded and the blood raced through his veins to settle low in his torso. When he heard her soft whimper he thought he would surely go mad with his own numbing desire, a desire she too was powerless to deny. Even if she did not want him.

Holding her as close as his own skin, he murmured, "I'm so damned worried about you." In that instant he knew that if anything ever happened to Maggie he would not want to go on living. But she was not his. Nor did she want to be his. She would soon offer herself to another man, another man who would relieve Edward of the burden of protecting her. Edward could not bear to think of her in another man's arms.

Nor could he bear to think of Fiona. It suddenly became glaringly clear to him that he was prepared to spend the rest of his life with a woman he did not love.

He cupped Maggie's beloved face in his hands and stared at her with moist eyes. He had to give her up. As a man of his word, he was unable to break with Fiona. "Forgive me," he said, his voice husky with emotion. "I had no right to kiss you."

Her bottom lip quivered. "Perhaps I should return to America."

Why, then, was he bringing her to Yorkshire? Why hadn't he been possessed of the good sense to put her on a schooner bound for America? Could it be the thought of never seeing her again was far too painful?

He nodded, then got to his feet and offered her a hand. As they began to stroll, Maggie did not link her arm through his, nor did she speak at all for the half hour it took to circle the lake.

They rode until six o'clock that night when they reached Dorkington, where they would put up for the night. Lord Warwick affected a great interest in studying his map during the journey. For her part, Maggie could not rid her thoughts of the scorching kiss. Nor could she forget his words that afternoon in Greenwich when he had offered for her. He had said many married people would never experience the sublime lovemaking they had shared. The shattering passion that surged between them was undeniable. He had only to touch her and her body opened like a flower, creating a deep, molten ache that only Lord Warwick—Edward, she thought with a secret, warming intimacy—could fill.

Would that another man—any other man—could ignite so searing a passion within her. She told herself she was not in love with Edward. She didn't even know who he really was. His own superior thought he might be capable of betraying his country. He was in love with another woman, and he was far too honorable to ever cry off an engagement.

Why, then, did the prospect of never seeing him again plunge her into such despair?

Returning to America would really be for the best. Better for him. Better for her. How was she to bear seeing him marry Fiona? But returning to America did not appeal. There was no Almack's there, no place to find so many eligible husbands.

She did need to find a husband, a man who was not promised to a pretty peeress. A man who one day might be able to arouse in her the passions that Edward had stirred.

Chapter 20

"Lord Warwick thinks we should return to America," Maggie told her sister at dinner that night. Edward was grateful no one could listen to their conversation. Not a single night during the journey had they been forced to share a private parlor, good fortune he attributed to the fact that persons of intelligence would wait until spring to make the arduous journey north. Traveling in January and February was always risky because of the dismal weather. In this instance, the risk had paid off. He could not remember a milder February, mild in the sense the weather was merely bitterly cold but not actually violent.

Miss Peabody stiffened, her mouth gaped open, and her eyes peering through those thick spectacles looked bigger than ever. "But I don't wish to return to America!"

"There's nothing to keep you here, since you're not interested in finding a husband," Maggie said.

Edward did not trust himself to meet Maggie's gaze. His actions that afternoon were unpardonable. A gentleman did not take such liberties with a woman he did not intend to marry. And he most certainly did not intend to marry Maggie.

"I have come to realize how utterly provincial America is," Miss Peabody said.

"In what way?" her sister asked.

"Intellectually."

"I beg to differ with you," Maggie said. "There were many intellectuals among our acquaintance in Virginia, though I admit our intercourse with them was not on a daily basis."

"London's the center of the world." Miss Peabody directed a worshipful gaze at Edward. "And Lord Warwick's library is far and away the finest I've ever encountered."

"I thank you," he said, eyeing the thick volume which reposed on the bench next to her. "I see you're reading Miss Burney's *The Wanderer.*"

She nodded, sending her spectacles slipping down the bridge of her nose, then she nudged them back. "I'm ever so grateful for the use of your library, for the price of all four volumes of Miss Burney's newest novel is something we never could have afforded."

"I'm very happy that others can enjoy my books. How are you liking *The Wanderer*?"

"I've read but the first volume and am actually rather disappointed. It's not nearly as fine as her *Evelina,* which I read when I was quite young and excessively enjoyed."

He wanted to laugh. Seventeen seemed to him quite young. "I believe your opinion of the work matches the consensus of those who've read it."

"Becky knows her literature—and poetry," Maggie said with pride. "She read *Paradise Lost* at age five—to give you some idea of her vast expertise."

How could Maggie stay so cheerful after what had occurred this afternoon? Did she feel none of the agonizing remorse that left him aching inside?

Miss Peabody shrugged. "I do have vast experience—of reading—to draw from." She faced him. "Did you like Miss Burney's latest work, my lord?"

"No," he said with a shake of his head. "In fact, I was

so disappointed in the first volume, I didn't read the others." He would gladly discuss literature all night if it would keep him from looking at Maggie, from remembering today's searing kiss.

"If you would like a light, enjoyable read I recommend *Waverly* by Walter Scott," Miss Peabody said. "I did not see it in your library."

"I daresay you know my library better than I do myself," he muttered. "Though I have read *Waverly*. The reason you didn't find it is because it's still in my bedchamber."

"And did you like it?" Miss Peabody quizzed.

"Very much."

"I thought," Maggie said with impatience, "that we were discussing our return to America."

Miss Peabody stomped her foot. "I refuse to go back."

"But your sister's in grave danger as long as she's in England," Edward said.

He watched the girl's lids lower in contemplation. The swooping dark lashes were so much like Maggie's. "Has it not occurred to you, my lord, that every port which conveys passengers to America will be watched?"

"Dear God! Becky's right!" Maggie said in a forlorn voice.

"Bloody hell," he hissed. "Why didn't I take you to Falmouth straight away?"

"Well, I'm very glad you didn't!" Miss Peabody said. "I don't believe I can ever set foot on a boat again!"

"She was dreadfully sick the entire crossing," Maggie said, patting her sister's hand.

"I'll own it's a most vexing set of circumstances we find ourselves in," Miss Peabody acknowledged, sending a somber look at her sister. "I truly am worried about you and should die if anything happened to you, but I'm persuaded we'll be safe at Windmere Abbey."

Maggie frowned. "We cannot stay there forever."

"I have every confidence Lord Warwick will think of something. He is a most intelligent man."

Edward scowled. "Because I possess a fine library?"

"Not only that," Miss Peabody said. "I know you're intelligent. One does not spend twelve hours a day in someone's company and not come to understand that person."

"A point I've lamented more than once," Edward said. "Your sister has come to know me far too well." He allowed his gaze to shift to Maggie for the first time that evening. The candlelight bathed her solemn face and glinted off her dark tresses. He wondered if the pink in her cheeks came from the chamber's toasty warmth. When her lashes lifted, he looked away.

"I, too, believe you'll think of something," Maggie said to him.

"Madame, I do not merit your trust! I was a bloody fool not to rush you to the first ship bound for America. I pledged to keep you safe . . ." His voice faltered. "And it seems I've failed you."

"You've done no such thing! I'm here, aren't I? And it's all thanks to you—you who single-handedly fought off four armed men who most certainly wished me harm."

"Of course his fighting off four armed men wasn't the most intelligent thing to do," Miss Peabody interjected. "No offense, my lord. We're frightfully happy that you behaved with such foolish disregard for your own life."

"I've been a blasted idiot!"

"You have not!" Maggie argued. "Tell me this, my lord. Is there someone else who can protect me better than you?"

She had him there. As inadequate as he felt, Edward knew there was no other living soul he would trust with Maggie's life. He shook his head ruefully.

"It seems, madame, that I'm to be your protector by default." Her eyes flashed with humor when they met his.

When they finished eating, Miss Peabody—book in hand—begged to take her leave.

Maggie agreed, then faced him. "I'll just run up and re-dress your wound before turning in. I know it's early, but I'm utterly fatigued. I daresay it is exhaustion after so many days on the road."

"And so many nights you've been afraid to go to sleep," he murmured.

She bit at her lower lip then lifted her solemn face to his.

"Put your woes on my shoulders," he said softly. "They're bigger—than yours."

"I would love to transfer my woes to someone!" she said lightly, then started for the stairs. He caught up with her. "I'll dress the wound myself tonight."

She spun around to face him. "With one arm? I think not!"

He could see there was no stopping her. With a grumble he went to procure another bottle of brandy and met Maggie in his bedchamber a few minutes later.

She had already moved a pair of wooden chairs across the floor's wooden planks to face the stone hearth and had set her medicinals on one of the chairs.

"I shan't be drinking that nasty stuff tonight," she said, eying the pair of glasses in his hand.

"Hellfire! I am!" He poured out a glass and promptly downed it.

Her step was so light, he had not heard her move to him. Then she was beside him speaking in her silky voice. "I'll help you remove that coat and shirt." She was so close he could smell the rose scent he always associated with her.

Bloody hell. His willpower was being sorely tested.

He removed his coat from the right side easily enough, but her assistance was needed for the left. He found himself closing his eyes so he wouldn't have to watch her as she eased him out of his clothing. *God give me strength.*

"Hold up your arms, and I'll help with the shirt," she said. Did she have any idea how seductive her voice was when she spoke so low?

He drew in a deep breath and went to raise his arms, but was unable to lift the left arm over his head. Of course, she didn't know how seductive she is, he told himself. She's merely lowering her voice out of courtesy to those who might be in the next room. From the looks of it, the walls in this inn weren't any too thick.

After she pulled the shirt from his right arm, she gently eased it from the left. "There, I hope that didn't hurt," she said.

Of course it hurt, but he wasn't going to act like a milksop over a trivial injury. "It's just a little stiff."

"If you'll sit down, I'll begin."

He dropped onto the chair. She had placed it too deuced close to the fire. That must be why he felt so heated. As she moved to him he noticed the blue shawl draped around her shoulders and the memory of first placing it on her that day in Greenwich swamped him. He shut his eyes against it, against so painful a memory.

"Hold the candle near the left arm, will you?" she asked once she had removed the old bandage.

"Does the arm look any better tonight?"

"I can't say that it does," she answered in a grim voice, "nor—I'm pleased to say—does it look worse." She poured her decoction onto fresh linen and began to dab at the infernal wound.

He kept his eyes shut, wincing against the pain.

"Is your brother really dead?" she asked as casually as she would inquire about the weather.

It was as if he had been walloped with a flagpole. He could not have been more taken aback had his brother—safe in India these past five years with his wife and growing brood—come strolling through the door.

The room was utterly silent, save for the soft crackle at the hearth, the north winds whistling outside the window. As she watched him for a reaction, he drew in his breath, tried to formulate his thoughts. He should never have lied to Maggie. She was too damned intelligent. "How did you know?" he asked.

The corners of her lovely mouth turned down. "I knowest thou too well."

She damned well did!

"Pray, what is your real name?" she asked as she started to bind the wound with strips of linen.

"Edward."

"I know that!"

His mouth firm, his eyes narrowed, he said, "My father was Sir Perry Stanfield. My brother is now the baronet, since my father died some three years ago. We were not related to the Lord Warwick at all. His title should be extinct."

"Does Lady Fiona know you're not really an earl?"

He nodded. "I could not have offered for her without her knowing precisely who she was marrying. Fiona's the only person with whom I've ever shared the truth, and must ask you not to tell anyone, even your sister."

Maggie cleared her things from the other chair and sank onto it. "What do I call you?"

"Continue using Lord Warwick."

"When it's just the two of us, I cannot."

"When it's just the two of us," he said in a husky voice, "you may call me Edward."

She was silent for a moment. "Then when Lady Fiona agreed to marry you, she knew she was not marrying an earl, knew she was agreeing to marry a man who had no hopes of succeeding to a title?"

"That's true. She could have married a duke, you know. Not having met her, I can see where you might have formed an unflattering opinion of her, may have thought her some arrogant peeress who snarls at her servants and won't associate with anyone who's not a blueblood. But I assure you nothing could be further from the truth. Malice of any kind is as alien to Lady Fiona as . . . as lying is to you."

Maggie gave a bitter laugh. "Though I'm exceedingly honest by nature—and given to blurting out my thoughts—you are well aware of deceits I've tried to propagate."

A smile curved his lip. "Any deceits you may have intended were born out of desperation."

"And your deceit? Why?" As she stared at him, he saw the disillusionment on her saddened face. And he knew he had lost something he would never be able to recover.

He shook his head. "That I cannot tell you. I was sworn to secrecy."

"And to the honorable Lord Warwick—or should I say Edward Stanfield?—his pledge is irrevocable." There was bitterness in her voice.

"What else have I to recommend me save my word as a gentleman?"

"Such a gentleman that even though it's Fiona you love, you offered to marry me because that was the gentlemanly thing to do—given the circumstances?"

"I'm not proud of what I've done to you." He got up, strode to the table where he had placed the brandy, and poured himself another glass of the abominable liquid. Two long gulps and the glass was empty. "The pity of it is," he said, his voice rough and full of emotion, "I'd do it all over again. Even today's kiss."

He watched her gravely as she tightened the shawl about her shoulders. "Then I'd best return to my room."

"Yes," he nodded as she got up. "You'd best go."

All the nights of the journey Maggie had lain in her bed listening to the forlorn wind outside her window and pictured the dead body of Andrew Bibble. She had been afraid to sleep, afraid to let down her guard for fear she would meet the same fate as the man in Greenwich. But she had let down her guard today with Edward, and tonight the memory of his kiss kept her awake. She might prevent herself from babbling her devotion, but how could she keep from responding to his scorching kisses?

Maggie was most vexed. She hadn't put up any resistance when his mouth had swooped down on hers. Her arms had only too eagerly slipped around him, her mouth too eagerly opened beneath his. Edward was bound to think her a harlot!

She did not know what she wanted him to think of her. She did not know what she thought of him. Never in her life had she been more confused. Oddly, she trusted him with her life—even though he had admitted he was a fraud. Why would an honorable man perpetrate such a deception? Could he be in the employ of the French?

Could Lord Carrington's suspicions of Edward be accurate? Were Edward to betray England, Maggie would have no other course but to betray Edward, even if he had risked his life to save hers. She had no love for Napoleon's aggression, or his megalomania.

Yet she could not believe Edward would do anything dishonorable.

She would close her eyes and remember the feel of his lips crushing against hers. With an ache in her heart she would recall his words tonight. *He would do it all over again.*

That's why she had to flee his room. Were he to touch her, she would have been powerless to deny him anything.

Even though he was bound to Maggie by strong carnal desire neither of them had the power to resist, he loved Fiona. Fiona was the only person he entrusted with the truth.

Maggie could only roll over and punch up her pillow and sigh. Nothing would stop Edward from marrying Fiona, but as the days of their journey mounted, it was clear that Edward's feeling for Maggie had strengthened. What she and Edward shared was much stronger than the undeniable hunger for physical intimacy. They had grown close in the way couples who shared their lives grew close. He had as good as admitted she knew him as no one else did, and she was aware that he knew her like no man ever had.

Given the depth of their unacknowledged feelings, Edward was bound to have misgivings about his plan to wed Fiona—misgivings he would never act upon. Maggie would never forgive herself if he entered his marriage to Fiona with only half a heart. She owed it to Edward to release him from any attachments he might developed for her.

She could do that only by making it clear she intended to marry another.

It suddenly occurred to her that Rebecca had gone to sleep. Raising herself on one elbow, Maggie peered over her sister's shoulder and smiled. Becky's face—spectacles and all—lay gently on her open book. Maggie slipped from the bed, tiptoed around to remove the spectacles, then eased the

book from beneath Rebecca's flattened cheek—all
without waking her sister. After extinguishing the
candle, Maggie padded through the inky darkness
and climbed back onto the bed.

The fire had long ago died, its smoldering embers
struggling to keep out the frosty night. She pulled the
counterpane up to her chin and listened to the lonely
howl of the wind outside. Was Edward, too, lying
awake down the hall? Would the throbbing pain of his
wound make getting comfortable impossible for him?
Oh, how she envied Fiona, who would lie beside him
for the rest of their days.

Edward informed them over breakfast the next
morning that this would likely be the last day of their
journey. "If there are no delays," he had said, "we
should arrive at Windmere Abbey around dusk."

Breakfast had been a somber affair. Even after they
had bundled themselves in the carriage, the winds
swooping against the rattling carriage doors, Edward's
dark mood did not improve.

Maggie allowed herself to wonder if he shared her
regrets that their journey was coming to an end, that
never again would the two of them be this close.

It was best, she told herself, that she implement her
plan now.

"You must tell me all about Harry Lyle, your lordship, for I should like to bestow my affections upon
him. Please say he's not to blame for my abduction."

He glowered. "I can tell you no such thing."

"I have a difficult time believing such a nice man
could be guilty of anything so underhanded," she said.

"Even if he's innocent, I doubt Lyle's in a position
to offer for any woman."

"A pity," she said with a sigh, pulling the rug around

her more tightly. Then her face brightened and she asked, "Does Lady Fiona have a brother, perchance?"

His eyes were as cold as agate when he replied. "She does."

"And is her brother married?"

"Neither of her brothers are married," he hissed. "Do you wish to snare the one who is nine and twenty or the one who's only twenty and still at Cambridge?"

Maggie meant to convince him she was a calculating female. "The elder, I should think. Is he not in line for a title?"

Cursing under his breath, Edward yanked the well-worn map from his pocket and began to study it.

Every time the coach hit a rough spot on the road, Edward would wince against the pain she knew was throbbing in his arm. Her thoughts drifted to Mr. Heart. If his leg had been amputated, he might still be alive today. Not that she actually knew the first thing about amputation, which required several strong men to hold the patient down. Nor was it an area of medicine in which she wished to acquire expertise.

Few survived it. She grew somber and wondered if Edward's arm would have to be amputated. She would have to watch it closely. But how could she? Traipsing into his bedchamber at Windmere Abbey would hardly be tolerated. With a firm set to her mouth, she decided she would have to tell Fiona of her betrothed's serious injury. If Fiona were the paragon Edward he said she was, surely she would see that he was properly cared for.

So the counterfeit countess had finally shown him her true colors, Edward reflected bitterly. As soon as she found out he was no earl, Maggie had lost all interest in him. Hadn't her desire for a title pressed her into marrying The Scoundrel? Edward tried to tell himself he was far better off without her.

Now he could dismiss his guilt and rekindle his love for Fiona. If his calculations were right, he would see her within the hour. He might even be able to coax a kiss from her. Just two weeks ago the thought of kissing Fiona would have made his heart beat erratically. But no more.

The anticipation of seeing her was sadly flat. He almost dreaded it. Always before he had hungered to see her sweet face, to hear her soft laughter as they slipped behind the yew hedge where he would draw her into his arms for a thorough kiss.

But now the only person he wanted to kiss thoroughly was Maggie, a cold, calculating, provocative vixen.

The country around Windmere Abbey was as well known to him as that of his family's Pickford Manor. He had first come to Windmere with Randolph, Fiona's elder brother, when he was no more than twelve. The familiar streets of Cranford Bog came into view, and his heart began to thump. They were but minutes away now from Windmere Abbey. He fleetingly wished he had taken Maggie straight away to Falmouth. His chest tightened at the hopelessness of never again seeing Maggie. Then he cursed himself for a fool.

His body tensed as the coach turned onto the long lane that would take them to Windmere. And to Fiona.

Chapter 21

Windmere Abbey, Maggie thought as she peered through the frosty window of their carriage, did not look like an abbey at all. She had expected a crumbling Gothic structure, but the mansion that stood proudly at the end of a long stretch of lawn was decidedly Palladian. Its columns and pediments and neoclassical symmetry were set off by a sandstone facade glowing golden in the late afternoon sun. The families who had lived there over the generations would have made their mark in the pages of English history. Blood that ran in Lady Fiona's veins, Maggie thought morosely, could no doubt be traced back to some noble defender of the crown.

Maggie let the curtain drop. During the next few minutes she fought her mounting nervousness. Would Fiona resent her dreadfully? Would Edward make a cake of himself over the woman he loved? Would Maggie be able to stand the pain of seeing him with the woman he loved?

"We're here," Edward said as the carriage came to a stop.

She could see from the grim set of his mouth he was no more happy about the visit than she. All of that would change once he beheld his bride-to-be.

Edward assisted Maggie and Rebecca from the carriage, then gave orders to a footman dressed in pale blue satin livery. Maggie drew in her breath as they approached the huge entry portico of Windmere Abbey.

The door suddenly swept open and an excited young lady rushed out to greet them. At first Maggie doubted the woman was Fiona. The lovely creature looked no more than eighteen, and Maggie knew Fiona was older than she. Perhaps it was the lady's slimness, the delicacy of her person, that made her seem more youthful, Maggie decided. She watched as Edward drew the lady's graceful hand into his and bent to kiss it. Pure adoration shone in the lady's eyes as they met Edward's.

It was Fiona. Maggie's chest felt heavy as her gaze swept from Fiona's pale blond curls to her exceedingly fair skin and sparkling blue eyes, then whisked over her slender elegance in the mourning gown of midnight black.

Fiona Hollingsworth was the most elegant, most beautiful woman Maggie had ever seen.

Maggie was aware that Edward was talking, but she felt, somehow, at the opposite end of a long tunnel that separated them.

"Allow me to present the Countess Warwick and her sister, Miss Peabody," he was saying to his betrothed.

Fiona's blue eyes locked with Maggie's, and for a fraction of a second Fiona stiffened, her icy glare sweeping over Maggie. Then she recovered, and a warm smile dimpled her lovely face. "I have been so happy you've come to Windmere Abbey. I have been completely bereft of female companionship," Fiona said.

Maggie curtsied. "It is good of you to have us."

Before they entered the abbey, they were joined by Fiona's father, a slender man in his early sixties who dressed in the mode popular a generation earlier, right down to his powdered hair. He needed only a tricorne hat to complete the picture.

"Warwick," he said to Edward with a great deal of amiability, "I cannot tell you how keenly we've been looking forward to this visit."

Then his glance skipped from Maggie to Rebecca.

"Lord Agar, allow me to present Lady Warwick and her sister Miss Peabody," Edward said.

Lord Agar was all that was courteous as he took each lady's hand and brushed his lips over their gloves. "Come, we must get you ladies out of the cold."

"You poor things," Fiona said as they swept into the great receiving hall with its glistening marble floors and glittering chandeliers. "Even through your gloves I could tell your hands were frigid. What's needed are a nice warm rooms. I've had fires burning in your bedchambers all day."

No doubt Fiona could not wait to dump them and have Edward all to herself. "How very kind of you," Maggie said. Her heart sank as Fiona laced her arm through Edward's, and they began to mount the broad, well-lit stairway.

Lord Agar stood at the base of the stairway and looked up at them. "I shall see you at dinner."

Maggie and Rebecca trailed behind Lady Fiona and Edward, close enough to hear their conversation.

"You'll stay in your old room," Fiona said to Edward. "I've put the ladies in the same wing."

Edward nodded, then asked, "Is Randolph here?"

"He's shooting in Scotland but should be back next week."

Maggie assumed Randolph was the brother nearest to Edward in age.

When they reached the second floor, Fiona turned to face Maggie, a radiant smile on her face. "This first room will be yours, my lady." She swept open the door.

Maggie stepped into the airy room.

"You'll want to rest before dinner," Fiona said, her cheeks dimpling with her smile. "Dinner's at six. Have you brought a maid?"

"No."

"Should you like me to send up a maid to help you unpack?" Fiona asked.

"I'll manage by myself," Maggie answered, closing the door.

Despite the gray day, light abounded in the room. All the cornices and moldings were painted a creamy white, and the silken draperies had been swept back from tall casements that flooded the room with somber light. Pale blue damask covered the walls, and a silk bedspread in the same blue draped over the full tester bed, and more blue silk hung as curtains gathered at the bed's four corner posts.

Before she could even remove her gloves, a footman brought her valise. As Maggie unpacked, she was filled with melancholy. She had not sufficiently prepared herself for Lady Fiona's complete devotion to Edward, for the possessive way she had tucked her arm into his, or for the warmth of the secret glances they exchanged.

No wonder Edward loved Fiona. What man wouldn't be captured by her fragile beauty, her sweet nature, and her family pedigree? She wasn't at all what Maggie had expected. Maggie had pegged her to be blond, but a robust, healthy-looking blond bursting with self-assurance. Instead Lady Fiona was so pale, so thin, so utterly delicate that she would elicit any man's innate sense of protectiveness. Edward would like that, Maggie realized with a little pain in her heart.

* * *

When they came to Edward's door, Fiona took both his hands and stood back to look at him. "Oh, Edward dearest, I've missed you so dreadfully."

He had not remembered she was so small, so exceedingly fair. Even her voice was not like what he remembered. It seemed more youthful than the voice of a woman who was five and twenty. "It's been a wretched four months for you," he said, his voice gentle.

"And I'm so wretchedly selfish. I know how fatigued you must be from the journey. I know you need to wash up and rest, but I cannot bear to part from you. There's so much I want to say."

She wanted to be alone with him, but for the first time in the many years he had been devoted to her, he did not wish to be alone with her. His heart thudded. "I assure you, rest is something I can do without. After so tedious a journey, the prospect of stretching my legs is most welcome. Where would you like to go?"

A winsome smile washed over her delicate face. "It doesn't matter—as long as I'm with you."

He took her hand and tucked it within the crook of his arm as they retraced the steps that had brought them to the second floor.

"We can go to the drawing room," she said. "There's a cozy fire there."

"As you wish."

A moment later she was closing the door to the gold and ivory room, backing herself into it and searching his face with smoldering eyes. "Please, Edward, put your arms around me." Her voice cracked, becoming suddenly childlike. "It's been so very long."

He took two strides and pulled her to him, her slender arms snaking around him as he held her close. He felt as if he were embracing a thirteen-year-old boy. Why had he never before noticed her absence of a bosom? Then she lifted her face. *She wants me to kiss her.* But all he could think of was the scorching kisses he had shared with Maggie. He could almost feel Maggie's soft tongue mingling with his, kissing her with a passion that was absent from his and Fiona's chaste kisses. His head lowered until he felt the brush of Fiona's lips. He held the kiss for a few seconds. Never before had he been so willing to terminate one.

And never before had Fiona kissed him with such passion.

After the kiss, she burrowed her face into his chest and smiled. "Oh, my dearest, I've missed you so bitterly. How many times I have wished that we had married before Mama's death."

"Things have a way of working out for the best. I'm sure you've been a great comfort to your father in his grief."

Her little head nodded. "Poor Papa, he's been far too mired in his grief."

"Perhaps having house guests will be good for him."

Her eyes glittered. "Oh, it will! He's been enthusiastically looking forward to your visit."

She angled back, then faced him. "Is your visit still to be kept in secret?"

Fiona might have an ethereal look about her, but she was a typical woman, through and through. She had not been able to wait even an hour before demanding an explanation of her intended's clandestine trip.

"I'd rather you not tell anyone of my presence here in Yorkshire." His brows drew down. "You're to say nothing of this, even to your father."

Her eyes wide, she nodded.

"Someone's been stalking the countess—someone who's up to evil. The night we fled London, four armed men tried to abduct her."

She gasped. "Who, pray tell?"

"We don't know."

"I daresay it's a spurned lover. The woman is breath-takingly beautiful. I'm very jealous that you've spent so much time with the exquisite creature."

His insides clenched. Fiona had no idea just how exquisite Maggie was. Already, he rued the end of their journey, the end of his intimacy with her. "I am betrothed to a woman who's breathtakingly beauti-ful," he said, a half-grin pinching one side of his face. "Just ask any of her myriad of suitors."

A smile played at her delicate lips. "Why would someone . . . The threats against the countess have something to do with that wretched position of yours at the Foreign Office, do they not?"

He nodded.

She watched him through narrowed eyes. "Did you injure yourself trying to extricate her from the mis-creants?"

"What makes you think I'd be that foolish?"

Her rosy little mouth lifted into a smile. "I've known you, Edward Stanfield, for a very long time. You're . . . you're the most gallant man I know."

Deuced awkward the way these women kept finding him so gallant and all. "As it happens," he said, "those mornings spent at Jackson's salon came to good use in thwarting the cutthroats."

"It's your arm, isn't it?" Her worried gaze dropped to his left arm.

"How did you know?"

"There was a hesitation in your movement when you drew me into your arms." Her eyes narrowed and her voice hitched. "Oh, my dearest, are you hurt very badly?"

"Not very."

"I'll have my old nurse look at it," she said. "She's awfully knowledgeable about illnesses and wounds and broken bones and such."

Not as good as Maggie. He laughed. "She would have

to be, given your brothers' propensity for getting into scrapes."

"Allow me to get you a drink."

God, but he *did* need a drink. "A glass of madeira would be most welcome."

She went to the decanter, poured out a glass, and handed it to him. "Come, let's sit down."

They sat on a silken sofa some ten feet away from the blazing fire, and he sipped his drink. For the first time today he felt warm.

"Now that you've come," she said, "you must help me with Papa. He's been most vexing."

"How so?"

"About our engagement. I've begged him to post the announcement in the newspapers, but he refuses to. One would almost think he didn't like you—when I know for a fact he's exceedingly fond of you."

"What does it matter if you post the announcement now? We can't marry until you're out of mourning."

"I should like to proudly tell the world you're to belong to me." Her eyes softened. "Besides, you cannot imagine how my suitors have contrived to use their condolences over my poor Mama's loss to secure a position in my heart. The sooner I can send them away, the better."

A month ago he would have fumed over Fiona's long line of suitors, but now he was strangely indifferent. "Why does your father say he won't post the announcement?"

"He doesn't say! He's being extremely vague. I've talked to Randy and Stephen about it, and they think Papa's transferring all the love he felt for Mama to me, that he does not wish to let me go."

"Your brothers are likely right. I suggest you humor your father until the end of your mourning period when it will be easier for him to accept your marriage."

"I know you're right. And I know I'm being ever so selfish. Do you suppose . . ." She set her dainty hand upon his. "Can you procure a special license so we can wed the day after I come out of mourning?"

He stiffened. "If that's what you'd like."

Chapter 22

"Fiona tells me you married old Lord Warwick before he died," Lord Agar said to Maggie at dinner that night. She had been placed to his right while his daughter presided over the opposite end of the table, Edward at her right. With diamonds sparkling in her silvery blond hair and a frothy snow white gown billowing about her graceful body, Fiona looked like a fairy princess, at least like Maggie's vision of what a fairy princess ought to look like.

Maggie tensed. She hoped Lord Agar would not question her about the old earl since she knew nothing about him. "That's true," she said, feeling guilty for lying.

"May I say the old codger showed remarkably good judgment in his selection of a wife?" Lord Agar said.

"That's very kind of you, my lord," Maggie said. She thought perhaps Lord Agar was a bit of a codger himself, he had so easily forgotten his mourning in order to shower her with his attention.

"Never could figure out why old Lord Warwick was so devilishly reclusive, but come to think of it, even when he was a young man, he was a loner. His last year at Oxford was my first. The fellow had already succeeded and was extravagantly rich, but kept to his rooms. Never socialized. Never even— Well, I don't need to discuss such a topic in the presence of you lovely ladies. Suffice it to say he thought he didn't need anyone."

"Yes," Maggie embellished, "my late husband was very lonely when I met him."

"Robbed the cradle, he did!" Lord Agar said. "I daresay you're younger than my Fiona."

Maggie directed her brightest smile on him. "I'm four and twenty."

"See!" he boomed. "You're a year younger than my daughter."

"I suppose my . . . husband treated me more as a daughter than a wife." Maggie detested lying but thought she might have a natural talent for it.

"How long were you married?" Lord Agar asked.

Thinking of her marriage to The Scoundrel, she said, "Two years."

"And no babies?"

Maggie felt the blood rushing to her cheeks.

"Papa!" Fiona said with exasperation. "Leave the lady be. Don't ask such questions." Sending Maggie a warm smile, Fiona said, "I do apologize for my father's inquisitiveness."

"There's nothing to apologize for," Maggie said.

"Papa, you must have Lady Warwick tell you about America. That's where she was raised."

"Is that so?" he asked. "Where in America?"

"Our home was in Virginia, though I must tell you my parents were English."

"Where were they from in England?"

"Bristol."

Lord Agar shook his head. "Don't know any Peabodies from Bristol." He filled his plate, then continued the discussion. "I expect the red savages run amuck in America."

Maggie could barely suppress a giggle. "Actually, I've never seen one."

"Is that so? I daresay you had a great many slaves, though."

She was sorry to admit the truth. "My father—as all the planters in Virginia did—owned slaves."

"Nasty business."

"I've always wished to go to America," Lady Fiona said, graciously redirecting the conversation, "but you ladies have quite changed my mind."

"Why?" asked Maggie.

Fiona gave a self-conscious little laugh. "Because I should feel quite ugly, indeed. Are all the women in America as beautiful as you and your sister?"

Maggie felt Edward's eyes on her and flicked her gaze to him, but he quickly looked away. "Actually," Maggie said, "I was wondering if all the ladies in Yorkshire are as lovely as you."

"Yes, Agar," Edward said, "I should think we're the most fortunate men in the three kingdoms to be dining tonight with such beautiful ladies."

"Yes indeed," Lord Agar concurred.

Maggie was pleased that she had chosen to wear the rose gown that draped off her shoulders and gracefully hugged the gentle curves of her body. Even Rebecca's efforts to pin up Maggie's hair in the Grecian goddess mode had been reasonably successful. All of this bolstered Maggie's sagging confidence, but not enough to compensate for the inadequacy she felt when she stared down the table at her elegant hostess.

"You must tell me about Windmere Abbey," Maggie said to Lord Agar. "It's not at all what the name conjures."

He smiled. "That's because the original abbey was pulled down in the early seventeenth century. My great-grandfather had this house erected in its place, but the old name stuck."

"And my grandfather," Lady Fiona said, "rebuilt

and added on in the Palladian mode toward the end of the last century."

"Have you a library?" Rebecca asked Lord Agar.

"Yes. My father had a new one built," Lord Agar said.

"It's the room we're most proud of," Fiona added.

Edward smiled at Rebecca. "If you like my modest library, you will fall in love with Agar's. It's on the end of the new wing—a full two stories in height with a great many windows to provide good reading light."

Through her spectacles that glistened beneath a glittering pair of crystal chandeliers, Rebecca's eyes widened as she turned to her host. "Oh, Lord Agar, I should be ever so happy if you would allow me access to your library."

He patted her hand. "I would be honored."

"Do you think you could take me there after dinner?" she asked.

"Lady Fiona may have need of you for other pursuits tonight," Maggie told her sister. Didn't genteel ladies play at the pianoforte and sing after dinner?

"I hope I'm not such a demanding hostess that I don't put my guests' interests first," Fiona said. "I perceive that Miss Peabody is enamored of libraries."

Maggie and Edward both broke out laughing.

"Miss Peabody delights in books, books of all kinds," Edward explained.

"And since my sister becomes queasy when reading in the carriage," Maggie said, "Rebecca is feeling rather deprived at the present."

"I daresay your deprivation is at an end, Miss Peabody." Fiona smiled at the young lady. "Have you come out yet?"

Swallowing her stewed eel, Rebecca shook her head.

Fiona's pale eyes began to dance. "Nothing would give me greater pleasure than to present you, Miss Peabody."

"Lady Fiona—when not in mourning—is the toast of the *ton*," Edward informed them.

Did the gorgeous Fiona have no faults? She was beautiful and kind and popular, too. Maggie saw that her sister was weighing the *ton* against the library, and the *ton* was a distant second. "Perhaps by the time you're out of mourning, Lady Fiona, my sister will be ready to come out," Maggie said. "She's not quite eighteen, so I believe it will not hurt to wait until next year."

Fiona gave Rebecca a benevolent smile. "Attendance at assemblies here in Yorkshire would be an agreeable way to introduce you to society without the anxiety."

Edward stiffened. "A good idea, but not this trip. The ladies—after so exhausting a journey—will require total peace and quiet."

Which, Maggie realized with appreciation, was Edward's way of keeping their presence here secret.

After dinner Lord Agar was only too pleased to show off his spectacular library. Even Edward's flattering description had not done it justice. Maggie could not decide if its most striking feature was the circular wall of windows at the west end or the barrel-vaulted ceiling that soared forty feet overhead. Another impressive feature was the catwalk that ringed the second-floor level. The room's rich dark woods, the deep claret of the Turkey carpets on the wide-planked floors, and the massive fireplace gave the room warmth despite its gargantuan dimensions. She watched for Rebecca's reaction.

"My lord!" Rebecca shrieked, "so many books! How many volumes have you?"

"Thirty thousand," he said.

"Not any more, Papa," Fiona said softly.

"Oh, yes, I sold off a couple of thousand volumes after losing my shirt on that African gold mine."

"I shouldn't think a few thousand would even be missed," Edward said.

Rebecca had walked up to a wall of books and was examining the titles. "Lord Agar?"

He turned to her. "Yes, my dear?"

"Would it be a terrible annoyance to you if I requisition the sofa by the windows for my own spot each day?"

"I would be most happy to have you take up the sofa every day for as long as you're here."

"This room," Rebecca announced dramatically, "was made for readers."

"I spend a good bit of time here each day myself," Lord Agar said, "but I've little time for reading, what with my correspondence and ledgers and all, but I'll be most happy for the company."

"Oh, I'm not good company," Rebecca said.

"Which is just as well," Maggie added, bestowing a smile on Lord Agar. "I assure you my sister will in no way disturb your important work."

He must have appreciated her reference to his work as important. Lord Agar smiled down at Maggie and offered his crooked arm. "Shall we repair to the saloon for whist? You do play, don't you?"

"Her ladyship is an uncommonly good whist player," Edward said.

Lord Agar covered her hand with his own. "In that case I claim her for my partner." Then, lowering his brows, he turned back to Rebecca. "Unless Miss Peabody should wish to play. Five's a deuced awkward number."

Rebecca, her nose in a book, was not even aware she was being spoken to.

"I believe my sister would prefer to spend the evening in your library, my lord," Maggie said, "if that is agreeable with you."

"Yes, quite."

Edward was angry with himself for boasting about Maggie's play at whist. He had never bragged about Fiona's play, and though she was too much a lady to express jealousy, the fleeting hurt he saw on Fiona's face wrenched at him.

They took their seats at the game table, Fiona opposite him and Maggie to his right. It was during the first hand his gaze fell on Maggie's graceful shoulders and the creamy skin that dipped beneath the full bodice of her rose-colored gown, and he realized it was the same gown she had worn the first time he ever saw her. He would never forget how magnificent she had looked that night standing below him at the base of the stairs, ordering his servants about, and he would never forget his instantaneous feeling that she was the loveliest creature he had ever seen.

He forced his gaze across the table to Fiona, who smiled at him, then returned her attention to her cards. Fiona wasn't any less pretty than she'd been the last time he saw her. She still exuded the elegance and fragile beauty that had won his heart so many years before.

It was he who had changed.

And that realization left him feeling as if he'd lost his oldest friend.

When Agar got up to replenish his brandy, Fiona spoke to Maggie. "I'm so very happy you've come, my lady. Your visit has been the source of much amusement to my poor father. This is the most animated I've seen him in the four months since we lost my mother."

Good Lord! Edward thought. Did Fiona think Maggie would be even remotely interested in Lord Agar as her newest conquest? Then he realized Fiona—and her father—would quite naturally believe Maggie attracted to wealthy old peers. The very idea of Maggie and Agar revolted him. Why, she was too . . . too what? he asked himself. He had initially thought her unimpressed by titles, disinterested in fortune. Hadn't she turned down Lord Aynsley? But now he did not know what to think after her behavior in the carriage this morning. Mercenary was probably what she was! His face clouded when Agar returned to the table and threw out a card.

Fiona was not a bad player. For a woman, she was quite good, actually. Whenever he had played with her in the past, Edward had thought she would much rather be talking to friends than concentrating on her cards.

"How did you find Hogarth Castle?" Fiona asked Maggie.

He could see the blank look on Maggie's face. Of course she would have no idea that Hogarth Castle was the Warwick country estate. "I believe the countess much prefers London," Edward said.

A look of relief washed over Maggie's face. "Yes, quite, though—due to my mourning, which I'm heartily glad to be out of—I've seen very little of London."

"Then you've not been a good host," Fiona scolded Edward. "Did you take her ladyship to the theatre?"

"We saw *The Tempest*," he answered.

"Were you able to go up to Richmond?" Fiona asked Maggie.

"No, but we did go to Greenwich one day," Maggie said as casually as she would utter a salutation.

God help him! It was hard enough sitting so close to Maggie, feeling the touch of her leg against his, peering at those lovely breasts, without having to be reminded of Greenwich and the most incredible lovemaking in his entire life. He felt the perspiration popping out on his brow. *Damnation—it was hot in here.*

"Do you know," Fiona said, "I have never been to Greenwich. Do you recommend it, my lady?"

Maggie shrugged. "It's hard for me to say because the weather was so very dreadful the day we went."

"But you were able to return to London the same day?" Fiona asked, her brows lowering. "The roads were passable?"

Edward felt as if he had been kicked in the gut.

"We just barely made it back," Maggie said calmly.

Damn Fiona! She was entirely too perceptive. "The worst of it was, Lady Warwick's unduly upset by thunderstorms."

Fiona gave Maggie a concerned look. "How awful for you!"

"Yes, it's dreadfully inconvenient. If I'm home I can bury myself beneath the covers of my bed for the duration of the storm," Maggie said with a laugh, "but if I'm away from home my fears render me an absolute burden to whomever I'm with."

"You were not a burden," Edward said, kindness in his voice. When he glanced across the table, the haunted look on Fiona's face troubled him. *She knows.*

Chapter 23

Randolph Hollingsworth returned to Windmere Abbey the following afternoon. To say that he was infatuated with Maggie would be an understatement, Edward reflected bitterly. If she had been attracted to Harry Lyle, she would undoubtedly be bowled over by Hollingsworth. Unlike the other members of his family, Randolph Hollingsworth was not short, nor was he slender. From Lady Agar's family he had inherited a goodly height, though he was not as tall as Edward, and a sturdy, well-muscled body suited to athletic endeavor. Like his sister, he was possessed of a full head of blond hair and displayed impeccable manners.

He was Edward's oldest friend and Edward had always been remarkably fond of him, but Edward found himself quite out of charity with Hollingsworth. The man was an irrepressible flirt who was uncommonly popular with the ladies. Including Maggie.

One look at Maggie's lovely face and dazzling figure, and Hollingsworth had been completely captivated. Edward had never known his friend to forgo riding or a round of billiards, but the man now refused to enjoy any activity from which Maggie was excluded. Uncharacteristically, he even rose before noon in order to take breakfast with Maggie!

In addition, he took long walks with her, stared at her with adoration throughout dinner—he insisted on sitting beside her—and selfishly claimed her as his whist partner nightly, forcing his poor, aging father to join Miss Peabody in the library night after night. Of course, being the lady she was and knowing how keenly her father enjoyed whist, Fiona urged her father to take her place as Edward's partner, but Lord Agar nobly bowed out, saying he would leave the game to the young people.

All of this made Edward rather short-tempered.

He was all too happy to see the last of February. With March came milder days, bluer skies, and an awakening landscape, which enabled them to spend more time outdoors. Except for Miss Peabody, who only left the library to eat and sleep.

Therefore, Edward and Fiona, along with Maggie and Randolph, had begun to take excursions. To fulfill Maggie's request, this day they rode in the Agar barouche to see the moors.

"I've always longed to see the moors," Maggie said, smiling up at Hollingsworth, who sat bundled beside her. "We don't have moors in America."

"Is that so?" Hollingsworth asked. "I would have thought there were moors everywhere."

The man sounded like a parrot of his slow-topped father. "I believe they're peculiar to England," Edward grumbled.

Fiona grew quiet. She seemed to be doing that a lot lately. Edward wondered how much she had been able to guess. He was sure she sensed that something about Maggie's background was fabricated. Did she also sense that he and Maggie had been intimate? Is that why Fiona's smiles were becoming less frequent, why she was becoming so bloody solemn?

He felt wretched. One of the things he had loved about Fiona was her good nature and sense of humor, neither of which he had seen for days. Was he to blame? Was he destroying that which he had loved?

"I'm surprised, old fellow," Hollingsworth said to him, "that the Foreign Office can do without you for this long."

Maggie gave a mock scowl. "After so many years of conscientious service, Lord Warwick deserves some reward."

"It is time you allowed yourself a holiday," Fiona said, setting her hand upon his. "How much longer will we be able to keep you?"

Would that he could look into the future. By now his adversaries would have had time to visit all of his country properties and would know he was not at any of them. Which could mean that as a last resort they would come looking for him at Windmere Abbey. He should not allow himself to get too comfortable here, but where would he take Maggie next? Where could he be assured she'd be safe? "I need to start thinking about returning."

"But surely not the countess," Hollingsworth protested. "You cannot expect a woman to make that grueling journey again so soon?"

Fiona's worried gaze swung from Edward to her brother. "I've been sworn to secrecy, but I'm sure Edward means to apprise you of the danger to Lady Warwick." She eyed Edward.

Anger raged on Hollingsworth's face. "What do you mean, the countess is in danger?"

Fiona looked like a scared child. Edward took pity on her and pulled her hand into his. "It's all right, my sweet. I have no secrets from your brother." He turned his attention to Hollingsworth. "The night we fled London, four armed men tried to abduct Lady Warwick."

"Good lord!" Hollingsworth said, spinning toward Maggie. "Were you hurt?"

"No, but Lord Warwick was." Her eyes softened as

she glanced at Edward. "How is the wound to your arm, my lord?"

"I'm happy to say I've had almost a full recovery, thanks to you and to the Hollingsworths' old nurse."

"Her ladyship cared for your wound?" Fiona asked, sliding her gaze to Maggie. She did not sound at all pleased.

How, Edward wondered, did one bandage a man's arm without said man removing his shirt? Fiona was learning too many things he would rather she not know.

"I fancy myself adept at healing," Maggie said. "It's something I picked up from my mother."

Fiona turned a bright smile upon Maggie. "Then I'm most grateful you were with Edward when he was injured."

"Not as grateful as I am that he was with me when those wicked men tried to grab me. Lord Warwick was really quite magnificent, fighting off four men single-handedly."

"Is that so?" Hollingsworth said, admiration on his face. "Were you armed?"

Edward shook his head.

"You fought them off with your bare hands?"

Edward shrugged. "At the end, I had help."

"After he had already disabled two of the men," Maggie praised.

"You still sparring with Jackson?" Hollingsworth asked.

"I am."

Hollingsworth's eyes narrowed. "Bloody glad I'll be to get back to London. I'm longing for a good session with Jackson. This mourning business is beastly." A few seconds later he stammered an apology. "Not that my mother's memory is not worth excessive sacrifice on our part, mind you."

"I'm glad you've brought up the subject of London,"

Edward said. "I may need you to go there. Be my eyes and ears until Mag—, the countess is out of danger."

His heart raw with pain, Edward watched Hollingsworth beam down at Maggie. Why in the hell did she have to wear the damned blue shawl? The memories it evoked tormented Edward.

"I'd do anything for the countess," Hollingsworth said.

Edward had once said he would trust no other person with Maggie's safety. He was wrong. He would trust Randolph Hollingsworth. The man was honest, patriotic, and he cared about Maggie. Edward could see that he would have to take him into his confidence, to tell him everything.

Even about Andrew Bibble.

As they drew near the moors, they left the barouche and began to walk, Maggie and Hollingsworth arm in arm in front of him and Fiona. The wind grew stronger, the terrain rockier, the landscape more eerily haunting. "It's lovely here," Maggie was saying, "in a melancholy way."

Edward had thought Maggie would love the verdant English countryside, but damned if he'd known Hollingsworth was going to try to take credit for it! In his smug, proprietary way, the man was acting as if he'd single-handedly brought on the spring! Damn him.

Fiona's hand dug into Edward's arm, and he turned to face her. "Please, let them go on," she said. "I wish to have you all to myself."

"I'm yours to command," he said grimly, taking a turn away from the moors. They walked some little way before she finally spoke again. "What's troubling you, dearest?"

His stomach knotted. "Nothing's troubling me, save that nasty business back in London."

She gave a false laugh. "It's I who should have

changed these past four months, but the most marked change is in you."

She was right, of course, but he could not very well tell her, *I've bedded another woman, a woman who's displaced you in my heart*. He had thought that if he could just see Fiona, everything would return to what it had been before Maggie. But nothing was the same. Everything was worse. He had never been more unhappy. He was poised to marry a woman he no longer loved. That woman was now so steeped in melancholy he scarcely recognized her. He longed for Maggie, a woman who neither loved him nor wanted him, a woman who made a habit of collecting men's hearts.

Fiona could be entrusted with some of the truth. "It's my position at the Foreign Office." He turned to her. "What I say dies here."

"Yes, of course," she said.

"I'm certain one of my most trusted colleagues is a traitor, but I don't know which of them is guilty."

"Surely not Harry Lyle!"

His face grim, Edward nodded. "I could be wrong, but I believe the spy is either Lyle or Lord Carrington."

"But it couldn't be Lord Carrington, either!"

He gave a bitter laugh. "Now you see why I've been so devilishly ill-tempered." Or, now she could see one of the reasons why he'd been such a grump.

She drew closer to him, her arm resting on his, her modest bosom rubbing against his upper arm. "Would that there was something I could do to help you."

He patted her hand. "It's nothing you need concern yourself with."

They were walking against a southerly wind that was so strong it blew the hood of Fiona's black cloak away from her face. Restoring it would have been a wasted effort. Her efforts were needed to traverse the rocky terrain. He turned to look back, but the moors were no longer in view. He could not see Maggie or Hollingsworth.

They soon came to an old crofter's hut which had been abandoned decades ago. To his surprise, Fiona ducked into the one-room building. He glanced up and saw that its wooden roof had almost completely eroded away. Then he sent Fiona a questioning look.

"I would like for you to kiss me," she whispered in her sweet melodious voice.

With every beat of his heart he wanted to love Fiona as he once had. Perhaps if he allowed himself to kiss her, the heated passions she had once stirred would return. He took two strides, settled steady hands upon her slim shoulders, then lowered his mouth to brush against hers. The woman he was prepared to spend the rest of his life with had decidedly different ideas about the potency of the kiss. Her slender body swayed against his and her breath was ragged as her arms encircled him, clinging to him, refusing to terminate the kiss. At that moment Edward hated himself. Her desire for him had never been so passionate, his for her never so impotent.

He stiffened and backed away, but she continued to cling to him. Her smoldering eyes met his and she spoke breathlessly. "I want to make love to you. Now. Here."

God in heaven! What had he done to the purest, finest woman he had ever known? "You can't know what you're saying. You're a lady——"

"A lady who's madly in love," she said, her voice heavy with passion.

He felt as if the very ground he stood upon had caved into oblivion. His hands grasped both her arms, and he backed her away from him. "I will not make love to you until we're married."

An unbelievable melancholy washed over her sweet face, and he felt like a monster.

* * *

As Maggie walked along the lonely moors, wind singing in her face, it suddenly occurred to her how remote this forlorn stretch of land was. Her heart beat erratically as she pictured Andrew Bibble's bloody body. Terror gripped her and she had an overwhelming desire to return to the safety of Windmere Abbey. "What are those yellow flowers?" Maggie asked Randolph, gripping his hand tightly.

"Gorse," he said. "You don't have them in America?"

"Not that I'm aware of." She had taken an immediate liking to Mr. Hollingsworth, and during the past several days had grown comfortable with him. Were she to draw up a list of attributes she sought in a husband, a pastime in which she frequently indulged, Mr. Hollingsworth would be in possession of every one. She had even begun to think he might offer for her.

Such a proposal, if indeed he did make it, would merit serious consideration. Edward was completely out of the picture now that Maggie had met Fiona. Lady Fiona was everything he had said she was and more, and Maggie liked her very much. Far too much to want to steal her fiancé.

That was not to say a little something did not die inside Maggie every time she saw Edward take Fiona's hand or speak softly to her.

Maggie and Mr. Hollingsworth were holding hands and he was smiling down at her, when completely out of the blue he proposed. "I don't like to think of Warwick taking you away. You're the first woman I've ever wished to marry."

Her heart stampeded. *Was that a proposal?*

He moved closer and delicately touched each of her cheeks. "Will you honor me by becoming my wife?"

Oh dear. "It's I who am honored, but I must tell you there is much about me that you don't know. There's the possibility that when you do know my history you may not wish to marry me."

He took her hand and pressed his lips into her palm. Not letting go of her hand, he gazed adoringly at her. "I don't think there's anything you could tell me that would make me love you less. You've bewitched me. You're the first thing I think of every morning, the last thing every night."

"I am exceedingly flattered," she said, pulling back her hand, "but I need time to consider your offer."

His huge shoulders sagged, a frown sliced across his face. "And I had hoped to procure a special license and wed you within a fortnight."

She gave a false little laugh. She would have to discuss this with Edward. Though she hated her bogus position, she would not reveal the truth to Mr. Hollingsworth until Edward gave her permission to do so.

A sudden gust of wind almost ripped away her most precious possession, the blue shawl. "We'd better go back," she said.

Chapter 24

Before dinner that night Maggie waited in the corridor outside Edward's chamber door. When he closed his door and looked up to see her standing there in an elegant pink gown, his face brightened.

"I should like to have a private word with you," she said, closing the gap between them.

"We can go to the orangery." That the orangery was on the opposite end of the house from the dining and drawing rooms should ensure that neither of the Hollingsworths would intercept them. Edward needed to be alone with Maggie. He wasn't sure why, and he wasn't sure what he was going to say to her when he did get her alone, but he had to be with her without the intrusion of Fiona or her damned brother.

Since night had fallen, they took their own candle to the orangery, where they were quite alone. The glass room had grown cold now that the sun had set, but still the rows of rose bushes gave off their sweet scent. *Maggie's scent,* he thought, his memories of that day in Greenwich the sweetest form of self-torture. He set down the candle and turned to face her, his heart hammering. The candlelight glanced off her dark hair, hair that had been swept back but which had escaped its pins to frame her face in limp ringlets. His gaze swept to the pink tinge in her cheeks, along the smooth column of her neck to the bare shoulders of satiny flesh he hungered to touch. God, he wanted to draw her into his arms, but he could see from her casual nonchalance that she had no wish to be her seductive self. Not that she was actually aware of how seductive she was, he conceded.

"I must tell you," she began, "that I exceedingly dislike being a fraud. Don't you think that Mr. Hollingsworth—and Lady Fiona, too—can be trusted with the truth about my background?"

Edward's heart sank. So the reason Maggie wished to be alone with him was in order to discuss her newest suitor. He nodded somberly. "I've been thinking along the same lines myself. The problem is Fiona. She's been perfectly comfortable with the relationship between you and me because she believes familial ties make me responsible for you. What would she think if she learned the truth?"

Maggie bit at her lip. "I daresay she would not be happy, and I shouldn't like to make her unhappy for I'm most fond of her."

Edward nodded. "I'd rather wait until such a time as the nuptials grow nearer to tell her, but I believe we need to tell her brother the full truth."

"I had hoped you would say that," she said.

Damn! Did that mean she and Hollingsworth were at the betrothal stage? That she wished to be completely truthful with the man she intended to marry? Had one of Edward's own family members been killed, Edward could not experience pain greater than what he felt now. His mouth went suddenly dry. His heartbeat hammered. "Has . . . has he offered for you?"

"Actually he has."

Acute pain lanced through him. It was a moment before he could respond, before he finally managed, "Please accept my felicitations. Hollingsworth's a good man."

"Oh, I haven't agreed to marry him."

Relief strummed through him.

"Yet," she added, slashing his hopes. "How could I possibly give my hand to a man who doesn't know who the hand belongs to? Oh, dear, I'm muddling things. Do I make any sense?" Those deep brown eyes of hers locked with his.

"Yes," he said. "Before you can consent to marry Hollingsworth you wish to tell him your true identity."

"Exactly! Also, don't you think he needs to know how dangerous it is to ally himself with me?"

"I've been thinking along those lines myself." *Except for the allying part.* "Hollingsworth's completely trustworthy, and I wouldn't worry about danger scaring him off. He's no coward. If you have no objections, I'd like to tell him everything. I'd like for him to go to London, attempt to learn as much as he can, and hopefully let us know when—or if—we can return."

"I think what you're suggesting's an excellent idea."

He allowed his hand to graze her shoulder. "Then let's go dine. I'll speak privately with Hollingsworth after dinner."

"Oh," she said, her entire demeanor somber, "there's one other thing I wished to tell you."

God give me strength! It was killing him not to draw her into his arms, not to brand her as his own. His brow hitched.

Her lashes lowered and she began to speak in a whisper. "I wished to relieve your mind—knowing how much you wish to marry Lady Fiona." She paused, still not meeting his gaze. She began to pull at the stitching in her gloves. "If you'll recall that day at the Spotted Hound and Hare, I told you if I found that I was with child I should wish to marry you." Now her lashes lifted and their eyes met.

He nodded. He could barely breathe. Barely think. Hope swelled within him.

"You will be happy to learn I've had my courses," she said, gazing back to her gloves.

"You've just destroyed my last hope," he muttered, turning on his heel and leaving her behind as he walked along the long stone corridor back to the woman he had pledged to marry.

Her trembling wouldn't stop all through dinner. Maggie tried to be agreeable to Mr. Hollingsworth, who voiced concern over her condition. "I daresay I'm just cold," she said, brushing off his concern.

His blue eyes raked over her bare shoulders and lowered to the tops of her breasts. "Allow me to get your shawl," he said.

The only shawl she possessed was the blue one Edward had procured for her, and she could not allow herself to see it, to feel it, for in her confused, upset state she would likely fall to pieces. "I'll be fine," she said.

Her nerves were so utterly shattered it was a wonder she could attend to half of the conversation. What had Edward meant about his *last hope?* Was his hope for a child so strong he no longer wished to wed Lady Fiona? Maggie drew in a long, steadying breath. Could he possibly wish she had been with child? Could he possibly . . . She drew in a deep breath. Could he possibly wish to marry her? Then, looking to the foot of the table and seeing Fiona's graceful countenance, she felt wretchedly guilty for wishing to deprive her hostess of the man she loved.

For that *is* what Maggie wished. Never mind if Edward was a fraud. Never mind that he could even be a traitor. Never mind that he was pledged to a very fine woman who did not deserve his infidelity. It was suddenly clear to Maggie that she did not care about any of those things. The only thing on earth that mattered to her was Edward and how dearly she loved him.

She looked at the roasted duck on her plate and promptly lost her appetite. Across from her Rebecca was speaking to Lord Agar. "Are you quite sure there's no catalogue of your library?" Rebecca asked.

Lord Agar gave a puzzled frown. "I know there should be one, but I'm sure there's not. Demmed if I know why."

Rebecca's eyes widened. "I've just had a splendid idea!"

Lord Agar settled his hand over Rebecca's. "What is your splendid idea, my dear?"

"I should like to undertake a cataloguing of the contents of your library," she said, nudging up her spectacles that had a habit of creeping down her pert nose.

Their host seemed utterly perplexed. "But you cannot be serious! That would take months to accomplish—not to mention that it's an effort that should be conducted by an employee, not by one's guest."

"I think you should allow me to," Rebecca said matter-of-factly. "The first reason being that I should adore the task, the second, it would be an agreeable way for me to repay you for your kind hospitality."

"I don't know what to say," Lord Agar stammered. "What you're proposing is a great deal of work."

"Work I should love," Rebecca insisted.

"But I'm not in a position to pay you—"

"You've paid me handsomely by allowing me to live here, by allowing me complete rein of your wonderful library."

"Papa," Fiona said, "I think Miss Peabody's proposal has merit, and if she doesn't mind, then you shouldn't."

Lord Agar gave Rebecca a sheepish look. "You truly don't mind?"

"Truly."

"Then I would be honored if you'd catalogue our books."

Maggie gave her sister a stern look. "But we can't simply move in with these kind people." In truth, she did not know how much longer she could stay here, how much longer she could bear to see Edward with Fiona.

"I don't mean to restrict you," Rebecca said to Maggie. "You're free to leave when you need to. I'm not a child you have to hover over any longer."

It suddenly dawned on Maggie that it was best to leave Rebecca at Windmere Abbey when she did decide to leave. To keep Rebecca with her would only jeopardize her sister. "No, you're no longer a child," Maggie conceded.

After dinner the ladies and Lord Agar repaired to the saloon where they played at the pianoforte and sang. The younger gentlemen were absent due to Edward's desire to see Mr. Hollingsworth's new saber. Only Maggie knew Edward was taking this opportunity to apprise Mr. Hollingsworth of her true identity. She wondered if either man would mention Mr. Hollingsworth's proposal of marriage.

"I don't know why you're so bent on seeing my new saber," Randolph complained as the two men walked along the long corridor of the east wing. "It bloody well looks like any saber you've ever seen before."

"My dear man, has it not occurred to you that I wish to speak privately with you?"

Randolph stopped. "It's about the business in London, is it not?" He turned to face Edward.

Edward nodded. "I believe the countess told you

she could not consent to be your wife until you knew her full identity."

"What business is it of yours what the woman I love told me in private! And I don't like your knowing the details of our intimate conversations—even if you are one of my oldest friends." His blue eyes began to glitter. "And what do you mean 'her true identity'? Are you trying to tell me she's not a countess?"

"That's exactly what I'm trying to tell you."

"But . . . she *was* married to your uncle?"

Edward shook his head. "She was married. Not to my uncle. Did you ever know a chap called Lawrence Henshaw?"

A smile broke out on his face. "Of course. He was the jolliest of fellows. In fact, the drunkest I ever got—" He stopped. "You can't be inferring Henshaw was her husband? He wasn't at all the type to settle down."

"Come," Edward said, "we need to have a drink and talk."

A moment later, brandy snifters in hand, they sat in fireside chairs facing each other in front of the former library's fireplace. No longer used to store books, the shelves here now displayed various sporting trophies and stuffed game that Lord Agar and his sons had caught.

"Well?" Randolph asked.

"She thought she was a countess. Turns out Henshaw was utterly devious. He fled England just ahead of the hangman's noose—"

"Did he not work with you at the Foreign Office?"

"He did." Edward's voice dropped. "He betrayed England to the French."

"Bloody bastard!"

"He went to America, claiming to be Lord Warwick, and won Maggie's hand."

"See here, I don't like you calling her by her Christian name! She's not betrothed to you!"

Edward gave a bitter laugh. "She's not betrothed to you, either."

Randolph grimaced. "She really married Henshaw?"

Edward nodded. "He's dead now."

"Is that so? Foul play?"

"I wondered the same thing, but apparently he died after a fall. To keep the story as short as possible, Maggie—for lack of another name I can call her—brought her sister to England, showing up at Warwick House, thinking it was hers."

"Why did you not boot her out?"

"I tried." He shrugged. "She cried. Then later Lord Carrington ordered me to allow her to stay. He thought she must have valuable information—likely a document—that was in her husband's possession."

"Did she?"

Edward shook his head. "But her second night in London—after I had told three men at the Foreign Office of her arrival—her rooms were searched and all Henshaw's things stolen."

"Good Lord, what if she'd been there?"

"Thank God she wasn't."

"Who were the three men?"

"Carrington, Harry Lyle, and a fellow named Charles Kingsbury."

"Don't know the Kingsbury chap." He pondered what Edward said for a moment. "One of those men was responsible for breaking into the lady's rooms."

"I'm aware of that."

"What did they get of Henshaw's?"

"A map of Hertfordshire with no markings on it. A volume of *Tom Jones* with no markings other than a name of someone other than Henshaw. A brief letter from a man in Greenwich named Andrew Bibble. Diamond spurs and a ring."

"What did the letter say?"

"Something about being forced to go into mourning for their mutual acquaintance."

"That's all?"

"No, there's more." Edward paused, drawing in a long breath. "The night after the theft at Maggie's chambers, Andrew Bibble was killed, his home in Greenwich ransacked."

"Good Lord!" Randolph's brows lowered. "Surely . . . these murderers aren't the same ones who tried to abduct . . . Maggie?"

Edward nodded gravely. "Apparently they did not find what they were looking for in Greenwich."

"So they still think she's got an important document?"

"Apparently."

"She doesn't, does she?"

"I've wondered the same thing. She swears she doesn't, and I believe her. That's not to say there's not something right under her nose that she doesn't recognize."

Randolph took a long drink. "So it's likely that one of those three men at the Foreign Office killed that bloke in Greenwich and could try to kill Maggie?"

"Most likely." Edward explained about the abduction attempt the night they went to the theatre and concluded by informing Randolph that the mole had identified Maggie to one of the henchman as wearing a white dress with silver.

"So that narrows it down to Carrington and Lyle," Randolph surmised.

"I was so upset that night I decided to come here straight away. I knew I could not go to one of my own properties for they'd be sure to find us immediately."

"By now they've had time to check on your holdings." Randolph's face tensed. "By God, they'll think to come here next!"

"That's what I'm afraid of. I wish to God now I'd shipped her back to America."

Randolph nodded. "She was safe there."

"So you can see I need you to go to London. You're great friends with Lyle. See what you can learn. I'll need you to secretly communicate with me."

"I'll leave first thing in the morning," Randolph said, "but I don't like Maggie staying here much longer. Carrington and Lyle both know about you and Fiona. They're bound to start snooping here."

"Perhaps we should leave with you."

"I don't want her in London," Randolph snapped.

"No, but we could stay outside of London. Doesn't your father have a farm in Hertfordshire?"

Randolph frowned. "Actually, he's in the process of selling it off to pay some debts, but it's still his for a few more weeks."

"We'll stay there then."

Chapter 25

It was a misty, gray dawn the following morning when Lady Fiona and Miss Peabody gathered around them as the Agar carriage pulled up in front of Windmere Abbey. Maggie's countenance was maudlin as she tearfully parted with her sister. "If something should happen to me," Maggie said as she captured Miss Peabody in a hug, "you're to have my jewels."

It was a good thing the younger sister had left off her spectacles for she began to bawl and kept having to rub her eyes to check the flow of tears.

Edward desperately wished to cheer up the child. "I vow to you, Miss Peabody, as long as I draw breath your sister will be unharmed."

It was too much to hope that the sisters' melancholy would not extend to Fiona. She rushed to Edward and drew his hands into hers, great tears pooling in those pale blue eyes. "Dearest, you will take care of yourself?"

"Did you think I wouldn't?" he asked, striving for levity.

Randolph Hollingsworth mumbled his farewell to his sister, pecked her on the cheek, and said, "We can be reached at Broadmeadows, but don't share that information with anyone." Then Randolph assisted Maggie into the carriage. Fiona's hands clutched Edward's tighter. "Could you spare me a private word?" she asked.

In a dismissive air, he kissed her hand. "I can deny you nothing."

He followed as she stepped away from the carriage a half dozen strides. Then with her face painfully solemn, she looked up at him and whispered. "I will ask you a single question and wish for an honest answer."

Nervous, he nodded. Did she wish to move up the date of the wedding, to marry before she was out of mourning? His chest tightened.

"Are you in love with the countess?"

Her question stunned him. Had he not treated Fiona with as much courtesy and respect as he ever had? He had never once since arriving at Windmere Abbey paid any particular attention to Maggie. He thought he'd done a stoic job of denying his strong attraction to the dark-haired beauty.

But his performance obviously had not been convincing enough.

He felt sick inside. "Nothing has happened that would make me not honor my pledge to you," he said.

"That is not what I asked," she said sternly. "Do you love her?"

"If I did it would not change my intentions toward you."

"Tell me what's in your heart, Edward," she said softly. "Are you in love with the countess?"

"Yes, dammit!"

To all outward appearances, she was cool and calm. Until her voice quivered when she responded. "Go with God, Edward. I must think on the matter." Then she turned her back on him and began to mount the steps to the house.

Why hadn't she released him? Did she still wish to wed him even though he did not love her? His thoughts drifted to so many of his acquaintance who had married for family and money and for anything but love—and, remarkably, once their lives were entwined most of them had grown to love one another. Is that what Fiona was hoping for?

He watched her move gracefully through the mist and enter the house. Was this how they would part, with him not knowing what his future held? He fought the urge to run after her. She would, of course, need time to consider her reaction to his declaration.

A soft rain began to fall, and he strode to the carriage, taking one last look up at the clouds before he joined Maggie and Hollingsworth inside.

Maggie, sitting beside Randolph, had made a remarkable recovery. "What, oh purveyor of clouds, do you forecast for today's weather?" she asked Edward, a smile lifting her face.

He was in no mood for frivolity. "Rain," he grumbled. Then he pulled out his map. It was beginning to tear along the folds, but he didn't care. His only interest in it was as a prop to keep him from having to converse with the others, to allow him to mull over the painful scene with Fiona.

"Did you know, Mr. Hollingsworth," Maggie said, "Lord Navigator is most obsessed with studying his map? Because of his unfaltering diligence, I daresay we can be assured of arriving at our destination in the quickest possible time."

Randolph lifted a brow and regarded Edward. "Do you know where Broadmeadows is?" Randolph asked Edward.

"Not precisely."

"Here, I'll show you."

Edward reluctantly released the fragile map.

"What is Broadmeadows?" Maggie asked.

"It's Lord Agar's farm on the outskirts of London," Edward answered.

"Is that where we'll stay?" she asked.

"You and Warwick will," Randolph said, pointing to a spot just north of London. "It's right about here."

Edward leaned forward to peer at it at the same time as Maggie. He smelled roses. And thought about a cozy bedchamber at the Spotted Hound and Hare. Then he snatched the map away from Randolph and glowered over it for the next hour.

"I think it very clever of you," Maggie said to Hollingsworth, "to leave the Warwick coach behind."

"Actually, it's Warwick who's the clever one," Randolph said. "He pointed out that the crest on his would be a dead give-away to anyone searching for you."

She nodded. "Anyone looking for me would also be looking for two women—one in spectacles—so as difficult as it was, it's a good thing I've left Becky behind."

"Indeed it is," Randolph said.

"Does the motion of a coach make you ill?" Maggie asked Hollingsworth a moment later.

"No. Why do you ask?"

She shrugged. "It happens to my poor sister. She can't read at all in a carriage." Maggie lowered her voice. "Though he won't admit it, I believe Lord Warwick also suffers from this ailment."

"I do not!" Edward protested.

"You don't have to be such a bear," Hollingsworth said.

"Oh, dear," Maggie said. "He needs to eat breakfast." She bent over the basket and began serving cold meats and hard-cooked eggs to her companions.

Edward quickly diverted his gaze from her cleavage.

"Lord Warwick's quite the ogre when his stomach is empty," Maggie said.

"Then perhaps we should have taken time for breakfast before leaving," Randolph said, shooting a hostile glare at Edward.

"No, I think his lordship was right. We can easily trim a half hour from the journey just by eating breakfast in the carriage," Maggie said.

"I'm for anything that will shorten the journey.

There's nothing I hate more than a long carriage ride." Randolph reached into his pocket and withdrew a miniature cribbage board. "Can I interest you in a game of cribbage after you eat, my lady?"

She tossed a glance at Edward, who refused to look up. "Perhaps Lord Warwick would prefer to play with you. I know he shares your disdain for carriage travel. I, on the other hand, can amuse myself simply by looking out the window."

The rain was softly tapping on the roof. If it intensified, Maggie was sure to become frightened. She needed a diversion far more than he. "No, you two go ahead and play," Edward said.

But a half hour later he was to regret his decision. Not only because he was bored to distraction, but more specifically because of the provocative way Hollingsworth set the cribbage board on his bulging thighs and swiveled toward Maggie, their knees wedged together. *Damn the man!* And if that wasn't bad enough, the besotted Hollingsworth gaped down the bodice of her dress whenever her cards captured her attention. *Damn him twice!*

Edward could feign interest in the damn map for only so long. Eventually he folded it and returned it to his pocket, then sat back and glared at the couple across from him. Not that he was aware he was glaring, of course.

Despite the dreariness of the weather, Maggie's spirits were high. She chatted amiably with Hollingsworth, and they laughed frequently. Edward tried to discern if she was being flirtatious but decided she was not. She was not even being her seductive self. She spoke to Hollingsworth no differently than she would have spoken to Fiona or to Miss Peabody.

But Hollingsworth was another story. He gazed adoringly at her as if he were a love-struck schoolboy. His thirst to win—and, no doubt, to impress her—was nothing short of ruthless. He kept asking her if she needed the rug, if she was comfortable. He complimented her play. He praised her eyes, likening them to fresh coffee beans. Edward only barely refrained from punching his smug face.

"Harry Lyle said the countess's eyes were haunting, like those of Anne Boleyn on the scaffold," Edward said. Hollingsworth needed to know he wasn't the only man courting Maggie.

"Which I must tell you I found exceedingly flattering," Maggie said. "Though I had quite forgotten that Anne Boleyn's eyes—at least in her paintings—are the exact shade as mine. I've always wished for eyes as blue as yours, Mr. Hollingsworth. Have you ever noted that more than half the people in the world have brown eyes? Blue eyes are not nearly so mundane."

Perhaps she *was* being her flirtatious self, Edward amended. *Damn Hollingsworth's blue eyes!* Edward snorted. "I daresay Atilla the Hun was possessed of blue eyes."

"And need I remind you, so is Fiona," Randolph said, glaring at Edward. Then his gaze returned to Maggie. "What's this about Harry Lyle? I shall be jealous."

"Lyle is one of the lady's many admirers," Edward said. "She had hoped to receive an offer from him the day we suddenly had to travel north."

Randolph's face clouded. "I shall no longer consider Lyle one of my best friends. The rat."

"I shouldn't like for you to malign Mr. Lyle," Maggie said, shooting a scowl at Edward. "He's a very nice man—unless—" She threw a glance across the carriage to Edward.

"Hollingsworth knows everything," Edward said.

"Everything?" She asked.

Edward nodded. "Even about The Scoundrel."

"The Scoundrel?" Randolph asked.

"The man I lamentably married," Maggie said. "The man whose death did not cost me a single tear."

"But, then," Edward said, "the countess does not shed tears when she's truly distressed."

With narrowed eyes, Hollingsworth looked from Maggie to Edward. "Are you sure you two have only known each other for a matter of weeks?"

It seemed impossible to Edward that he had known Maggie for only a month. How could she have infused herself into his mind and heart—and even his soul—in so short a time?

"I daresay Lord Warwick wishes he could turn back the clock to a time before he'd ever met me," Maggie said with a little laugh.

Would he, if he could? How much less complex his life would have been had Maggie not charged into it, shaking up his heretofore predictable existence. But were he in a position to reorder his life, Edward would not change a thing. Not the day in Greenwich. Not his tortuous longing for Maggie. Every minute with her was a fleetingly precious gift. "Never that, my lady," he said, remorse in his deep voice.

The farther south they went, the bluer the skies became. For Maggie's sake, he was grateful. He didn't like to think of her being frightened out of her wits. Especially when he would be powerless to comfort her.

That night at the inn Maggie begged to be excused as soon as she had eaten. Influenced by her sister, she told them she was desirous of curling up in her bed with a book.

But Edward shot a skeptical glance at her. "You're at liberty, my lady, to read in the carriage. Correct me if I'm wrong, but you do not suffer from your sister's ailment."

"You're correct, but owing to the fact I prefer to be accommodating to those I'm with, I choose not to be a bore during the trip." She stepped toward the stairs, then turned back. "Mr. Hollingsworth has brought pasteboards. Tomorrow the three of us should play loo or some such game. It will make the journey go faster."

"I certainly have no objections to that," Edward said.

For her part, Maggie could not terminate the journey fast enough. Sitting across from Edward's brooding countenance all day had been sheer torture. How fortunate Lady Fiona was.

Given her profound feelings for Edward, Maggie was not at all sure if she should offer any encouragement to Mr. Hollingsworth. In her words and actions with him today she had been able to maintain an impersonal distance. He was far too fine a man to marry a woman who could not give him her whole heart, and as long as Edward lived, Maggie would never be able to purge him from her heart.

But marriage really was her only option, and Randolph Hollingsworth was the finest of her suitors.

She removed her blue shawl and lovingly draped it over the back of a wooden chair. Then she undressed and put on a thin wool nightshift and climbed beneath the covers. After she extinguished the candle she lay in the darkness, listening to the forlorn sounds of the wind and the sputtering fire in her hearth and pondered her own hopeless situation.

Then she came to a decision. She would give encouragement to Randolph Hollingsworth.

It was really for the best. For Edward and for her. She prayed she would make Mr. Hollingsworth a good wife.

Chapter 26

"Do you like cats, Mr. Hollingsworth?" Maggie asked the following day.

Much to Edward's consternation, she and Hollingsworth shared a carriage seat again. He did not know why Randolph could not sit beside him and give the lady the seat to herself.

Randolph grimaced. "Can't tolerate the beasts. Why do you ask?"

Her brows lowered. "Oh, dear, you're just like Lord Warwick. He's not enamored of my cat."

"The longer I was with the animal," Edward countered, "the less objectionable he became."

Maggie pouted. "Then why did you not allow me to bring him?"

"Had we the luxury of bringing an additional carriage, he could have ridden with the servants, but you must own traveling with an animal is problematic."

"Not with Tubby. He behaved perfectly during our crossing of the Atlantic. He's such a cuddler, and I miss him so dreadfully." She feigned a scowl at Randolph. "I could never live without my cats."

Dear God, was she planning on wedding Hollingsworth, then?

Randolph patted her hand. "I'm sure your cat would be all that's delightful."

"Oh, he is!" she said with a sigh. "And he's possessed of the most adorable personality."

In his observations of the animal, Edward had seen no evidence of that but he would not provoke Maggie by disagreeing with her.

"I have a hard time believing the creature has a personality," Randolph said. "Now a dog is a different matter altogether. My dogs are uncommonly intelligent. You could not help but to become attached to them, my lady."

"But they're so . . . big!" she said. "I like a pet who can curl up beside me when I sleep."

The vision of Maggie, Tubby and Hollingsworth lying together in a bed was more than Edward could stand. He took perverse pleasure in picturing Hollingsworth with two black eyes.

Hollingsworth frowned and muttered, "Don't see how anyone could sleep with an animal."

Though Edward had always shared that opinion, he now thought he could share a bed with a gorilla for the sake of sleeping with Maggie.

But he must not allow his thoughts to go there. He tossed out a card. "Shall we continue the game?"

Edward had to admit playing cards made the journey seem to pass much more quickly.

Over the next several days they played every card game that could be played with an odd number of participants, and the days flew by.

The favorable weather also accelerated their progress, and they made the trip to Broadmeadows in one less day than the journey to Windmere Abbey had taken.

It was mid-afternoon when his father's coach pulled up to the stone house at Broadmeadows, and as much as he hated to leave Maggie, Randolph said his

farewells and continued on to London. He and Warwick had discussed exactly how he would proceed
once he got to the capital.

He was in a very good humor as his horse pounded
along the country lanes. Though he'd not been able
to speak privately with the countess, he was confident
she favored his suit. After her reserve during the first
day of their journey, she had warmed to him. She
complimented his play at cards. She liked his blue
eyes, and she had even solicited his opinion on felines. In the future he would have to speak more
favorably of the damned creatures. Randolph would
be deuced glad when all this business was wrapped up
and Maggie could become his wife.

Riding his mount was a distinct improvement over
being cooped up in a carriage, especially when the
weather was so deuced fine. No summer day could be
preferable to this with the greenest of meadows slop-
ing up to meet skies as blue as a robin's egg.

He reached the Foreign Office at four o'clock and
went straight to Harry Lyle. The man was huddling
over a map when Randolph entered the office.

"Where's Warwick?" Randolph asked.

Lyle spun around, recognition instantly registering
on his features. "I had hoped you could tell me. Have
you come from Yorkshire?"

"I have."

"And Warwick's not there?"

"Of course he's not! Why would I seek him here if
I'd just left him?"

Lyle's shoulders slumped. "I've been deuced worried about them."

"Them?"

"Warwick was last seen with the Countess Warwick,
an extraordinary beauty."

It was difficult for Randolph not to acknowledge
Maggie's beauty and even more difficult not to flaunt

his own impending engagement to her. "Countess? But Warwick's pledged to my sister! Unofficially, of course. He surely can't have gone off and married someone else."

"No, no! This countess is the . . . the widow of his late uncle."

"I thought the old lord died a bachelor."

Lyle shook his head. "The codger upped and married the beauty before he died."

"Is that so? When do I meet this purported beauty?"

"That's the problem. She's disappeared, and so has Warwick. I'm devilishly worried they've been murdered."

Randolph sank into a chair. "Dear God! What makes you think this?"

He watched Lyle's reaction. The man seemed genuinely upset. "No one's seen them since we all attended Almack's together several weeks ago."

A gaunt looking young man entered the office, standing just inside the door, listening to their conversation. Harry did not notice him at first. Randolph frowned and tossed a glance at the intruder. The man could certainly use the services of a good tailor.

"Can I be of service to you?" Harry stiffly asked the man.

He stammered. "I . . . I, uh, wish to trouble you for a code book. It seems I've left mine at home. I'll just take Warwick's. By the way, any word from him?"

"No, dammit," Harry said.

Randolph stood and introduced himself.

"Sorry," Harry said. "Mr. Hollingsworth, allow me to introduce you to Mr. Kingsbury. Charles Kingsbury."

"Your servant," Randolph said, inclining his head.

They waited until Kingsbury left the office to resume their conversation. "Is he trustworthy?" Randolph asked.

Harry shrugged. "I wish I knew the answer to that."

"Have you looked for Warwick at Hogarth Castle?"

"We've looked at every one of Warwick's properties and were planning to seek him next at Windmere Abbey."

"We?"

"Lord Carrington is just as upset as I. We fear that Warwick and the countess were abducted. Carrington's kicking himself that he didn't requisition some Horse Guards to protect them."

"Why in the bloody hell would a civilian merit the Horse Guards?"

"The countess was suspected of being in possession of important documents that could be sought after by our enemies."

"Then it looks as if the enemy's got the earl and countess."

Lyle's voice was grave when he answered. "Yes, it does. Damn it!" The man was almost in tears.

"Is that Randolph Hollingsworth?"

Randolph whipped around to face Lord Carrington, then stood and bowed. "Your servant, my lord."

"Have you come from Yorkshire?"

"I have, but Warwick's not there. Lyle's been telling me about the disappearance."

Lord Carrington, too, looked genuinely worried. "If anything has happened to them, I'll never forgive myself. I should have had them guarded every minute."

Randolph found himself wondering if Lord Carrington, too, had become enamored of Maggie. Was no man immune to her charms? He supposed Warwick was, given that he was pledged to Fiona, but he could not completely discount him. For many days there had been a particularly tortured look on Warwick's face as he had gazed across the carriage at Maggie.

"If they ever return I will see to it they're never again left unprotected," Lord Carrington said.

Isn't this what Warwick had hoped for? To be able to return to London and promised safety? Randolph shook his head. "Nasty business."

"Yes, it is," Lord Carrington said, "but there is a glimmer of hope."

Harry spun toward him. "They're alive?"

"I believe they might be," Lord Carrington said gravely. "I've just come from Newgate Prison where I spoke to a band of miscreants who confessed to trying to abduct the countess the night she went to Almack's. I don't have the name of the man who hired them, but I'm told he was dressed as a gentlemen and spoke with a French accent."

"What do you mean 'tried to abduct the countess'?" Harry asked. "Was she able to escape?"

"Apparently so," Lord Carrington said.

"Thank God!" Lyle exclaimed. Then as if he were thinking aloud, he said, "And, fearing for her safety, Warwick would quite naturally go into hiding with her!"

Harry Lyle may not have known Maggie for long, but it was obvious to Randolph she had added Lyle to the string of men who had fallen in love with her.

"Just where do you think you're going?" Edward asked Maggie, who was tying on a bonnet as she stood inside the front door of Broadmeadows.

"For a walk. It's far too lovely a day to be indoors."

How could she so carelessly disregard her own safety? "I must insist on accompanying you."

"Surely you're not worried I'll be abducted at Broadmeadows!"

"If I've learned a single thing throughout this ordeal it's to be prepared for the worst."

She waited while he sheathed his saber and strapped it on, then they left the house, her arm tucked into his.

Warmed by the sun, they began to stroll along the rolling meadows behind the stone farmhouse.

"How do you find Broadmeadows?" he asked.

She sighed. "I love it here. If only Rebecca and I had a nice little place like this, then I'd not be in such haste to marry. The pity of it is, had I not married The Scoundrel my father would have left enough for us to purchase a similarly situated farm."

"He was that well off?"

"Not vastly wealthy but comfortably well off."

"Then I don't see why your brother couldn't be more generous with what his father left."

"That's because you're generous by nature. James is not. It's really quite disappointing that he did not inherit our father's benevolence. It's my belief James must have taken after his mother, and she must have been quite wicked." A moment later Maggie amended her statement. "Not to say that James is wicked, precisely. I'm being most uncharitable by speaking so unflatteringly about my own flesh and blood."

"You don't have to apologize for telling the truth."

They came to a tidy peach orchard and were able to walk in the shade. Off in the distance beyond the orchard the land dipped down to a deep blue lake that glistened like sapphires beneath the sun's bright glow. They had not spoken for several minutes now. He wasn't even sure he wanted to talk with her. He did not wish to hear her praise Hollingsworth. In the silence that closed around them like a shell he could allow himself to forget he was pledged to Fiona, forget that Maggie wasn't his.

Maggie sighed. "It's so beautiful today. I vow I don't see how anyone could possibly prefer being indoors. There's not even a wind—nor a cloud in the sky—" Her smiling face lifted to his. "Much to your consternation, I daresay."

He could not repress a grin. "You're wrong if you

think I have some kind of attachment to clouds. I assure you a day like today is exactly what I most wish for. Clouds or no clouds."

"Maggie," he said solemnly a minute later, his voice husky.

She tilted up her head, her delicate brows raised.

"Lord Agar's selling Broadmeadows. Let me buy it for you and your sister. I wish for you to marry because you want to, not because you have to."

There was a softness in her eyes and the unmistakable flicker of remorse in her voice when she responded. "See what I mean about your generosity? I do thank you for the offer, but you know I cannot accept. Besides you've got to consider Lady Fiona's feelings. As kindhearted and charitable as she is, you cannot expect her to stand by silently while you spend large amounts of money on an unmarried woman."

Of course she was right. Besides, even if he had taken great risks to claim the Warwick title and the lands and money that went with it, he was not assured of possessing these things for the rest of his life.

He frowned. "I don't like to think of you being in a hurry to marry Hollingsworth. This time your marriage will be forever, and I shouldn't like you to form an alliance you'll regret."

"I'll own I've only known Mr. Hollingsworth for a week, but you must admit one gets to know another quite well after being confined with them in a carriage for many days."

Edward's pulse leaped. "And you find Hollingsworth's presence not objectionable?" he asked, his gut wrenching.

"I find Mr. Hollingsworth a most worthy gentleman."

"Do you . . . are you falling in love with him?" His

hand fisted. His heart pounded in his chest, thundered in his ears.

She did not answer for a moment. His breath stilled. "You're being impertinent to ask so personal a question," she finally said.

So he was. "Forgive me. I had no right."

By now they had cleared the orchard and were heading toward the lake. "Oh look, Edward! Baby ducks!"

He could not repress a smile when he looked up to see a mother duck waddling along the bank of the lake, some five ducklings waddling behind her. "No doubt you miss Tubby all the more," he said kindly.

"Indeed I do."

Would that he could bring the fat, furry creature to her. There was nothing Edward would not do to keep the blush on her cheeks, a smile on her lovely mouth.

They walked until they came to a yew hedge which separated Lord Agar's property from his neighbor's, then they turned around to return to the farmhouse.

"Were you aware that Lord Agar has apparently suffered some financial setbacks?" she asked.

"Not until this last visit. He's had to sell some of his books, and now Broadmeadows."

"Apparently he lost a great deal of money in an African gold mine."

"Not only that," Edward said, "he'd previously lost heavily on the exchange." Was Maggie concerned that if she married Hollingsworth, his father's fortune would be gone before he inherited? Such greed was not consistent with what Edward knew of Maggie's character. Besides, hadn't she just refused his offer of Broadmeadows?

"I feel wretchedly sorry for Lord Agar," she said. "He's still suffering from the loss of his wife, and now this. Such a pity. If we win the war do you think the exchange will prosper?"

"Undoubtedly." *We win the war.* No one but a patriot to England would say that.

As they continued back Edward was aware of a deep melancholy hanging over him. Despite that the day was as glorious as any he'd ever known. Despite that the woman he loved was at his side. He was possessed of the oddest feeling the Almighty was bestowing these wondrous things upon him only to reinforce that he would be denied them for the rest of his life. Today might be the last time he was ever alone with Maggie, the last time he would ever feel her arm on his. He felt as if he were bleeding inside.

When they reentered the house, the matronly housekeeper informed him that a post for Lord Warwick had been delivered. Edward strode to the hall sideboard and saw a letter addressed to him in Fiona's hand.

Chapter 27

His heart thumped as his glance swung from the letter in his hand to Maggie. She stood on the third step of the stairway, her hand on the wooden bannister and the blue shawl draped over her shoulders as she smiled down at him. Sun streaming in through the sidelights dappled her dark hair, bringing out a reddish glimmer. Her cheeks were tinged with pink and she was so utterly beautiful, his breath caught. "I'll run along now and wash and change for dinner," she said.

He waited a moment before seeking his own room, which was next to hers. Once the chamber door was closed behind him, he strode to the window and opened the green damask draperies, flooding the chamber with the waning afternoon sunlight. Then he sank into an armless wooden chair and opened the letter.

My Dear Lord Warwick,

Since it is unlikely you'll be taking the arduous journey north in the near future, I have taken a coward's path in terminating our betrothal by means of this letter. I should have cried off before you left Windmere Abbey, but under the circumstances I was too rattled to think clearly.

> *It is fortuitous that our engagement was never pub-*
> *licly announced. Neither of us need claim any blame*
> *for the lapse in judgment that resulted in the secret be-*
> *trothal.*
>
> *As you must know, I have no wish to marry a man*
> *whose heart does not belong to me, though I confess*
> *that I gave the matter consideration.*
>
> *If you really love the beautiful countess, you must let*
> *her know before she accepts my brother's offer. I believe*
> *with all my heart that you two belong together.*
>
> > *F.*

His hand shook as he refolded the letter. After all these weeks of shouldering inexpiable guilt, he should feel some relief. But, oddly, he did not. That Fiona had released him did not absolve him from the onerous hurt he had inflicted upon her. She would never again be the happy, confident girl he had fallen in love with so long ago. No one more than she deserved a man who would love her above all else, but would that fragile heart of hers ever again trust a man?

Though Edward loved Maggie more with every beat of his heart, he had no reason to believe she returned his affection. Hadn't she already refused his offer of marriage? Was she not on the verge of accepting Hollingsworth's offer?

Why did his sister not think Maggie belonged with Hollingsworth? Could Fiona have seen something in Maggie's intercourse with Edward that warranted her belief they belonged together? Something Edward himself had not observed?

His shoulders slumped. He had no hope. All his observations of Maggie with Hollingsworth convinced him she would accept the man's offer.

A numbing grief darker than any he had ever experienced slashed through him. How did one live when one's heart had been ripped away?

* * *

They were almost finished with the second course when Mr. Hollingsworth, dressed in dusty riding clothes, strode into the dining room that night. Maggie was very happy for the interruption. Edward was in one of his brooding moods and had barely spoken a word through dinner.

"Won't you have a seat?" she said.

Randolph shook his head. "I couldn't possibly in these clothes."

"Then I'll prepare you a plate and bring it to the drawing room so you can nibble while you tell us everything you learned today," she said.

An hour later Randolph had changed into dinner dress, and the three of them sat on well-worn, slip-covered sofas in the drawing room. Edward and Maggie sipped on brandy while Randolph ate from the plate in his lap.

"Since you've returned so quickly, I'm assuming you learned something today," Edward said, his voice grave.

Randolph, finishing off a bite of sturgeon, nodded. "I believe it's safe for you to return to Warwick House."

Maggie's glance flicked to Edward. His brow crinkled. "I'm not exposing Maggie to harm based on 'your belief.' You'd better have something stronger to go on."

"Lord Carrington has promised to have Horse Guards watch Warwick House around the clock in order to ensure the lady's safety," Randolph said. "He laments that he did not do so earlier."

"As do I," Edward said.

Edward's gravity nearly broke her heart. A stray

tuft of his dark hair spilled onto his forehead, and she fought the desire to gently sweep it away, to flow into his arms and alleviate his woes, woes she had heaped upon his too-generous shoulders.

"There's one thing more," Randolph added, setting down his fork. "Carrington's finally been able to apprehend the cutthroats who tried to abduct the countess. They're in Newgate."

A sigh swooshed from her lungs. "I am so relieved."

"Has he found out who hired them?" Edward asked.

Randolph shook his head. "Not by name, but they claim the man who negotiated with them spoke with a French accent."

A smile lifted her face. "Then we can exonerate Lord Carrington and Mr. Lyle from culpability!"

"So it would seem," Randolph said.

Edward drew in his breath. "As much as I would like to believe them guiltless, we need to proceed with caution."

Randolph regarded Maggie with a tender gaze. "I couldn't agree with you more, but the lady cannot like the idea of spending her life in hiding and seclusion."

"Not just my life," Maggie said, "there's also my sister's life to consider."

Mr. Hollingsworth cleaned his plate and set it on the tea table in front of him, then he went to the decanter and filled a glass with brandy. "Here's what I propose," he said as he returned to his seat. "You and the countess quietly return to Warwick House, where you will have seen to it that your footmen are armed. Then, once she's safely ensconced in the hopefully impenetrable house, you inform Lord Carrington of the countess's return and demand protection by the Horse Guards."

"There's some merit to what you propose," Edward said. "A daytime arrival at Curzon Street—in your father's coach—should be unexpected and, therefore, safe." His eyes locked with Maggie's. "Would such a plan be agreeable to you?"

The very thought of returning to London terrified her. That's where men with knives had tried to grab her—men who had likely killed Andrew Bibble. The vision of his bloody dead body still came to her. She would have been perfectly happy to spend the rest of her life here at Broadmeadows. But that wasn't an option. She sucked in a deep breath. "If returning to London will hasten a return to normalcy, I will have to approve it."

Edward's eyes softened. "Are you afraid, Maggie?"

"I've never stopped being afraid," she said in a thin, nervous voice, "ever since that awful night we fled London."

Edward spoke gently. "Will you feel safer here at Broadmeadows?"

"I suppose I'll never feel entirely safe until The Scoundrel's document—or whatever it is they seek—is found."

"That might never be found," he said.

"One day it will surface," she said. "Of course we have no assurances that day will come during our lifetime." She gave a nervous little laugh.

"I thought you would wish to return to London," Randolph said, giving her a puzzled look.

A pity Randolph Hollingsworth did not understand her like Edward did, since in all likelihood she would be spending the rest of her life with Mr. Hollingsworth.

A pity he wasn't Edward.

"I don't like having to watch my back," she said, "to always have to wonder if I'm being followed, wonder if I'll live to see the next day." She looked into her glass and swished it up to the rim. "Returning to London will hopefully bring closure to so tenuous an existence."

Edward's lips thinned. "We're staying at Broadmeadows."

"Think what you're saying, Warwick!" Randolph said. "Are you prepared to put your life on hold in order to protect the countess? Will she ever feel safe walking along the meadows or through the orchard or rowing on the lake?"

"He's right," she said. "We must return to London."

"May I remind you, madame, of the consequences of making another rash decision?" Edward said.

He was, of course, referring to her disastrous marriage. "If it will alleviate your fears," she said, "I promise to sleep on the matter tonight. If I'm of the same mind in the morning, we should return to Curzon Street tomorrow."

Edward's brown eyes flared with anger. "As you wish."

"Can I interest you in cards?" Randolph asked with a shrug and a smile.

Maggie shook her head. "It's been an exhausting day. I'm going to bed, but might I suggest you play chess with Lord Warwick? He's exceedingly fond of the game."

Edward declined. Though Randolph Hollingsworth was his oldest friend, Edward had no wish to be in his presence longer than necessary. He neither wished to be reminded that it was Hollingsworth and his muscled body and blue eyes that Maggie was prepared to spend her life with, nor did he like to think he was so selfish a creature that he had come to despise so old a friend for no reason other than sheer jealousy.

So he grabbed a cigar, threw on his greatcoat, and stormed from the house. He strolled the width and breadth of the parterre garden, which had been neglected for some time. Not only were the weeds thigh high, but the once-neat grids now spilled over onto the paths. The orange-red glow of his cigar stood out from the night like a star in the inky sky, the nightingale's sweet lullaby penetrating the night's eerie silence.

He kept thinking about the last paragraph in Fiona's letter. He must act with haste if he wished to secure Maggie's hand. The very idea of taking her for his own gave him a heady rush, like downing an entire snifter of brandy in one long guzzle.

Then just as swiftly as he had been filled with hope, he sank into despair. If she had ever given him a single sign, if she'd ever laughingly flirted with him as she did with Hollingsworth, he would risk the humiliation of her rejection. But save for that day in Greenwich when she had been terrified out of her wits, she had never in any way expressed even a sliver of desire for him.

Then the memory of that one kiss during their walk around the lake on the journey north gave him a ray of hope. She had not been outraged when he had yanked her into his arms and kissed her with such passion. In fact, she had kissed him back with an intensity that equaled his own. His breath grew short as he remembered the feel of her arms closing around him. He was sick inside to think he had been the one who ended the kiss but knew he would do it again under the same circumstances: his betrothal to Fiona.

God, but they were good together, he and Maggie. A man could live a lifetime and never experience lovemaking as sublime as they had shared that day. She could never respond to another man with the passion she lavished upon him.

It was only now dawning on him that her storming into Warwick House that night had been their destiny. He had not known it then, nor did he think she knew it now, but he was certain their lives had been predestined to meld together for all of eternity.

And he could not risk letting her get away.

He crushed out his cigar on the flagstone path and returned to the now-darkened house, disappointed that he would not be able to see her tonight, not be able to tell her what was in his heart.

Chapter 28

After carrying her valise down the stairs without any assistance, Maggie threw open the front door and greeted Edward and Randolph when they returned from their morning ride.

Edward's unhappy gaze raked over her traveling costume and valise. "It would seem, madame, that you've made up your mind."

She nodded. "How long before you gentlemen can be ready to leave?"

"Only a minute to throw our clothing into a bag," Randolph said.

A few minutes later they were back in the Agar coach where Mr. Hollingsworth had once more insisted on sitting beside her. She chastised herself for being in such a hurry. This morning would have provided the perfect opportunity to single out Mr. Hollingsworth and tell him she favored his suit. So why hadn't she?

Because of Edward. Despite that he would marry Fiona, despite that Maggie liked Fiona very much, despite that Maggie's chances of engaging Edward's affections were next to nil, she loved him. She could not dispel the memory of him saying *It was my last hope.* Perhaps he *did* care for her, at least a little. To accept any man other than Edward would be to slam the door on her overflowing heart. She would have to close that door, but she was not ready just yet to condemn herself to a life without love.

As their carriage rattled along the bumpy country lane, she watched Edward as he stared out the window. He was so utterly masculine. It wasn't just the saber at his side or the riding boots and buff-colored breeches that stretched across muscled thighs that made him look so rugged. His virility went so much deeper than those things. The dark line of stubble on his jaw, the high cheekbones flaring to darkly somber eyes, the rigid clamp to his lips, the confident set of his shoulders, all these things melded to create the most desirable man she had ever known.

"I see, my lord," she said to him, "that you've begun to manage competently without your valet."

He faced her with laughing eyes. "I'm a bit less lethal, but I'll still be as happy to see Cummings as you'll be to see Tubby."

Just thinking of her cat made her giggle. "I cannot wait to see my little fluff muffin."

A quizzing look on his face, Randolph asked, "Tubby? Fluff muffin? I take it you're referring to your cat."

"She is," Edward said flatly.

When they rode into Mayfair a few hours later, Mr. Hollingsworth and Edward drew their swords. And when the coach turned onto Curzon Street, Edward guarded the right side of the carriage, Randolph, the left.

"I see nothing suspicious," Randolph said.

Edward's eyes swept from one end of the block to the other. "Nor do I."

A few minutes later they were safely inside Warwick House, and Tubby was affecting a bored look as Maggie made a great fuss over him. She and Tubby climbed the stairs to Sarah's third floor chamber, but did not find her there.

"Ye'll find Miss Sarah taking tea with Mr. Wiggins," one of the upstairs maids informed Maggie. "They've become quite chummy during your ladyship's absence."

How kind the butler was!

But as soon as Maggie found them belowstairs, sitting around a pine table adjacent to the kitchen, she knew Wiggins was not just being kind. The way the elderly butler adoringly gazed across the table at Sarah convinced Maggie he was attracted to her! "A fine lady's maid like yourself," he said to her, "should not feel guilty that she's not helping with the cooking and cleaning. It wouldn't do at all to spoil those lovely hands of yours."

Unnoticed, Maggie paused to observe Sarah. Her loyal servant looked a decade younger. The toll from the ocean voyage must have been greater than Maggie thought. Now that Sarah had rested for several weeks, pink colored her cheeks again and her blue eyes glittered as she looked at Mr. Wiggins. She had not been as healthy looking in years.

Wiggins saw Maggie first. He sprang to his feet and began to apologize for not personally greeting them.

"It's perfectly all right, Wiggins," Maggie said. "Besides, his lordship's already gone to the Foreign Office. Please, resume your tea. I merely wished to let Sarah know I've returned."

Sarah pushed away from the table. "I'll just come right up and unpack and your things and Miss Becky's."

Maggie put her hands on the other woman's shoulders and smiled. "You'll do no such thing! Rebecca stayed in Yorkshire, and I'm in no hurry to unpack. Please, finish your tea."

"Good Lord!" Harry Lyle said to Edward. "Where in the hell have you been?" The relief in his voice and the smile tweaking at his mouth convinced Edward his friend was genuinely happy to see him.

"I'm not at liberty to say," Edward answered.

"Were you or were you not attacked the night we all went to the theatre?"

"We were. Fortunately, we were able to escape."

"Then you went into hiding?"

"We did."

Harry sighed. "I don't see why you couldn't have sent me word you were unhurt. You don't know how deuced worried I've been."

Worried about Maggie. Edward set a firm hand on his shoulders. "Sorry, old fellow."

Harry scowled. "I had planned to ask for the countess's hand the day you went missing."

Edward's chest tightened.

"She is well?" Lyle asked.

"She is."

"Did she return to London with you?"

"She's at Warwick House. I've come to demand she be protected."

"Lord Carrington's pledged to assign Horse Guards to protect the countess."

"I want them this afternoon."

"You'll need to take it up with Carrington."

"He's in?"

Harry shrugged.

A moment later Edward strode into his superior's office. "My dear man, it is so very good to see you!" Lord Carrington exclaimed. Though his demeanor was as friendly as Harry's, he seemed less surprised. "We have searched for you high and low. It wasn't until yesterday I learned of the men who threatened you, and you can be assured they're being severely dealt with."

"You've spoken with them?"

"One of them. They're being held at Newgate.

Though the man assured me you had fled, I wasn't confident he told the truth. You cannot believe men like that, you know. Is Henshaw's widow safe?"

Edward nodded. "She's in London. I wish you to detail Horse Guards to protect her immediately."

Lord Carrington gave a faint smile. "So you've already spoken with Lyle?"

"Briefly. I was anxious to see you, to secure protection for the widow."

"Of course, I'll be happy to accommodate your request even though her would-be abductors are in prison."

"The man who employed them isn't!" Edward growled.

"You've got a valid point there. I have spoken with the Duke of York, who assured me I could have a small contingent of Guards."

"Good."

"Now sit down and tell me everything."

When Lord Carrington came to call that afternoon, two uniformed Horse Guards stood at the rear of Warwick House while four of their fellow officers protected the front entrance.

"Lord Warwick is in the library," Wiggins informed him.

"Oh, it's not Lord Warwick I wished to see. Please advise Lady Warwick that Lord Carrington is calling upon her."

Wiggins showed him into the saloon, then went to fetch Maggie, who entered the room a few minutes later.

Lord Carrington stood up and crossed the room, sweeping into a bow before Maggie, taking firm possession of her offered hand, and pressing his lips to it. "I cannot tell you how worried I have been about you, my lady."

"I cannot tell you how worried I've been about me!"

she said with a little laugh, moving to the pair of settees. "Won't you sit down, my lord?"

As they sat on the matched sofas she said, "I'm very much in your debt, my lord, for posting the Horse Guards outside."

"I wish to God I'd thought to do it earlier, but I can't cry over spilled milk. I vow that from now on there won't be a repeat of what happened the night those men tried to abduct you. Now you shall have protection around the clock."

"I'm very grateful." She found herself wondering what Lord Carrington had looked like as a younger man. Not that he was *that* old. She pegged him to be over fifty and under sixty, though he was probably the best looking man of that age she had ever seen. He was thin and perfectly dressed and neat and urbane.

And he was staring at her in a way that made her exceedingly uncomfortable.

"Tell me, my lady, have you uncovered anything since our last meeting?"

She only now remembered that he wished her to spy on Edward. "Nothing, your lordship. Nothing about my late husband. Nothing to discredit Lord Warwick."

"I see." He continued to stare at her.

"Allow me to order tea."

"No, thank you. I shan't be long. I must confess, my lady, I was in a great haste to come see you before your suitors learn of your return. I should like to make an offer for your hand in marriage."

Surely she had not heard him correctly! The marquis had never shown any partiality to her before, nor had he ever struck her as a man who would ever wish to marry. "I beg your pardon?"

"I suppose my offer strikes you as being completely unexpected."

"Then I *did* hear you correctly!"

He laughed. "I surprised myself with the depth of

my feelings for you, my lady. It wasn't until you went missing and I feared the worst that I came to realize how greatly I valued you."

"But, your lordship, we've only been together a few times! You can't possibly know enough of me to wish to make me your wife."

"To be perfectly honest, I never thought I'd ever want to make any woman my wife, but I am fifty-five years old and suddenly regretting that I've no heir. It's only in the past few months I've decided to seek a young bride of good family. When I met you, I began to think that perhaps you were the woman I've been waiting a lifetime for."

She was completely stunned. His desire for an heir must be far stronger than his desire for her. Which was actually a strong argument in his favor!

Though she had been prepared to accept Mr. Hollingsworth or Mr. Lyle, had he offered, she had felt wretchedly guilty for using men who thought themselves in love with her when she would never be able to return their affection.

But no such problem existed with Lord Carrington for she did not believe he was in love with her. She could not hurt him.

It was really rather like a business offer he was making. He wished for an heir and a wife to be a lovely ornament; she wished for security.

"I'm greatly flattered, my lord, but you must know your declaration has been a shock. I shall need time to consider it."

"Of course, my dear. Though I had hoped for affirmation today, I did not expect it."

"Affirmation of what?" asked Edward as he strode into the saloon.

Maggie's heart thumped.

Lord Carrington got to his feet and faced Edward. "A private matter."

Chips of ice in his eyes, Edward gazed from the marquis to Maggie.

"I was just leaving," Lord Carrington said. His head inclined. "Your servant, Warwick." Then Lord Carrington rounded the tea table and came to stand before Maggie, who offered her hand. He pressed it tightly as his mouth touched her glove. "Allow me to say how happy I am that you've returned, my lady."

"Allow me to say how much I appreciate the Horse Guards," she said with a smile.

Once he was gone Edward's icy glare met hers. "Have you bewitched Carrington now?"

Her pulse thundered. "What do you mean?"

"Did Carrington ask for your hand?"

"As a matter of fact, he did."

Chapter 29

Unleashed rage pounded through his veins. The gall of Carrington to tempt Maggie with his title and vast fortune! And damn Maggie with her sensuous ways! Edward scowled at her. Why did she have to look so deuced pretty in that blue-green dress that barely covered her lovely breasts? What man could be immune to such beauty? He turned his fury on her. "It would seem you've done well for yourself by waiting, madame."

She met his gaze with defiance. "What makes you think I'll accept his offer?"

"What woman would not wish to be a marchioness?"

Her jet black eyes locked with his and he perceived an intensification of her own anger. "Not only that," she said in a cold voice, "did you not tell me Lord Carrington is enormously wealthy?"

It was all he could do not to slam his fist into the wall. "As I said, madame, you've done well for yourself." He stormed to the decanter, poured himself a glass of Madeira, and drained the glass.

"I would have thought you'd be happy for me to turn down Mr. Hollingsworth so you won't have to suffer my presence at Lady Fiona's family gatherings."

He swiftly poured another glass and drank it, then turned to face her, his eyes glittering with rage. "I shall not be attending Hollingsworth family gatherings. Lady

Fiona has exercised her better judgment and decided not to marry me."

Maggie's face went white. She started to tremble, then sank back onto the silken sofa. "How long have you known this?" she asked in a shaky voice.

"Since yesterday's post."

The heavy rise and fall of her breasts, the splintering of her voice indicated she was upset. "I'm very sorry for you, Edward. I know how much you love her."

He gave a bitter laugh. "Then you don't know me as well as Fiona does."

"What do you mean by that?"

A harsh shake of his head was his only response. When he had gone to sleep the night before he had vowed to risk humiliation by declaring himself to Maggie. Wasn't the slim prospect of claiming her for his own wife worth the fear of rejection? But that slim prospect now seemed as unobtainable as securing a handful of stardust.

He turned his back on her to pour himself another drink when he heard her deep, wrenching sobs and whirled around to face her. She made no effort to check the torrent of tears which flowed down her delicate cheeks. He had come to know her so thoroughly he knew these tears were genuine, yet he could not conceive of what would have upset her so greatly that she lost all control of her emotions. Not a tear had been shed when her room was searched, not when the cutthroats tried to abduct her, not when she had been terrified by the thunderstorm, not even when she'd viewed Andrew Bibble's dead body. But now, sitting in the saloon hazily lit by the afternoon's waning sun, she crumpled into a fragile, woeful creature.

He wanted to rush to her, to cradle her within his arms and murmur healing words. Instead, he stiffened and lashed out at her. "Pray, what ploy is this, madame?"

Her sobs grew louder and her graceful shoulders shuddered as she completely lost her composure.

He could not bear it. To hell with his damned pride! He rushed to her, dropped to one knee and set his hands to her trembling shoulders. "What's the matter, Maggie?" he asked in a gentle voice.

She collapsed against his chest. Her cries grew even more woeful as her tears soaked through his shirt.

He drew her into his arms, breathing in her rose scent, and murmuring. "What is it, love? Why are you crying?"

Her arms tightened around him and she cried harder. "I'm s-s-s-so wicked," she managed between sobs. "I loved you *e-e-e-ven* knowing you were pledged to Fiona."

In that instant, he experienced a bliss so profound, so complete, he could have wept with joy. His eyes moistened as he held her so close he was afraid of hurting her. "My God, Maggie, how could you not have known how much I love you? Fiona knew."

She drew away to put enough distance between them to peer into his eyes. "Truly Edward? Do you really love me?"

Unshed tears pooled in those dark eyes of hers, and he thought she had never been more beautiful. He gave a false laugh. "So much that I wished to do murder to Harry Lyle, Randolph Hollingsworth, and Lord Carrington."

"Oh, Edward, dearest!" Her voice softened as her hand stroked his cheekbone. "I could not care for any of them—not when my heart ached for the love of you."

He removed her hand from his cheek and pressed a kiss to the inner hollow at the base of her wrist. The sound of her ragged breath was an aphrodisiac. He crushed his lips into hers, plunged his tongue into her mouth as his hands greedily moved over her body.

Without him even being aware of what was happening, Maggie slid from the sofa, her knees pressing to the floor, to the carpet so that her torso melted into his. His hand splayed over her hips, pressing her into his throbbing erection as they began to move together like a single pulsebeat.

He was able to free a breast from her stays, to cup it, to suck a rigid pink nipple into his mouth as she began to whimper.

For that moment in time he forgot everything—forgot that it was broad daylight, that a servant could walk in on them at any minute, that his knees ground into the floor. His love for her consumed him; his need for her obliterated everything else.

His heart caught as she began to softly weep. "What have I done to you?" he asked, his voice raw with emotion, as he eased her away so he could stare into her tear-filled eyes.

She swatted away a racing teardrop and drew in a ragged breath. Then she set a gentle index finger to his lips. "Continue whatever it is you're doing to me," she said breathlessly. "Don't ever stop. I need to feel you against me, inside me."

The sudden realization that he loved her too dearly to sully her with a quick mating on the floor or to possibly expose her bare body to any eyes but his own brought him to his senses. He caressed her face with cupped palms. "Will you come to my bedchamber?"

Her eyes smoldering with passion, she nodded.

He stood and offered her his hand, and together they left the saloon and began to mount the stairs.

She wished to climb slowly, to maintain a fragile hold on her dignity, but she found herself unable to rule her actions, actions that had become subservient to her passion. She clutched his arm and fairly stampeded up the seemingly never ending stairway. Her very breasts felt heavy, swelled; between her legs, she was hot and wet. Her breathing grew heavy and labored.

They finally reached the second floor and sped past Rebecca's room, then Maggie's, then at last came to Edward's door. As impatient as she, he knew his hand was trembling as he twisted the knob and entered the chamber. Once they were within the room, he firmly closed the door and bolted it, then turned to her. His eyes like those of a man drugged by opium as he hungrily drew her into his arms.

Every part of her body awakened to his sensual onslaught as her body bowed into his and his hands glided possessively over her. Everywhere his hand touched ignited flames of molten desire, and when his hand cupped her most intimate place she fleetingly thought she would surely go mad if she couldn't feel him buried deep within her.

She yanked his shirt from his breeches and ran her hands beneath it and along his rock-hard abdomen. Then she allowed her hands to move further down until her fingers coiled around his swollen shaft.

With a groan, he removed her hand and began to rip at the buttons of her dress. She helped him lift it off, then remove her shift, and she watched hungrily as his shaky hands fumbled to unlace her stays. When her breasts sprang free, he sucked in a deep breath. "Oh, God, Maggie," he groaned as he swept her into his arms and carried her to the huge bed.

He stood there beside the bed and looked down at her naked body with hungry eyes. She gazed at him, at his rumpled shirt, still wet from her tears, half tucked into his tight-fitting breeches, half out, and her heartbeat accelerated when her gaze dropped to the erection inside his clothes.

He quickly freed himself of his clothing, and she gloried in his sheer maleness as the rugged length of his body stretched out beside her and he hauled her

into his arms. Her hands possessively stroked his muscled back, her knee slid languidly up and down his
granite thigh as they began to pulse into one another.
She delighted in the feel of his engorged shaft thrust-
ing between her legs.

"I'm going to make you mine," he growled into her
ear. "By God, I'll never let you get away." His long, elegant fingers, began to stroke the slippery warmth
where her thighs widened. She bucked beneath him,
surging and retreating and so utterly ready for all he
had to give.

Satisfied that she was ready for him, he eased her
onto her back then settled himself over her. Even before he entered her, she began to shudder and had no
command over the sounds that came from her mouth.

She was glad it was still daylight, glad that she could
watch this man she had come to love so thoroughly as
he eased himself into her, rivulets of sweat pouring
from his brow as he drove into her. As she watched
him, a subtle fusing occurred. She was no longer de-
tached, no longer a person separate from him. His
cries were her cries; his pleasure, her pleasure. They
called out each other's names as he pounded into her.
They shuddered together as wave after wave of numbing pleasure slammed into them.

He finally collapsed back onto the bed, drenched
and breathing as if he'd just run uphill. Her cheek
moved to the center of his chest, where his heartbeat
roared in her ear. Waves of their shared pleasure still
lapped at her as she closed an arm around him.

"Forgive me for putting the cart before the horse,"
he said, panting. "You will marry me. I'll not let you
deny me, Maggie mine."

"I won't deny you anything. In fact," she said, pressing her lips to his, "I'd follow you to the ends of the
earth no matter what person's name you were stealing."

A possessive hand cupped her breast. "If you're to

be my wife," he said in a ragged voice, "I owe you an explanation about the Warwick business."

"You don't have to tell me anything, my love. My faith in you is boundless and blind."

He chuckled. "Nevertheless, I shall tell you." He dropped a kiss onto the crown of her head. "I shall first have to explain about the previous Lord Warwick. His father and grandfather had pledged their lives in service to the king. Clandestine service. The third earl, my predecessor, dedicated his life to King George. While everyone thought Lord Warwick was hiding himself at Hogarth Castle, he actually paraded about the continent performing services for the king—always under assumed identities. He was likely the most successful agent ever to infiltrate the French. Unfortunately, they eventually found him out."

"They killed him?"

Edward's thumb feathered over a taut nipple. "No. He outsmarted them. He told them that if he met an untimely death, information he had obtained about French double agents would be turned over to Napoleon. It was a bluff, but because these men weren't without guilt, they fell for it."

She propped herself on one elbow and gave him a quizzing look. "I don't see how you enter the picture."

"When Lord Warwick died of natural causes at the age of sixty, Lord Carrington—who had been apprised of the old earl's activities—urged that I take on the role of Warwick's heir. It was his opinion the French would believe that my purported uncle might have entrusted me with the information about the double agents, information the French would be desperate to get their hands on."

"That sounds like an extremely dangerous ruse."

"I knew the dangers when I accepted, but I also knew I might be able to entrap double agents. It seemed worth the risk. Like the real Lord Warwick, I was unmarried and would not therefore jeopardize a family."

A chill spiked along her spine. "It seems to me the odious Lord Carrington painted a target upon your chest."

He chuckled. "In a way, I suppose he did." Then she suddenly remembered that Lord Carrington's account vastly differed from Edward's. "But Lord Carrington told me before the trip north that he'd just learned of your duplicity. He cast suspicions on your character."

Edward chuckled as his hand splayed over her bare hip. "So he was trying to prejudice you against me even then? It's a rugged cross I must bear—being in love with the most sought-after woman in London."

Could Lord Warwick really have fancied himself in love with her before they went to Yorkshire? "What about the Warwick ruse? Have any French spies approached you?"

"It's the damnedest thing. I've not been approached in these nineteen months since I took on the false identity."

"You think they realized the former Lord Warwick was bluffing?" Her hand softy stroked his mat of chest hair.

"I don't know what to think."

"Perhaps the French double agent planted a servant in your house, a servant who's been conducting a search all these months, trying to find the information. Have you any French men in your employ?"

"No."

She settled her head against his chest again. "Are your servants retainers of the old Lord Warwick?"

"No. He never stayed at Warwick House and was rarely at Hogarth Castle. His only old retainers are still at Hogarth."

"So all your servants here have been hired since you 'ascended'?"

"All of them," he said, his mouth a grim line.

"Oh, my darling, it's all too complicated. Can you not just revert to being Mr. Stanfield? Mr. Stanfield who does not have a target painted on his chest."

He rolled to his side, drawing her with him. Her hand came up to stroke his jaw. "Under the circumstances, I should infinitely prefer being Mrs. Stanfield," she murmured.

This was the Maggie he had fallen in love with. She didn't give a tuppence about wealth or titles. She loved him, Edward Stanfield. He knew it as surely as he knew the sun had just set, blanketing his chamber with velvety darkness.

He regretted all the tortured weeks that had led up to this moment, resented anything that had kept Maggie from his arms. But he knew those weeks had only fed the bud of affection opened that day in Greenwich, by allowing them to get to know one another on a level separate from the physical. Their blossoming love had roots that went deep.

Her sweet rose scent evoked memories of a cozy bedchamber at the Spotted Hound and Hare, memories of the most exquisite lovemaking a man could ever know. He had not thought he would ever again experience anything so sublime, yet he found it again this afternoon, and it was even more exquisite this time because of the knowledge she returned his love.

"I would like to be plain Mr. Stanfield, to take my precious wife and flee from danger, to protect you and love you till the end of our days."

"We could go to America," she said hopefully.

He drew her into his arms. "Would that we could, my love, but we'll never be free until we find the villain who threatens our happiness." His lips covered hers softly, thoroughly, as hers parted beneath his. He felt himself growing hard again as he began to trace a path of kisses to the softness beneath her chin, down the smooth curve of her neck, along the swell of her breasts. He weighed a breast in his cupped hand, then drew the nubbed nipple into his mouth as she began to moan and arch against him.

Beneath his touch her body became a fine instrument and he a virtuoso whose deft hands could make it sing.

Once again he mounted her. This time he entered her in one swift, sure move. And once again she took him to a place no woman had taken him before, a place of fractured light and intoxicating pleasure.

Long afterward as she lay in his arms she whispered, "You'll never know how much I wanted to accept your offer that day in Greenwich."

He smoothed away the damp hair from her beloved brow. "Then why did you refuse? I thought you hated me."

"I thought you loved Fiona—that to you I was nothing more than a compliant body."

"You're so very much more than that. Even before that day," he said with a bitter laugh, "you had succeeded in purging Fiona from my mind. I was obsessed by you, my maddening wench."

"You truly didn't love her then?"

"After I met you I began to wonder if what I had once felt for her had ever been love."

"But . . . I'll vow there was something between you and her. Once. I believe she loved you very much."

"I'm sorry for any hurt I may have caused her." He drew in his breath. "Especially when I told her it was you I loved."

"So that's why she released you?"

He nodded, tugging her against his chest.

Her hand traced sultry circles on his back. "I vow I'll make up for all the anxiety I've caused you."

"You already have," he murmured.

A knock sounded at his chamber door.

"What is it?" he growled, not moving.

"Mr. Hollingsworth is calling on the countess, and I can't find her," Wiggins said.

"She's out!" Edward snapped. "And she won't be back for dinner."

"Very well, my lord."

"And Wiggins?"

"Yes, my lord?"

"I'm not here, either."

Chapter 30

The pounding on Edward's bedchamber door awakened her the following morning.

"What is it?" Edward barked, planting his elbow into the mattress and raising up to cast his glance at the locked door. There was just enough light in the room for her to see the dark line of stubble on his jaw. Her eyes lit upon his bare chest that funneled to a trim waist, her languid gaze dipping to the thick black hair surrounding that most special part of him. She was almost overcome with the intensity of her love for him, the thrill of her possession.

"Miss Sarah is frantic with worry, your lordship," Wiggins said. "Lady Warwick did not return last night."

Edward threw Maggie an amused glance and shrugged. "I've ruined you," he whispered playfully.

"I'd advise you not to tell him I've been beneath you all night," she whispered, her hand moving to stroke the rugged plane of his cheek, her eyes dancing.

"Then you don't want it known you've been here?"

"Of course I want it known! I'd shout if from the Tower of London."

He smiled and drew her close. "Tell Miss Sarah not to be alarmed," Edward shouted to the unseen butler. "Lady Warwick has been sealing the marriage agreement with her future husband."

"Very good, my lord."

"And Wiggins?"

"Yes, my lord?"

"That future husband happens to be your employer."

"Very good, my lord."

Giggling, Maggie collapsed into Edward's arms. His powerful hands glided over her smooth, bare flesh, lighting little fires anew wherever he touched. They had lain with one another for twelve straight hours. There was no part of her body he had not reverently touched, had not pressed his lips to. Consumed only by their blazing need for each other, they had forgone dinner and feasted instead upon each other's bodies.

He drew her close and murmured in her ear. "You'll never be rid of me, Maggie mine, not until I'm in a narrow cell six feet below the earth."

She tucked her face into his chest, her hand sliding down the length of his taut stomach muscles, then lower to close her fingers along the velvety length of his lush shaft. Something he just said sparked a long ago memory, a memory buried so deep she had forgotten it. *Narrow cell.* Coffin. Why was the term so significant? Sudden realization spiked through her and she bolted up.

"Edward! I've remembered it!"

"Remembered what?" he groaned.

"The Scoundrel's clue!"

Edward jerked to a sitting position. "Good Lord, Maggie, what is it?"

Her hand flattened against her temple. "How could I have not remembered!"

Facing her, he clasped hands to both her shoulders. "Remembered what, love?"

"The poem!"

"What poem?"

"The one The Scoundrel made me memorize."

"Good Lord! When was this?"

"When we first married. He begged that I memorize a silly stanza—not that it was silly, really. Actually, it was quite morbid. But being a new bride, I was eager to please my husband."

The solemn look on Edward's face caught at her heart. Of course he wouldn't want to be reminded that she had once belonged to another man. "Do you remember it still?" he asked.

She nodded. "I have an excellent memory."

"I want you to go to my desk and write it down."

Her nudity did not cause her a moment's embarrassment. She strode to his French desk, sat down, picked up the quill, and began to write.

Beneath those rugged elms, that yew-tree's shade,
Where heaves the turf in many a mouldering hill,
Each in his narrow cell forever laid,
In the long-forgotten kirkyard at Rufton Mill.

His hand cupping her shoulder, Edward watched as she wrote. "It's oddly familiar," he said. "I can't believe Henshaw composed it. It's too good."

"That's what I thought," she said with a laugh. "It's always seemed vaguely familiar to me too, but for the life of me I can't remember why, can't grasp the significance." She caught his hand and looked up at him, adoration firing her eyes. "Do you suppose it's some kind of code?"

"Since Henshaw was a cryptographer, it's quite likely," Edward said, pulling his wrinkled breeches from the floor and stepping into them. Then he returned to the desk and snatched the poem.

After withdrawing from the chair, Maggie went about dressing in her crumpled gown while Edward sank into the chair and took up the plume. She came to stand over him as he began to crack the code. He replaced the initial letter in every word that started with a consonant. Then he would replace the re-placement consonants. *Shade* became made, blade, paid, braid, prayed, weighed, played, laid, and slayed. Then he underlined *blade*, which she realized was a noun. Of course, he would be looking for a thing rather than an action. Before long, he had filled three pages with columns of the replacement words and was so intent on what he was doing he did not seem to realize she was even there.

"I would help you if I had any notion of how to proceed," she said, setting her hands to his shoulders.

He gazed up at her. "Oblige me by writing to Hollingsworth."

Why did he want her to write to Randolph Hollingsworth? Then apprehension dawned on her. "You wish me to inform him that I cannot accept his offer?"

"I do."

"Shall I tell him I'm to marry you?"

"Seeing that he doesn't know I'm no longer engaged to his sister, I think not. You could say your affections are otherwise engaged."

"How long before we let others know—about us?"

A frown settled on his face. "As much as I wish to shout it from the Tower of London, I think perhaps we should wait."

"I don't wish to wait," she said with a pout.

He drew her hand into his. "Not for long. Allow me time to apprise Hollingsworth that Fiona has cried off."

"Should you like me to also write to Lord Carrington?"

Edward muttered a curse. "I should like you to place an announcement on the front page of the *Times* to let all the men who've fallen in love with you know you belong to me."

"You can't be serious!"

He chuckled. "No, I wasn't, but I'm not sure how to proceed with Carrington. I can't get a read on his offer. Not that you're not the loveliest, smartest, most desirable woman ever to walk this earth, but I'm not convinced of his devotion to you."

"I feel the very same."

"Let's think on it for a few days."

She pulled up another chair and sat beside him to compose her letter to Randolph Hollingsworth.

"I don't know what to do about Harry Lyle," Edward mused. "He, too, plans to offer for you."

"Could you not just tell him about us? Isn't he your best friend?"

"He won't be after I tell him."

"He'll come around."

She finished her letter and paused to read it.

My Dear Mr. Hollingsworth,

Allow me to say how flattered I am over your offer of marriage. The woman who marries you will be most fortunate indeed. That woman, however, cannot be I. I regret that I was not more honest with you. I should have told you I was already in love with someone else, someone whose affections I had no hope of securing, and because of that I seriously considered marrying you. Circumstances have blessedly changed, and I find that that magical door that was once closed to me is now open.

After she finished with the letter, she watched Edward fill a fourth page with columns, then he leaned back and studied all four pages, only to end up cursing and wadding up all the pages and tossing them across the room.

"I'm going to need my code book," he finally said.

"I take it that it's at the Foreign Office?"

"It is," he said, frowning and getting up from the chair.

"While you're gone I believe I'll sneak into my chamber and change into fresh clothing."

His eyes glittering as he looked at her, he hauled her into his arms and held her firmly. "Oblige me by wearing the rose dress you wore that first night."

"I should like to do anything that will please you."

Gentle lips brushed over hers.

Sarah, her hands hitched to her hips and a scowl on her face, was waiting in Maggie's sunny bedchamber. "I've been frantic all night worried about you, and here you were right under this very roof behaving the strumpet with the lord and master!"

Maggie only smiled. "I'm sorry I didn't alleviate your fears, dearest, but when one's being a strumpet, it's rather difficult to extricate oneself."

Sarah regarded Maggie through narrowed eyes, a tell-tale hint of a smile at her lips. "I knew that first week that Lord Warwick was the man for you, but you, my pretty little one, don't always exercise good judgment in your selection of men."

"So you're saying I exercised good judgment this time?"

"I believe you have."

Maggie smiled. "Come help me into my rose gown. His lordship asked me to wear it especially for him."

In her looking glass Maggie watched Sarah, her gray head bent, fasten the row of buttons at the back of the gown. "How fortunate for you that I'm to end up with Lord Warwick! Now you won't have to leave Mr. Wiggins."

A deep red blush climbed into Sarah's sallow cheeks.

Maggie's eyes twinkled with mischief as she turned to face Sarah. "Can there perhaps be *two* strumpets under this roof?"

The maid's blush turned darker but she only shrugged.

Smiling, Maggie dropped into the chair in front of her dressing table, and Sarah began to arrange her hair.

"The rose is my favorite gown on you, too," Sarah said.

"A pity I can't wear it every day!"

A moment later Sarah asked, "Will Miss Becky be returning soon?"

"I don't believe so. We'll have the devil of a time prying her from Lord Agar's library—which she has volunteered to catalogue."

"I was wondering what I should do with Lord Warwick's library books that are still in her chamber."

"I believe I should like to see them."

Sarah nodded. "You had two gentleman callers yesterday."

"Who else—besides Mr. Hollingsworth?"

"A Mr. Lyle."

"Oh, dear."

"Why are you *oh dearing*?"

Maggie sighed. "Because Mr. Lyle wishes to offer for me. Oh! By the way I need you to post a letter to Mr. Hollingsworth."

Sarah stood back and glared at Maggie, her eyes narrowed. "I take it the letter to Mr. Hollingsworth is to decline his offer?"

Maggie nodded sheepishly.

An hour later Harry Lyle had come and gone. Maggie was satisfied she had let him down gently. After he proposed, she merely said, "Were I not planning on marrying another, I would have been most happy to consider your suit."

"May I know whom you plan to marry?" he had asked.

"After some minor details are worked out, I shall be happy to inform you," she had said.

Now that he was gone, Maggie settled down on the bench before the saloon's pianoforte and began to pick out a tune.

"Here are those books Miss Becky was reading," Sarah said, sweeping into the room with a stack of four books.

Maggie got up and came to examine the titles of each book. A slender volume of poetry seemed precisely what she wished to read today. She took it and went to read beside the window.

The first poem that captured her attention was Thomas Gray's "Elegy Written in a Country Churchyard." She set back and began to read. When she reached the fourth stanza she bolted up. *My God!*

It was a modification of The Scoundrel's poem! But realizing the poem was likely written before The Scoundrel was born, it was The Scoundrel who had done the adaptation.

The most significant modification was the complete rewriting of the last line. What originally read *The rude Forefathers of the hamlet sleep* had been changed to *In the long-forgotten kirkyard of Rufton Mill.* Could Rufton Mill be a real place? A place where The Scoundrel had hidden his document—or whatever it was he had?

She hurried to Edward's library to seek a map of England.

That's where she was when Lord Carrington called. "Oh, my lord, how fortuitous that you've come now! I may have discovered where my late husband hid whatever it was that he had." She proceeded to tell him about the poem.

"Would you be so good as to write it down?" he asked.

She went to Edward's broad Tudor desk and copied it, then presented it to Lord Carrington.

His eyes flashed with warmth.

"Do you know of a place called Rufton Mill?" she asked.

"I do, my lady. It's not far from here. Shall we go?"

"Should we not wait for Ed—for Lord Warwick?"

"We can be back before he returns."

"Allow me to fetch my pelisse and bonnet," she said.

Sarah and Wiggins were softly speaking in the broad hallway when Maggie swept through. "If Lord Warwick returns before I," Maggie said, "tell him I've gone to Rufton Mill with Lord Carrington."

Chapter 31

Damn it! Edward flung his code book across the room. Four short lines and he couldn't break the damn code. He had been sitting at his desk in the Foreign Office for the past hour, plagued by a maddening suspicion the damned poem was not in code, by the fuzzy memory of another poem he was powerless to recall.

A pity Harry Lyle was not here. He was a master at cryptography.

Another niggling thought kept eating away at Edward, but he was unable to give it shape and substance. He only knew that it had something to do with Lord Carrington.

Stuffing the stanza into his pocket—not that he needed it since he now knew it from memory—Edward stormed from the building.

At Warwick House, he went straight to the saloon, suspecting that Maggie might be receiving callers there. But she wasn't there. The sight of an open book on top of the pianoforte caught his attention. He strode to it and began to read Gray's "Elegy Written in a Country Churchyard."

Even before he got to the fourth stanza, he knew why Henshaw's stanza had been so familiar. As soon as he realized the significance of the Rufton Mill substitution, he stormed to his library to consult his map.

Rufton Mill must be a place! A place where Henshaw hid his damned document.

He was deuced angry at himself for not realizing sooner that Rufton Mill was a real place. Though he had never been there, he had heard of it before—not that he could not recall when or where.

For the next half hour he searched his maps but could not find Rufton Mill. Then that hazy memory that had been swimming around in his feeble brain rose to the surface, and he knew where he had heard of Rufton Mill. The previous Lord Warwick was buried there!

In a drawer of his desk he rifled through a stack of papers until he found what he was looking for. Rufton Mill was located in Kent, just outside Hogarth Castle.

He debated on whether he should tell Lord Carrington. Something about Lord Carrington— something beside the man's unexpected interest in Maggie—screamed a warning. But hadn't the fact the men in Newgate Prison identified a Frenchman as the evil-doer behind Maggie's abduction exonerated Lord Carrington?

Then Edward realized that he had only Lord Carrington's word to go by. His pulse thundering, he flew from the library, through the house and raced to the mews.

He helped his groom quickly saddle a mount. He had no wish for his gig. Speed was what was called for.

He sped through Mayfair, then along The Strand, his horse's hooves clattering over the cobblestones as he rushed to Newgate Prison. Since he'd had some minor dealings with the Newgate official, the man recognized him immediately.

"Good afternoon, Lord Warwick," the man said.

Even the official's office was not free from the prison's foul stench. "It is a matter of some urgency that I speak with the prisoners Lord Carrington questioned yesterday."

The man shot him a puzzled look. "But, your lordship, I have no recollection of Lord Carrington being here any day this week."

Edward's heart drummed. "You've been here every day?"

"Every day."

"Is there someone else who may have assisted Lord Carrington?"

"No, my lord."

Edward cursed. "If you should find that Lord Carrington's been here, please send word to me at Warwick House on Curzon Street." Edward did not hear the man's response. He was racing from the building.

His heart thundered as he galloped back to Warwick House. What if Carrington were with Maggie right now? What evil was the man plotting?

They had been driving in Lord Carrington's carriage for an hour, the maze of narrow London streets now behind them. Maggie was growing uncomfortable. "Is this mill not in London, my lord?"

"No, my dear, it's not."

"But you said we could be back before Edward returned." She was so out of charity with Lord Carrington she did not care that she had addressed Edward by his Christian name.

"And so we will."

She had the distinct feeling he was lying to her. "I wish to turn around now. I should never have come off without Lord Warwick."

"Oh, but we are so close, my lady."

She wedged herself into a corner of the carriage and glared at the man across from her. "That's what you said a half hour ago—and a half hour before that. Just where is this Rufton Mill?"

"Actually, it's in Kent."

"In Kent! I may not be knowledgeable about English geography, but I know that's well south of London! I believe, my lord, you've lied to me."

He shrugged. "Just a mild prevaricration, my dear. Can you blame me for wishing to steal away some little time with the woman I hope to marry?"

Odious man! She folded her arms in front of her, her eyes shooting daggers at him. "I don't think I have any desire to wed a man who can't be truthful."

Ignoring her, he lifted the curtain to peer from the glass.

"Truthfully, my lord, how much longer?" She didn't like to think of Edward worrying about her.

He turned cold blue eyes on her. "Truthfully, we should be there at dusk."

"At dusk! But that's a good two hours away! How could you have been so devious as to tell me it was but a short distance? I thought we were going to some little mill a couple of miles from Mayfair."

His voice was harsh when he answered. "You cannot blame me for your own erroneous interpretation."

She was almost overcome with a raging urge to slap the man across his smirking face. Instead she wedged even further into her corner, refusing to speak to the horrid man.

It was some little while before dusk when Lord Carrington's coach rattled up to an overgrown cemetery and lurched to a stop. Not waiting for him or his coachman to open the door, she bolted from her seat, threw open the door, and leaped down to the soft earth.

She tossed a curious glance to three rough-looking men on horses who drew up behind the marquis's coach.

Her pulse exploded when she saw the man with a

patch over his eye. The man who was missing a front tooth.

As his horse drew up in front of Warwick House, Edward sighed with relief. Thank God Carrington's carriage wasn't there. He leaped from his mount, gave the reins to the ostler, then flew up the steps to throw open the door just as Wiggins came striding toward him.

"Where, Wiggins, can I find my future countess?" Edward could barely suppress a grin at the intoxicating thought that Maggie would be his wife.

"She has gone off with Lord Carrington, my lord."

It was as if a cannonball had hurled into the pit of Edward's stomach. His very breath was trapped in his chest. "Dear God," was all he could manage.

Wiggins's brows creased with concern. "Is something wrong, my lord?"

"Did she tell you where she was going?"

"Actually her ladyship did give us her destination, but I can't seem to recall the place. Not anywhere I've ever heard of."

"Who else did she tell?" Edward demanded.

"Miss Sarah."

"Fetch her at once!" But as Wiggins went to the climb the stairs Edward was too impatient to wait. Like a banshee, he screamed out her name. "Sarah!"

She came running along the second-floor hallway, and from the top of the stairs answered. "What is it, my lord?" Her face had gone ashen as she bent over the railing to look down at him.

"Where has your mistress gone?" Edward demanded.

She pursed her lips. "Now let me see. I believe it was to some mill."

A string of vile curses strung from Edward's mouth

as he spun around and raced to the library where he stored his pistols. He took one from the case and slammed it into a pocket, then he hurriedly strapped on his saber before storming from the house—only to almost knock down Randolph Hollingsworth.

"Where in the hell are you going in such a huff?" Hollingsworth asked.

"Carrington's got Maggie," Edward said in an anguished voice. "And he's the one."

Hollingsworth issued an oath. "I'm coming with you!"

Edward looked down at the sword at Randolph's side. "We've got to hurry!"

Chapter 32

As soon as she saw the those vile men she understood everything. That Lord Carrington had completely fabricated the Newgate Prison story. That Lord Carrington was the man who employed the cutthroats, the man who ordered Andrew Bibble's death. That Lord Carrington, for reasons completely unclear to her, had betrayed his country. Now she understood why he had so desperately tried to cast suspicion onto Edward.

Stark, white-hot fear on her face, she whirled to the marquis. "Why have you brought me here?" *Oh God.* She knew why. Her chest tightened, her pulse pounded. *He's going to kill me.* "I'm not the only one who knows about the poem," she taunted before she realized her implication of Edward would likely cost his life, too.

"You told Warwick?" he snarled.

She stiffened. "No. Someone else."

His gaze flicked from her to the man with the eye patch. "Find a shovel, will you?"

They were going to kill her and bury her here, and no one would ever know what happened. She looked around to see if any houses were nearby, but clumps of trees obliterated any view of the surrounding countryside for as far as she could see.

"Tie her up!" Lord Carrington ordered.

She picked up her skirts and began to sprint into the crumbling cemetery. She sped past eroded gravestones and over clumps of overgrown weeds, running as fast as her legs could power her. Then her foot plunged into a rut. Her ankle twisted, and she tumbled on top of a neatly kept grave.

As her face collided with the soft earth, she saw the name on the tombstone. *Third Earl Warwick, 1751-1811.* She tried to hoist herself up, but one of the men lunged at her and caught her wrist. Pain splintered through her arm as the man yanked her up, twisting the wrist within a brutal grip while the other men stepped forward and began to tie her hands behind her.

"Where's Logan?" the marquis demanded. "He should have been able to procure a shovel by now!"

A moment later, One Eye returned, lugging a shovel. When he reached the late Lord Warwick's grave, Lord Carrington ordered him to start digging. "Start around the headstone," he said.

As soon as One Eye drove the spade into the ground, they heard the sound of clanking metal. A minute later a metal box was unearthed. "I'll take that," Lord Carrington said.

"'Tis light as a feather," said the man with the eye patch. "I'll wager there's no gold sovereigns in it."

Lord Carrington's flashing eyes flicked from the box to his hired henchmen. "Do you fellows know how to read?"

"Why ye be askin' us foolish questions like that?" One Eye asked. "We ain't no fancy pants to be sittin' around no school room."

"Just as I thought," Lord Carrington said in a guttural voice. "Why don't you gents just step away for a few minutes."

The three men backed up ten paces.

"Back to the horses!" Lord Carrington screamed visciously.

There was fear on their faces as the men complied.

Once they were out of earshot, the marquis opened the box and withdrew a document bearing a regal-looking seal. "My eyes are not what they used to be," he said, facing Maggie. "Oblige me by reading this."

"Oblige me by untying my hands!" she spit out at him.

"I think not. I'll hold it for you." He drew closer and unfurled the vellum that stretched to over a foot in length. She saw that it was written in French, in large bold letters. Her glance dropped to the signature. *Napoleon, Emperor of France.*

"Read it! Damn you!"

She translated as she read. "*On the twelfth of August in the year eighteen-seven it is agreed that in payment for invaluable services rendered not without personal risk and in recognition of diligent loyalty to the Emperor of France, Albert Black, Fourth Marquis Carrington, will be placed on the English throne at such time as the British Isles come under French rule.*"

She looked up at him, hatred in her eyes. "You're the devil himself!"

"The devil, madame, was your late husband. He stole this document from me. He was just as guilty as I of helping the French, only he wasn't as smart. Warwick—or Stanfield as he was then—found him out, but as long as Henshaw had possession of the document I had to see to it that Henshaw lived."

"So that's why you insisted I stay in London! You knew eventually I'd lead you to this."

"And you did," he said smugly. "Now tell me who else knows about the poem."

"I had three gentlemen callers after you left yesterday afternoon. I shared it with all of them."

His eyes glittered with rage. "And with Warwick?"

"Of course, he knew about it, too."

There was a menacing look on his face as he stared at her. "I don't believe you. I don't think anyone else knows about the poem."

"You're wrong! Besides, I wrote it down and sent copies of it to several important people."

He struck her face. The force of the blow tore something in her neck. Her eyes watered and a thread of blood began to ooze from her nose.

He shoved the document back in the metal box, and called for the henchmen to return.

It suddenly occurred to her that he did not wish the cutthroats to know the importance of the document. She met One Eye's glance. "You would never have to do another day's work," she said, "if you steal his lordship's box."

Lord Carrington stepped up and slapped her again. Then again.

Then One Eye pulled him off of her. "Maybe we just better have that box, yer lordship."

Carrington drew a pistol from his pocket and turned it on them.

All of them.

Edward and Randolph rode harder and faster than any money winner at Newmarket had ever run. They twice changed to fresh horses. Edward's only hope of rescuing Maggie was in beating that luxurious coach Carrington always traveled in, a difficult feat to be sure, given that the carriage had an hour's head start. But it was just possible his and Randolph's fleet mounts could overtake the cumbersome coach-and-four.

While changing horses at the first posting inn, Randolph eyed Edward warily and asked. "Am I to assume you've broken your pledge to my sister?"

So Randolph knew he loved Maggie. "Actually, it was your sister who broke the pledge to me. A most intelligent move on her part."

"Intelligent, given that you're in love with another woman."

Edward's gaze dropped. "I shouldn't want to live if anything happened to Maggie." Then he promptly mounted his horse and dug in his heels.

He cursed his own staggering stupidity. His relief that the men who threatened Maggie were behind bars had stripped away his usual caution. Why hadn't he demanded to see them straight away? Why had he not warned Maggie not to trust Carrington?

And, God in heaven, why had he left Maggie unprotected today? Why had he not shared his suspicions of Carrington with her before he rushed off to Newgate? He had shared everything else with her—except that which was most critical.

He took his fury out on the horse that was already giving him all it had to give. Poor creature.

As they neared Hogarth Castle he castigated himself for not previously familiarizing himself with the castle's environs. Where in the hell was Rufton Mill? Carrington likely knew.

And that knowledge—the knowledge that the vile marquis had dragged her there for his own evil purposes—drove thunderous, raging fire through Edward's veins. He had never wished to kill a man. Until today.

In the distance he saw the turrets of Hogarth, and his stomach tumbled. He prayed he would be in time. He sped past the lane that led to the castle, past the gatekeeper's house, desperately searching for Carrington's shiny black carriage. He rounded a lush bend in the road, and his heart nearly stopped. Some hundred feet off the road, Carrington's coach-and-four was parked, another trio of mangy horses surrounding it. He and Randolph surged ahead.

Then he saw her. His instant relief that she was still alive plummeted when he saw that her hands were tied behind her, blood staining that incredible face. Beside her was the ruffian with the eye patch, Carrington barely a foot away.

And he was holding a pistol.

Rage thundering through him, Edward jumped the low rock fence that surrounded the graveyard, his horse pounding toward the circle of men as he shouted curses at them in a ploy to distract their attention from Maggie.

As he drew within six feet of them he leaped from the fleetly moving animal.

Just as Carrington aimed his pistol.

The musket ball grazed Edward's ear as he powered toward Carrington, unsheathing his saber, Maggie's shrieks filling the acrid air. Carrington threw down the smoking pistol, his eyes widening with fear. "Get this man!" he yelled to his henchmen as he stumbled backwards.

But the other men did not move.

Edward lunged toward Carrington, who tried to run backward, afraid to take his eyes off his attacker. He stumbled again and fell on his back as Edward drove his sword through Carrington's coat, pinning him to the soft earth, but not connecting with Carrington's flesh. Behind Edward, Randolph was handling the other three men who were not foolish enough to resist an armed man, but at this moment Edward's only thought was to murder Carrington.

The marquis's pale blue eyes glittered not with fear but with hatred. "Do me the goodness of driving your sword through my heart," Carrington pleaded. "All is lost."

Edward's menacing gaze swung from his impaled

sword to Carrington's desperate face. He did not speak, did not move. He thought of Andrew Bibble and was consumed with the overwhelming urge to do to Carrington what Carrington had done to Bibble. His hand gripped the hilt of the sword and he drew it away, his eyes never leaving Carrington's. Then his boot dug into the ground, and he kicked dirt onto Carrington's face.

Turning his sword on the other men, Edward ordered them to untie the lady. The sight of her welted face tore at his heart. With cold eyes he watched the one-eyed man unfasten the cords at Maggie's wrists, wrists slashed by the cord. "Now tie Lord Carrington," Edward ordered, sickened by Maggie's injuries.

But before the men could comply, Carrington yanked a dagger from his pocket and drove it into his own heart.

Maggie screamed a blood-curdling yell. Though Edward wanted to draw her into his arms and hold her, he could not drop the sword. Not while three miscreants were ever ready to pounce on it.

"See if he's dead," Edward ordered the one-eyed man.

The man stooped down and pressed his filthy hand to Carrington's bloody wrist. "Aye, that 'e is. Good riddance it be, too."

Edward's glance flicked to Randolph. "Oblige me by tying up these men while I keep my weapon on them."

Only when their hands were firmly tied behind them did Edward allow himself to drop the sword and draw Maggie into his arms.

Chapter 33

She had really humiliated herself. If only those dark clouds had not come up. But they had. Right when they were waiting for Mr. Hollingsworth to get back from rounding up the local magistrate. Right there, bunched above the cemetery at Rufton Mill. The rain and thunder and those things that drove her to act like a ninny waited just until dear Mr. Hollingsworth and the addled magistrate came striding through the huddle of gravestones. Then the clouds exploded.

When the roaring thunder shook the ground and lightning flashed white into the blackened sky, Maggie let out a scream. No dainty scream, but a loud wail that was in perfect harmony with the terrified look on her face.

Though the other men observed her as one would a mad dog, her darling Edward was really quite wonderful about it all. Not saying single word, he opened one side of his generous great coat and hauled her beneath it, closing it around her and directing his attention to the gentlemen. "Thunderstorms seem to have a mortifying effect upon my future wife," he explained.

He entrusted Mr. Hollingsworth to wrap up all the wretched business with Lord Carrington and the brutes while he hastened through the already muddy mire to settle her in Lord Carrington's carriage, instructing the coachmen to drive them to Greenwich.

"Greenwich?" she had asked, looking at Edward as if he'd just launched into a fit of lunacy, even though it was she who acted the lunatic.

He had drawn her into his arms. "We're returning to the Spotted Hound and Hare."

She had never felt so closely connected to anyone as she was to Edward at that moment. Who else would understand her yearning to be in that cozy bedchamber of the Spotted Hound and Hare? No one else could ever have spent so glorious an afternoon as she and Edward had shared there.

Even though the menacing weather continued all the way to Greenwich, Edward's diversions wildly succeeded in keeping her mind off her treacherous situation, those diversions being kissing, stroking, freeing her breasts, freeing his—well, all sorts of delicious things, actually.

By the time they arrived at the Spotted Hound and Hare, her dress was enormously wrinkled, her hair spilled from its pins to hang willy-nilly about her bruised face, and there was a wet circle on her dress just over the part that covered her nipple where Edward's mouth had pleasured her. She was extremely grateful for pelisses.

The innkeeper and his aproned wife, smiles as broad as the River Thames on their faces, rushed to greet them. "I was just tellin' the missus we'd not be seein' the likes of our fine lord and lady again and here ye comes—just like that other day—and it be rainin' again, too!"

"There's no finer place to be on a rainy day, I was just telling my lady," Edward said, his sparkling eyes full of mischief. "I would be most obliged if we could have our same room."

The woman led them through the firelit parlor. "Ye'll be wanting a nice pot of 'ot tea, too."

"Yes, later," Edward said. "For now we will be most happy for a dry place to rest."

Maggie was happy he had forestalled their hostess. She had no need for tea when there was Edward to warm her.

Once they were in their room, he framed her face with his hands and spoke huskily. "You don't know how I've longed to be here again. With you."

Her hands tugged at his shirt to dislodge it from his pantaloons, his hand swept down her bodice. Then there was a tangle of arms and legs flying until each of them was stripped bare and panting, their clothing strewn across the room. She felt the intensity of his gaze as it lingered over her body, felt as if he were about to devour her. "Were you to be presented to the queen, you could not be more beautiful than you are right now," he said in a deep, low voice.

She thought he looked pretty magnificent, too. Her glance flitted over his powerful chest and the smooth muscles of his elongated torso, and her breath caught when she saw his huge arousal, then her gaze dropped to his long sinewy legs that were dusted with dark hair. It was getting more difficult to breathe without whimpering.

Their hungry eyes locked, she began to giggle her pleasure, then they hurled themselves onto the bed, Edward planting his thighs on each side of her as he stared down into her sultry face and hungrily swept her into his arms, growling his satisfaction. He kissed her long and deep and with incredible tenderness.

Her breath was ragged when his lips traced a moist path along her neck and up the slope of her breast, then she began to moan when his lips parted to close over her nipple. And when his mouth went lower still she found herself arching to meet his lips, his tongue as they delved into her slickness. He spread her legs wider, wedging his head deeper, stroking her pearly bud with strong flicks of his heated tongue. She began to pulse against him, her eyes shut tightly as she thrashed up and down and from side to side. A profound heat consumed her as she flew to another place, a place where she and Edward were a universe of two. She began to shudder uncontrollably. He watched with smoldering eyes as she pulsed and trembled, and he gently wiped the moisture from her brow as she called out his name.

"I can't wait any longer, love," he whispered hoarsely. "I want you to ride me." He flopped onto his back and she climbed on top of him, spreading her legs wide as she took him deep inside. This time she kept her eyes open and with an intoxicating feeling of possession watched the man she loved convulse beneath her, watched the dazed satisfaction on his face, felt his warm seed flooding her and was engulfed in the torrent of their love.

One final, deep, heaving surge and the bed collapsed beneath them. As their mattress crashed to the wood floor, he crushed her to him and they both laughed. "The Earl of Warwick's bed, I believe, is more durable," he said, stroking her silken flesh. "First thing tomorrow I get a special license. I've an unquenchable urge to make you my wife, Maggie mine."

"I'm possessed of an unquenchable urge to become Mrs. Edward Stanfield."

EPILOGUE

Six months later . . .

As it happens, she did not become Mrs. Stanfield.

Once the Regent learned of Edward's role in unmasking Lord Carrington's treachery, he saw to it that every possible honor was heaped upon Edward. Edward was elevated to Lord Carrington's position as Foreign Secretary, and the lands and title of the Warwick earldom were also bestowed upon him.

Edward pensioned off Wiggins, who now lived with his new wife in a cottage near Hogarth Castle, and Miss Rebecca Peabody had returned to Warwick House to commence cataloguing Edward's library.

Once the transfer of the Warwick title was official, Edward cupped his hand over his wife's beloved, swelling belly. "Think you the fifth earl resides in your womb, love?"

She brought his hand to her lips. "If not this babe, then perhaps the next will be a male. We have many years ahead, and making babies is devilishly fun!"

His heart swelled every time he was with his Maggie. She had loved him just as fiercely when he had no prospects of being an earl. No man could be more loved than he; no woman loved more than she. "From this day forward, you are no longer my counterfeit countess," he said—and then he kissed her.

ABOUT THE AUTHOR

After careers in journalism and in teaching English, Cheryl Bolen published her first book (*A Duke Deceived* with Harlequin Historical) in 1998 and was named Notable New Author. Six more Regency-set historicals and one novella have followed. Her books have been translated into Norwegian, Italian, French, Portuguese, Swedish, Dutch, Polish, and Japanese.

Cheryl and her professer husband live in Texas and are the parents of two sons who claim to be grown. An antiques dealer, Cheryl travels to England whenever writing deadlines permit.

Readers can write to her website, www.cherylbolen.com.

More Regency Romance
From Zebra

More Historical Romance From
Jo Ann Ferguson